The Beekeeper of Aleppo

Brought up in London, Christy Lefteri is the child of Cypriot refugees. She is a lecturer in creative writing at Brunel University. *The Beekeeper of Aleppo* was born out of her time working as a volunteer at a Unicef supported refugee centre in Athens.

The Beekeeper of Aleppo

CHRISTY LEFTERI

MANILLA PRESS

First published in Great Britain in 2019 by
ZAFFRE
This paperback edition published in 2020 by
MANILLA PRESS
An imprint of Bonnier Books UK
80-81 Wimpole Street, London, W1G 9RE
Owned by Bonnier Books
Sveavägen 56, Stockholm, Sweden

Copyright © Christy Lefteri, 2019

All rights reserved.
No part of this publication may be reproduced,
stored or transmitted in any form by any means, electronic,
mechanical, photocopying or otherwise, without the
prior written permission of the publisher.

The right of Christy Lefteri to be identified as Author of this
work has been asserted by her in accordance with the
Copyright, Designs and Patents Act, 1988.

This is a work of fiction. Names, places, events and
incidents are either the products of the author's
imagination or used fictitiously. Any resemblance to
actual persons, living or dead, or actual
events is purely coincidental.

A CIP catalogue record for this book is
available from the British Library.

ISBN: 978–1–83877–001–3

Also available as an ebook and an audiobook

14

Typeset in Janson MT by Palimpsest Book Production Ltd, Falkirk, Stirlingshire
Printed and bound in Great Britain by Clays Ltd, Elcograf S.p.A.

Manilla Press is an imprint of Bonnier Books UK
www.bonnierbooks.co.uk

For Dad
Also, for S

1

I AM SCARED OF MY WIFE'S eyes. She can't see out and no one can see in. Look, they are like stones, grey stones, sea stones. Look at her. Look how she is sitting on the edge of the bed, her nightgown on the floor, rolling Mohammed's marble around in her fingers and waiting for me to dress her. I am taking my time putting on my shirt and trousers, because I am so tired of dressing her. Look at the folds of her stomach, the colour of desert honey, darker in the creases, and the fine, fine silver lines on the skin of her breasts, and the tips of her fingers with the tiny cuts, where the ridges and valley patterns once were stained with blue or yellow or red paint. Her laughter was gold once, you would have seen as well as heard it. Look at her, because I think she is disappearing.

'I had a night of scattered dreams,' she says. 'They filled the room.' Her eyes are fixed a little to the left of me. I feel sick.

'What does that mean?'

'They were broken. My dreams were everywhere. And I didn't know if I was awake or asleep. There were so many dreams, like bees in a room, like the room was full of bees. And I couldn't breathe. And I woke up and thought, please don't let me be hungry.'

I look at her face, confused. There is still no expression. I don't tell her that I only dream of murder now, always the same dream; it's only me and the man, and I'm holding the bat and my hand is bleeding; the others aren't there in the dream, and he is on the ground with the trees above him and he says something to me that I can't hear.

'And I have pain,' she says.

'Where?'

'Behind my eyes. Really sharp pain.'

I kneel down in front of her and look into her eyes. The blank emptiness in them terrifies me. I take my phone out of my pocket, shine the light of the torch into them. Her pupils dilate.

'Do you see anything at all?' I say.

'No.'

'Not even a shadow, a change of tone or colour?'

'Just black.'

I put the phone in my pocket and step away from her. She's been worse since we got here. It's like her soul is evaporating.

'Can you take me to the doctor?' she says. 'Because the pain is unbearable.'

'Of course,' I say. 'Soon.'

'When?'

'As soon as we get the papers.'

I'm glad Afra can't see this place. She would like the seagulls though, the crazy way they fly. In Aleppo we were far from the sea. I'm sure she would like to see these birds and maybe even the coast, because she was raised by the sea, while I am from eastern Aleppo where the city meets the desert.

When we got married and she came to live with me, Afra missed the sea so much that she started to paint water, wherever she found it. Throughout the arid plateau region of Syria there are oases and streams and rivers that empty into swamps and small lakes. Before we had Sami, we would follow the water, and she would paint it in oils. There is one painting of the Queiq I wish I could see again. She made the river look like a storm-water drain running through the city park. Afra had this way of seeing truth in landscapes. The painting, and its measly river, reminds me of struggling to stay alive. Thirty or so kilometres south of Aleppo the river gives up the struggle of the harsh Syrian steppe and evaporates into the marshes.

I am scared of her eyes. But these damp walls, and the wires in the ceiling, and the billboards – I'm not sure how she would deal with all this, if she could see it. The billboard just outside says that there are too many of us, that this island will break under our weight. I'm glad she's blind. I know what that sounds like! If I could give her a key that opened a door into another world, then I would wish for her to see again. But it would have to be a world very different from this one. A place where the sun is just rising, touching the walls around the ancient city and, outside those walls, the cell-like quarters and the houses and apartments and hotels and narrow alleys and an open-air market where a thousand hanging necklaces shine with that first light, and further away, across the desert land, gold on gold and red on red.

Sami would be there, smiling and running along those alleys with his scuffed trainers, change in his hand, on his way to the store to get milk. I try not to think about Sami. But Mohammed? I'm still waiting for him to find the letter and money I left under the jar of Nutella. I think one morning there will be a knock at the door, and when I open it he will be standing there and I will say, 'But how did you get all the way here, Mohammed? How did you know where to find us?'

Yesterday I saw a boy in the steamed-up mirror of the shared bathroom. He was wearing a black T-shirt, but when I turned around it was the man from Morocco, sitting on the toilet, pissing. 'You should lock the door,' he said in his own Arabic.

I can't remember his name, but I know that he is from a village near Taza, beneath the Rif mountains. He told me last night that they might send him to the removal centre in a place called Yarl's Wood – the social worker thinks there's a chance they will. It's my turn to meet her this afternoon. The Moroccan man says she's very beautiful, that she looks like a dancer from Paris who he once made love to in a hotel in Rabat, long before he married his wife. He asked me about life in Syria. I told him about my beehives in Aleppo.

In the evenings the landlady brings us tea with milk. The Moroccan man is old, maybe eighty or even ninety. He looks and smells like he's made of leather. He reads *How to Be a Brit*, and sometimes smirks to himself. He has his phone on his lap, and pauses at the end of each page to glance down at it, but no one ever calls. I don't know who he's waiting for and I don't know how he got here and I don't know why he has made such a journey so late in his life, because he seems like a man who is waiting to die. He hates the way the non-Muslim men stand up to piss.

There are about ten of us in this rundown B&B by the sea, all of us from different places, all of us waiting. They might keep us, they might send us away, but there is not much to decide anymore. Which road to take, whom to trust, whether to raise the bat again and kill a man. These things are in the past. They will evaporate soon, like the river.

I take Afra's abaya from the hanger in the wardrobe. She hears it and stands, lifting her arms. She looks older now, but acts younger, like she has turned into a child. Her hair is the colour and texture of sand since we dyed it for the photos, bleached out the Arabic. I tie it into a bun and wrap her hijab around her head, securing it with hairpins while she guides my fingers like she always does.

The social worker will be here at 1 p.m., and all meetings take place in the kitchen. She will want to know how we got here and she will be looking for a reason to send us away. But I know that if I say the right things, if I convince her that I'm not a killer, then we will get to stay here because we are the lucky ones, because we have come from the worst place in the world. The Moroccan man isn't so lucky; he will have more to prove. He is sitting in the living room now by the glass doors, holding a bronze pocket watch in both of his hands, nestling it in his palms like it's a hatching egg. He stares at it, waiting. What for? When he sees that I'm standing here, he says, 'It doesn't work, you know. It stopped in a different time.' He holds it up in the light by its chain and swings it, gently, this frozen watch made of

bronze

was the colour of the city far below. We lived in a two-bedroom bungalow on a hill. From so high up we could see all the unorganised architecture and the beautiful domes and minarets, and far in the distance the citadel peeking through.

It was pleasant to sit on the veranda in the spring; we could smell the soil from the desert and see the red sun setting over the land. In the summer though, we would be inside with a fan running and wet towels on our heads, and our feet in a bowl of cold water because the heat was an oven.

In July the earth was parched, but in our garden we had apricot and almond trees and tulips and irises and fritillaries. When the river dried up, I would go down to the irrigation pond to collect water for the garden to keep it alive. By August it was like trying to resuscitate a corpse, so I watched it all die and merge into the rest of the land. When it was cooler we would take a walk and watch the falcons flying across the sky to the desert.

I had four beehives in the garden, piled one on top of the other, but the rest were in a field on the outskirts of eastern Aleppo. I hated to be away from the bees. In the mornings I would wake up early, before the sun, before the muezzin called out for prayer. I would drive the thirty miles to the apiaries and arrive as the sun was just rising, fields full of light, the humming of the bees a single pure note.

The bees were an ideal society, a small paradise among chaos. The worker bees travelled far and wide to find food, preferring to go to the furthest fields. They collected nectar from lemon blossoms and clover, black nigella seeds and aniseed, eucalyptus, cotton, thorn and heather. I cared for the bees, nurtured them, monitored the hives for infestations or poor health. Sometimes I would build new hives, divide the colonies or raise queen bees – I'd take the larvae from another colony and watch as the nurse bees fed them with royal jelly.

Later, during harvesting season, I would check the hives to see how much honey the bees had produced and then I would put the combs into the extractors and fill the tubs, scraping off the residue to collect the golden liquid beneath. It was my job to protect the bees, to keep them healthy and strong, while they fulfilled their task of making honey and pollinating the land to keep us alive.

It was my cousin Mustafa who introduced me to beekeeping. His father and grandfather had both been keepers in the green valleys, west of the Anti-Lebanon range. Mustafa was a genius with the heart of a boy. He studied and became a professor at Damascus University, researching the precise composition of honey. Because he travelled back and forth between Damascus and Aleppo, he wanted me to manage the apiaries. He taught me so much about the behaviour of bees and how to manipulate them. The native bees were aggressive from the heat, but he showed me how to understand them.

When the university closed for the summer months, Mustafa joined me full-time in Aleppo; we both worked hard, so many hours – in the end we thought like the bees, we even ate like the bees! We would eat pollen mixed with honey to keep us going in the heat.

In the early days, when I was in my twenties and still new to the job, our hives were made of plant material covered with mud. Later we replaced the trunks of cork trees and the terracotta hives with wooden boxes, and soon we had over five hundred colonies! We produced at least ten tonnes of honey a year. There were so many bees, and they made me feel alive. When I was away from them it was like a great party had ended. Years later, Mustafa opened a shop in the new part of town. In addition to honey, he sold honey-based cosmetics, luscious sweet-smelling creams and soaps and hair products from our very own bees. He had opened this shop for his daughter. Though she was young at the time she believed that she would grow up to study agriculture, just like her father. So, Mustafa named the shop *Aya's Paradise* and promised that one day, if she studied hard, it would belong to her. She loved to come in and smell the soaps and smother the creams on her hands. She was an intelligent girl for her age, I remember once how she said, 'This shop is what the world would smell like if there were no humans.'

Mustafa did not want a quiet life. He always strove to do

more and learn more. I've never seen this in any other human being. However big we got – even when we had big customers from Europe and Asia and the Gulf – I was the one who looked after the bees, the one he trusted with this. He said I had a sensitivity that most men lacked, that I understood their rhythms and patterns. He was right. I learned how to really listen to the bees and I spoke to them as though they were one breathing body with a heart, because, you see, bees work together. Even when, at the end of summer, the drones are killed by workers to preserve food resources, they are still working as one entity. They communicate to one another through a dance. It took me years to understand them, and once I did, the world around me never looked or sounded the same again.

But, as the years passed, the desert was slowly growing, the climate becoming harsh, rivers drying up, farmers struggling; only the bees were drought-resistant, 'Look at these little warriors,' Afra would say on the days when she came with Sami to visit the apiaries, a tiny bundle wrapped up in her arms, 'Look at them still working, when everything else is dying!' Afra always prayed for rain, because she feared the dust storms and the droughts. When a dust storm was coming we could see, from our veranda, the sky above the city turn purple, and then there was a whistle deep in the atmosphere, and Afra would run around the house closing all the doors, bolting all the windows and shutters.

* * *

Every Saturday we would go to Mustafa's house for dinner. Dahab and Mustafa would cook together, Mustafa measuring every ingredient, every spice, meticulously on the scales, as if one tiny mistake would ruin the whole meal. Dahab was a tall woman, almost the same height as her husband, and she would stand beside him and shake her head, as I'd seen her do with Firas and Aya. 'Hurry up,' she would say. 'Hurry up! At this rate we will be eating this Saturday's meal next Saturday.' He hummed while he cooked, and stopped every twenty minutes or so to smoke, standing in the courtyard beneath the flowering tree, biting and sucking on the end of his cigarette.

I would join him, but he was quiet at these times, his eyes glistening from the heat of the kitchen, his thoughts elsewhere. Mustafa began to fear the worst before I did, and I could see the worry in the lines of his face.

They lived on the bottom floor of a block of flats, and the courtyard was enclosed on three sides by the walls of the neighbouring blocks, so that it was always cool and full of shadows. The sounds from the balconies above tumbled down towards us – scraps of conversations, music, the faint murmur of television sets. There were vines in the courtyard, laden with grapes, and a trellis of jasmine covering one wall, and on another a shelf of empty jars and slices of honeycomb.

Most of the courtyard was taken up by a metal garden table positioned right beneath the lemon tree, but there were bird feeders along the edges and a small vegetable patch in a square of soil, where Mustafa tried to grow herbs. Mostly they wilted because there was not enough sunlight. I watched my cousin as he pressed one of the lemon blossoms between his thumb and forefinger and breathed in the scent.

At these times, during the quiet of a Saturday evening, he began to overthink things, to contemplate; his mind could never rest, was never still. 'Do you ever imagine what it would be like to have a different life?' he asked me on one such evening.

'What do you mean?'

'It scares me sometimes to think how life can go one way or another. What if I was working somewhere in an office? What if you had listened to your father and ended up in his fabric shop? We have a lot to be grateful for.'

I didn't respond to this. While my life could easily have taken a different turn, there was no chance that Mustafa could have ended up in an office. No, his dark thoughts came from somewhere else, as if he had already become afraid of losing everything, as if some echo from the future was reaching back and whispering in his ear.

Much to Mustafa's annoyance, his son Firas would never get up from the computer to help with the meal. 'Firas!' Mustafa would call, heading back to the kitchen, 'Get up before you become glued to that seat!' But Firas would stay on the wicker chair in the living room, in his T-shirt and shorts. He was a lanky boy of twelve with a long face and slightly overgrown hair, and when he smiled, in defiance of his father, for a moment he resembled a Saluki hunting dog, the type you find in the desert.

Aya, who was just a year older than her brother, would hold Sami by the hand and set the table; by this time he was three and he trotted about like a little man on a mission. She would give him an empty plate or a cup to hold so that he would feel that he was helping her. Aya had long golden hair, like her mother, and Sami would pull at her curls whenever she bent down and giggle as they sprang back up. And then we would all get involved, even Firas – Mustafa would drag him from his chair by a skinny arm – and we would take steaming plates and colourful salads and dips and bread to the table in the courtyard. Sometimes we had red lentil and sweet potato soup with cumin, or kawaj with beef and courgettes, or stuffed artichoke hearts or green bean stew, or parsley and bulgur salad, or spinach with pine nuts and pomegranate. Later, honey-soaked baklava and lugaimat dough balls dripping with syrup or preserved apricots in jars that Afra had prepared. Firas would be on his phone and Mustafa would snatch it from his hands and put it in one of the empty honey jars, but he would never really get angry with his son – there was a certain humour between them, even when they were in battle with each other.

'When will I get it back?' Firas would say.

'When it snows in the desert.'

And by the time coffee was on the table, the phone would be out of the honey jar and back in Firas's hands. 'Next time, Firas, I will not put it an *empty* jar!'

As long as Mustafa was cooking or eating, he was happy. It was later, when the sun had set and the scent of the night jasmine engulfed us, especially when the air was still and thick, that his face would drop and I knew that he was thinking, that the stillness and darkness of the night had again brought whispers from the future.

'What is it, Mustafa?' I said, one evening when Dahab and Afra were loading the dishwasher after dinner, Dahab's booming laugh sending the birds up past the buildings and into the night sky. 'You don't seem yourself lately.'

'The political situation is getting worse,' he said. I knew he was right, though neither of us really wanted to talk about it. He stubbed out his cigarette and wiped his eyes with the back of his hand.

'Things will get bad. We all know it, don't we? But we're trying to continue living like we did before.' He stuffed a dough ball in his mouth as if to prove his point. It was late June, and in March of that year the civil war had just begun with protests in Damascus, bringing unrest and violence to Syria. I must have looked down at this point, and maybe he saw the worry on my face, for when I glanced up again, he was smiling.

'I'll tell you what, how about we create more recipes for Aya? I have some ideas – eucalyptus honey with lavender!' And his eyes gleamed as he began considering his new soap product, calling Aya to bring his laptop outside so that, together, they could work out the exact composition. Although Aya was only thirteen at the time, Mustafa was determined to be her teacher. Aya was busy playing with Sami – how the child loved her! He was always desperate to be close to her, always scanning for her with his large, grey eyes. They were the colour of his mother's eyes. Stone. Or the colour of a newborn baby's eyes before they change to brown, except his didn't change, and they didn't turn bluer either. Sami would follow Aya around, pulling at her skirt, and she would pick him up, high in her arms, to show him the birds in the feeders, or the insects and lizards that crawled over the walls and across the concrete patio.

With each recipe, Mustafa and Aya would consider the pigments and acids, the minerals in each type of honey, in order to create a combination that *worked perfectly*, as he put it. Then they would calculate the sugar density, granulation, tendency to absorb moisture from air, immunity from spoilage. I would give suggestions, and they would accept them with kind smiles, but it was Mustafa's mind that worked like the bees. He was the one with the ideas and the intelligence, while I was the one who made it all happen.

And for a while on those evenings, with the apricot sweets and the smell of night jasmine, Firas on his computer and Aya sitting beside us with Sami in her arms while he chewed her hair, and Afra and Dahab's laughter reaching us from the kitchen, on those nights, we were still happy. Life was close enough to normal for us to forget our doubts, or at least to keep them locked away somewhere in the dark recesses of our minds while we made plans for the future.

When the trouble first started, Dahab and Aya left. Mustafa convinced them to go without him. As his fears began to be confirmed, he very quickly made plans, but he needed to stay a while longer to see to the bees. At the time I thought he was being too hasty, that his mother's death when he was a child – which had haunted him for as long as I knew him – had somehow made him overprotective of the women in his life, and as a result Dahab and Aya were among the first to leave the neighbourhood and were fortunately spared from what was to come. Mustafa had a friend in England, a professor of sociology who had moved there some years ago on account of work, and this man had telephoned Mustafa and urged him to make his way to the United Kingdom; he was convinced the situation would get worse. Mustafa gave his wife and daughter enough money to see them through the journey, while he stayed in Syria with Firas.

'I can't just abandon the bees, Nuri,' he'd said one night, his large hand coming down over his face and his beard, as if he was trying to wipe off the sombre expression he always wore now. 'The bees are family to us.'

Before things became really bad, Mustafa and Firas would join us for dinner in the evenings and we would sit on the veranda together and watch the city below and hear the rumble of a distant bomb, see the smoke rising into the sky. Later, as the situation worsened, we started to talk about leaving together. We would gather around my illuminated globe in the half darkness of early evening while he traced with his finger the journey Dahab and Aya had made. It had been easier for them. In a thick leather wallet, Mustafa had the names and numbers of various smugglers. We went through the books, checking the finances, making calculations about the possible cost of our escape. Of course it was hard to predict, smugglers changed their rates on a whim, but we had a plan, and Mustafa loved plans and lists and itineraries.

They made him feel safe. But I knew this was just talk; Mustafa wasn't ready to leave the bees.

One night, late in the summer, vandals destroyed the hives. They set fire to them, and by the time we got to the apiaries in the morning they were burned to char. The bees had died and the field was black. I will never forget the silence, that deep, never-ending silence. Without the clouds of bees above the field, we were faced with a stillness of light and sky. In that moment, as I stood at the edge of the field where the sun was slanting across the ruined hives, I had a feeling of emptiness, a quiet nothingness that entered me every time I inhaled. Mustafa sat down on the ground in the middle of the field with his legs crossed and his eyes closed. I walked around scanning the ground for live bees and stamped on them because they had no hives or colony. Most of the hives had crumbled completely but a few stood like skeletons with their numbers still visible: twelve, twenty-one, one hundred and twenty-one – the colonies of grandmother, mother and daughter. I knew because I had split the hives myself. Three generations of bees. But they were all gone now. I went home and tucked Sami into bed, sitting for a while beside him as he slept, then I went to the veranda and watched the darkening sky and the brooding city below.

At the bottom of the hill was the Queiq. The last time I saw the river it was full of rubbish. In the winter they fished out the bodies of men and boys. Their hands were tied. Bullets in their heads. That winter day in Bustan al-Qasr, in the southern neighbourhood, I watched them pull the bodies out. I followed them to an old school, where they were laid out in the courtyard. Inside the building it was dark and there were lit candles in a bucket of sand. A middle-aged woman knelt on the floor next to another bucket, full of water. She was going to clean the faces of the dead men, she said, so that the women who loved them would recognise them when they came searching. If I had been one of the dead men in the river, Afra would have climbed a mountain to find me. She would have swum to the bottom of that river, but that was before they blinded her.

Afra was different before the war. She used to make such a mess all the time. If she was baking, for example, there would be flour on every surface, even on Sami. He would be covered in it. When she painted, she made a mess. And if Sami was painting too, it was even worse, as though they had shaken loaded brushes at the room. Even when she spoke she was messy, throwing words out here, there, taking them back, throwing out different ones. Sometimes she even interrupted herself. When she laughed, she laughed so hard the house would shake.

But when she was sad my world was dark. I didn't have a choice about this. She was more powerful than I. She cried like a child, laughed like bells ringing, and her smile was the most beautiful I've ever seen. She could argue for hours without ever pausing. Afra loved, she hated, and she inhaled the world like it was a rose. All this was why I loved her more than life.

The art she made was amazing. She won awards for her paintings of urban and rural Syria. On Sunday mornings we would all go to the market and set up a stall, just opposite

Hamid, who sold spices and tea. The stall was in the covered part of the souq. It was dark and a bit musty there but you could smell cardamom, cinnamon, aniseed and a million other spices. Even in that dim light, the landscapes in her paintings were not still. It was like they were moving, like the sky in them was moving, like the water in them was moving.

You should have seen the way she was with the customers who approached the stall, businessmen and women, mainly from Europe or Asia. At these times she would sit, very quietly, Sami on her knee, her eyes fixed on the customers, while they moved closer to a painting, lifting their glasses, if they wore them, then stepping back, often so far back they bumped into Hamid's customers, and then they would freeze there for a long time. And often the customers would say, 'Are *you* Afra?' And she would reply, 'Yes, I am Afra.' And that would be enough. Painting sold.

There was a whole world in her, and the customers could see this. For that moment, while they stared at the painting and then looked at her, they saw what she was made of. Afra's soul was as wide as the fields and desert and sky and sea and river that she painted, and as mysterious. There was always more to know, to understand, and as much as I knew, it wasn't enough, I wanted more. But in Syria there is a saying: inside the person you know, there is a person you do not know. I loved her from the day I met her, at my cousin Ibrahim's eldest son's wedding, at the Dama Rose Hotel, Damascus. She was wearing a yellow dress, with a silk hijab. And her eyes, not the blue of the sea, or the blue of the sky, but the inky blue of the Queiq River, with swirls of brown and green.

I remember the night of our wedding, two years later, and how she had wanted me to take off her hijab. I removed the hairpins, gently, one by one, unwrapping the material and seeing for the first time her long black hair, so dark, it was like the sky above the desert on a night with no stars.

But what I loved most was her laugh. She laughed like we would never die.

When the bees died, Mustafa was ready to leave Aleppo. We were about to go when Firas went missing, so we waited for him. Mustafa would hardly talk during this time, his mind completely preoccupied, imagining one thing or another. Every so often he would make a suggestion about where Firas might be. 'Maybe he has gone to find one of his friends, Nuri,' or, 'Maybe he can't bring himself to leave Aleppo – he is hiding somewhere so that we will stay,' or, one time, 'Maybe he has died, Nuri. Maybe my son has died.'

Our bags were packed and we were ready, but the days and nights passed with no sign of Firas. So Mustafa worked in a morgue in an abandoned building, where he would record the details and cause of death – bullets, shrapnel, explosion. It was strange to see him indoors, shut away from the sun. He had a black book, and he worked round the clock, writing down with the stub of a pencil the details of the dead. When he found identification on the corpses, his task was easier; other times he would record a distinguishing feature, like the colour of their hair or eyes, the particular shape of their nose, a mole on their left cheek. Mustafa did this until that winter day when I brought his son in from the river. I recognised the teenage boy dead on the slabs in the courtyard of the school. I asked two men with a car to help me take the body to the morgue. When Mustafa saw Firas, he asked us to lay him down on the table, then he closed his boy's eyes and stood for a long time, unmoving, holding his hand. I stood in the doorway while the other men left, the sound of an engine, the car pulling away, and then there was stillness, such stillness, and the light came in from the window above the table where the boy was lying, where Mustafa was standing holding on to his hand. For a while there was no sound, not a bomb or a bird or a breath.

Then Mustafa moved away from the table, put on his glasses and carefully sharpened the small pencil with a knife, and, sitting down at his desk, he opened the black book and wrote:

Name – My beautiful boy.
Cause of death – This broken world.

And that was very the last time Mustafa recorded the names of the dead.

Exactly a week after this, Sami was killed.

2

THE SOCIAL WORKER SAYS SHE is here to help us. Her name is Lucy Fisher and she seems impressed that I can speak English so well. I tell her about my job in Syria, about the bees and the colonies, but she doesn't really hear me, I can tell. She is preoccupied with the papers in front of her.

Afra won't even turn her face towards her. If you didn't know she was blind you would think that she was looking out of the window. There's a bit of sun today and it's reflecting off her irises, which makes them look like water. Her hands are clasped together on the kitchen table and her lips are sealed tight. She knows some English, enough to get by, but she won't talk to anyone except me. The only other person I heard her speak to was Angeliki. Angeliki, whose breasts were leaking with milk. I wonder if she managed to find her way out of those woods.

'How is the accommodation, Mr and Mrs Ibrahim?' Lucy Fisher with the big blue eyes and silver-rimmed glasses consults her papers as if the answer to her question is in them. I'm struggling to see what the Moroccan man was talking about.

She looks up at me now and her face is a burst of warmth.

'I find it very clean and safe,' I say, 'compared with other places.' I don't tell her about these other places, and I definitely don't tell her about the mice and cockroaches in our room. I fear it would appear ungrateful.

She doesn't ask many questions, but explains that we will soon be interviewed by an immigration officer. She pushes her glasses up the ridge of her nose and reassures me in a soft and precise voice that once we receive the papers to prove we are claiming asylum, Afra will be able to see a doctor about the pain in her eyes. She glances at Afra and I notice that Lucy Fisher's hands are clasped in front of her in exactly the same way. There is something about this that I find odd. Then she hands me a bunch of papers. A packet from the Home Office: information about claiming asylum, eligibility, notes about screening, notes about the interview process. I skim through and she waits patiently, watching me.

To stay in the UK as a refugee you must be unable to live safely in any part of your own country because you fear persecution there.

'Any part?' I say. 'Will you send us back to a different part?'

She frowns, pulling at a strand of her hair, and her lips tighten as if she has eaten something horrible.

'What you need to do now,' she says, 'is get your story straight. Think about what you're going to say to the immigration officer. Make sure it's all clear and coherent and as straightforward as possible.'

'But will you send us back to Turkey or Greece? What does persecution mean to you?' I say this louder than I meant to and my arm begins to throb. I rub the thick line of tight flesh and red tissue, remembering the edge of the knife, and Lucy Fisher's face is blurred, my hands are shaking. I undo the top button of my shirt. I try to keep my hands still.

'Is it hot in here?' I say.

She says something I cannot hear, I see only that her lips are moving. She is standing up now, and I can feel Afra shifting in her seat beside me. There is the sound of running water. A rushing river. But I see a sparkle, like the edge of a very sharp knife. Lucy Fisher's hand turning the handle of the tap, walking towards me, placing the glass in my hands and lifting it up to my face as if I am a child. I drink the water, all of it, and she sits down. I can see her clearly now and she looks frightened. Afra places her hand on my leg.

The sky cracks. It is raining. Torrential rain. Worse even than Leros where the land was saturated with rain and sea. I realise that she's spoken, I hear her voice through the rain, I hear the word *enemy*, and she stares at me, frowning, and her white face looks flushed.

'Excuse me?' I say.

'I said we're here to help you as much as we can.'

'I heard the word *enemy*,' I say.

She thrusts her shoulders back and purses her lips, she

glances again at Afra, and in the spark of anger that fires up her face and eyes, I see what the Moroccan man was talking about. But it's not me she's angry with; she can't really see me.

'All I said was that I'm not your enemy.' Her voice is apologetic now, she shouldn't have said that, it slipped out, there is pressure on her, I can see it in the way she tugs at that strand of hair. But the words ring out still in the room, even as she packs her things together, even as she speaks to Afra, who now nods her head very slightly at her, if only to acknowledge her presence.

'I hope you are OK, Mr Ibrahim,' she says as she leaves.

I wish I knew who my enemy was.

Later, I step out into the concrete garden and sit on the chair beneath the tree. I remember the humming of the bees, the sound of peace, I can almost smell the honey, lemon blossoms and aniseed, but this is suddenly replaced by the hollow smell of ash.

There is a buzzing . Not a collective sound like thousands of bees in the apiaries, but a single buzz. On the ground by my feet there is a bee. When I look closely I see that she has no wings. I put my hand out and she crawls onto my finger, making her way onto my palm – a bumblebee, plump and furry, such soft pile, with broad bands of yellow and black and a long tongue tucked under her body. She is crawling over the back of my wrist now so I take her inside with me and sit in the armchair and watch her as she nestles into my hand, preparing to sleep. In the living room the landlady brings us tea with milk. It's busy in here tonight. Most of the women have gone to bed, apart from one, who is talking in low whispers to a man beside her in Farsi. I can tell from the way she is wearing her hijab loose over her hair that she is probably from Afghanistan.

The Moroccan man slurps the tea like it's the best thing he's ever tasted. He smacks his lips together after each gulp. He checks his phone occasionally, then closes his book and tap-taps it with his palm like it's the head of a child.

'What's that on your palm?' he says.

I hold out my hand so that he can see the bee. 'She has no wings,' I say. 'I suspect that she has the deformed wing virus.'

'You know,' he says, 'in Morocco there is a honey road. People come from all over the world to taste our honey. In Agadir there are waterfalls and mountains and plenty of flowers that attract people and bees. I wonder what these British bees are like.' He leans in closer to take a better look, lifts his hand as if he is about to pet her with his finger like she's a tiny dog, but changes his mind. 'Does she sting?' he says.

'She can.'

He moves his hand to the safety of his lap. 'What will you do with her?'

'There's not much I can do. I'll take her back outside. She won't live very long like this – she's been banished from her colony because she has no wings.'

He looks out through the glass doors into the courtyard.

It is a small concrete square with flagstones and one cherry tree in the middle.

I get up and press my face against the glass. It is nine o'clock and the sun is just setting. The cherry tree is tall and black against the glowing sky.

'Now it's sunny,' I say, 'but in three minutes it will rain. Bees don't come out in rain. They will never come out in rain, and here it rains seventy per cent of the time.'

'I think English bees are different,' he says. When I turn to face him he is smiling again. I don't like it that he finds me amusing.

There is a bathroom downstairs and one of the men has gone to use the toilet. His stream in the toilet bowl sounds like a waterfall.

'Bloody foreigner,' says the Moroccan man, getting up to go to bed. 'Nobody stands up to urinate. Sit down!'

I go out into the courtyard and place the bee on the flower of a heather plant by the fence.

In the corner of the room there is a computer with Internet access. I sit down at the desk to see if Mustafa has sent me another message. He left Syria before me and we have been emailing each other throughout our journeys. He is waiting for me in the north of England in *Yorkshire*. I remember how his words kept me moving. *Where there are bees there are flowers, and where there are flowers there is new life and hope.* Mustafa is the reason I came here. He is the reason that Afra and I kept going until we got to the United Kingdom. But now all I can do is stare at the reflection of my face on the screen. I do not want Mustafa to know what has become of me. We are finally in the same country, but if we meet he will see a broken man. I do not believe he will recognise me. I turn away from the screen.

I wait there until the room empties out, until all the residents with their foreign tongues and foreign manners have left and the only sound is the traffic in the distance. I imagine a beehive swarming with yellow bees, and that when they exit they head right up into the sky and away to find flowers. I try to picture the land beyond, the highways and the streetlights and the sea.

The sensor light suddenly comes on in the garden. From where I'm sitting in the armchair facing the doors, I can see a shadow, something small and dark dashing quickly across the patio. It seems to be a fox. I get up to take a look, and the light goes off. I press my face against the glass, but the thing is larger than a fox and standing upright. It moves and the light flashes on again. It is a young boy with his back to me. He is looking through a gap in the fence, into the other garden. I knock hard on the glass but he doesn't turn. I search for the key and find it hanging on a nail behind the curtain. When I approach him, the boy turns to face me, as if he has been waiting for me, looking at me with those black eyes asking for the answers to all the questions in the world.

'Mohammed,' I say softly, in case I scare him away.

'Uncle Nuri,' he says, 'See that garden – there's so much green in there!'

He steps aside so I can take a look. It's so dark that I can't see any green. Only the soft shadows of bushes and trees.

'How did you find me?' I say, but he doesn't answer. I feel that I need to be cautious. 'Would you like to come in?' But he sits down on the concrete, legs crossed, and peeks through the hole in the fence again. I sit down beside him.

'There is a seaside here,' he says.

'I know.'

'I don't like the sea,' he says.

'I know. I remember.' He is holding something in his hand. It's white and I can smell lemons, though there are no lemons here.

'What is that?' I say.

'A flower.'

'Where did you get it?' I open my palm and he places it there. He tells me that he picked it off the lemon tree in

Aleppo

was all dust. Afra wouldn't leave. Everyone else had gone. Even Mustafa was desperate to go now. But not Afra. Mustafa's house was on the road that led to the river and I would walk down the hill to visit him. It wasn't a long walk but there were snipers and I had to be careful. The birds were usually singing. The sound of birdsong never changes. Mustafa told me this many years ago. And whenever the bombs were silent, the birds came out to sing. They perched on the skeletons of trees and on craters and wires and broken walls, and they sang. They flew high above, in the untouched sky, and sang.

As I approached Mustafa's house I could hear, even from a distance, the faint sound of music. I always found him sitting on the bed in his half-bombed room, vinyl playing on an old record player, biting and sucking at the end of his cigarette, the smoke rising in clouds above him, on the bed beside him a purring cat. But on this day when I arrived, Mustafa was not there. The cat was asleep in the spot where he used to sit, its tail curled around its body. On the bedside cabinet, I found a photograph of the two of us that was taken the year we opened the business together. We were both squinting into the sun, Mustafa at least a foot taller than I was, the apiaries behind us. I knew we were surrounded by bees, though they weren't visible in the picture. Beneath the photograph was a letter.

Dear Nuri,

Sometimes I think that if I keep walking, I will find some light, but I know that I can walk to the other side of the world and there will still be darkness. It's not like the darkness of the night, which also has white light from the stars, from the moon. This darkness is inside me and has nothing to do with the outside world.

Now I have a picture of my son lying on that table, and nothing can make it fade. I see him, every time I close my eyes.

Thank you for coming with me every day to the garden. If only we had some flowers to put on his grave. Sometimes in my mind he is sitting at the table and he is eating lakhma. With the other hand he picks his nose and then he wipes it on his shorts and I tell him to stop being like his father, and he says, 'But you are my father!' and he laughs. That laughter. I can hear it. It flies above the land and disappears into the distance with the birds. I think this is his soul, it is free now. O Allah keep me alive as long as is good for me, and when death is better for me, take me.

Yesterday I went for a walk to the river, and I watched as four soldiers lined up a group of boys.

They blindfolded them and shot them, one by one, and they threw their bodies in the river. I stood back and watched all this and I imagined Firas standing there among them, the fear in his heart, knowing that he would die, the fact that he could not see what was happening and could only hear the gunshots. I hope he was the first in line to die. I never thought I would ever have such a wish. I shut my eyes too and listened, and in between the gunshots and the thuds of falling bodies, I heard a boy crying. He was calling for his father. The other boys were silent, too afraid to make a sound. There is always one person in a group who has more courage than the rest. It takes bravery to cry out, to release what is in your heart. Then he was silenced. I had a rifle in my hand. I found it last week on the side of the street, loaded with three bullets. So I had three shots and there were four men. I waited until their guard was down, till they sat on the bank of the river smoking cigarettes and put their feet in the water where they had thrown the bodies.

My aim was good. I got one in the head, one in the stomach, the third in the heart. The fourth man stood and held his hands up and when he realised I had no shots left, he fumbled for his gun and I ran. He saw my face and they will find me. I have to leave tonight. I must get to Dahab and Aya. I should not have waited this long to leave, but I didn't want to go without you and abandon you here in hell.

I cannot wait here to say goodbye. You must convince Afra to leave. You are too soft, too sensitive. This is an admirable quality when it comes to working with bees, but not now. I will be making my way to England, to find my wife and daughter. Leave this place, Nuri, it is no longer home. Aleppo is now like the dead body of a loved one, it has no life, no soul, it is full of rotting blood.

I have a memory of the first time you came to my father's apiaries in the mountains and you were standing there surrounded by bees, without protective gear, your hands shielding your eyes, and you said to me, 'Mustafa, this is where I want to be,' even though you knew your father wouldn't be happy. Remember that, Nuri. Remember the strength you had then. Take Afra and come and find me.

Mustafa

I sat down on the bed and cried, sobbed like a child, and from that day I kept the photograph and letter in my pocket, but Afra wouldn't leave, so I would go out every day and forage in the ruins for food and return with a gift for her. I'd find so many odd bits, broken or unbroken pieces of people's lives: a child's shoe, a dog's collar, a mobile phone, a glove, a key. Interesting to find a key when there are no doors to open. Come to think of it, even stranger to find a shoe or a glove when there is no longer a hand or a foot to fit it.

These were sad gifts. Nonetheless I'd offer them to her, place them on her lap, and wait for a reaction that never came. But I would keep trying. It was a good distraction. Every day I went out and found a new thing. One day, I found the best gift of all: a pomegranate.

'What did you see?' she said to me as I stood by the door.

She was sitting on the camp bed, where Sami used to sleep, facing the window, with her back against the wall. She reminded me of a cat, in her black hijab, with that white stone face and large grey eyes. No expression at all. I could only understand how she was feeling from her voice, or when she picked at her skin so hard she made it bleed.

The room smelled of warm bread, of normal life. I began to speak but stopped, and she turned her ear to me, a slight twitch of her head.

I saw that she'd made bread again. 'You made khubz?' I said.

'I made it for Sami,' she said. 'Not for you. But what did you see?'

'Afra . . .'

'I'm not an idiot, you know. I haven't lost my mind. I just wanted to make him some bread. Is that OK with you? My mind's sharper than yours, don't forget that. What did you see?'

'Do we have to do this every time?'

I watched her. She locked her fingers together.

'So . . . the houses,' I began, 'they're like carcasses, Afra. Carcasses. If you could see them you would cry.'

'You told me that yesterday.'

'And the grocery store, it's empty now. But there's fruit still in the crates where Adnan left them – pomegranates, and figs, and bananas, and apples. And they're all rotten now, and the flies, thousands of them swarming in the heat. But I rummaged through and I found a good one. And I brought it for you.' I walked towards her and placed the pomegranate on her lap. She took it, feeling its flesh with her fingers, turning it around, pressing it against her palms.

'Thank you,' she said. But there was no expression at all. I'd hoped the pomegranate would reach her. Before she'd spend hours peeling and deseeding them. She'd cut one in half, push out the centre a bit, then start whacking it with a wooden spoon, and when she'd filled the glass bowl to the top, she would smile and say she had a thousand jewels. I wished she would smile. But that was a stupid wish, and a selfish one. She had nothing to smile about. It would have been better to wish for this war to end. But I needed something to hold on to, and if she smiled, if by some miracle she smiled, it would have felt like finding water in the desert.

'Please tell me.' She wouldn't give up. 'What did you see?'

'I told you.'

'No. You told me what you saw yesterday. Not what you saw today. And today you saw someone die.'

'Your mind's playing tricks on you. It's all that darkness.' I shouldn't have said that. I apologised, once, twice, three times, but her face didn't change.

'I know from the way you were breathing when you came in,' she said.

'And how was I breathing?'

'Like a dog.'

'I was perfectly calm.'

'As calm as a storm.'

'OK, so when I left the grocer's,' I said, 'I took a bit of a detour. I wanted to see if Akram was still here, and I was on the long road that leads to Damascus, just past the bank, by that bend where that red loading van used to stop on Mondays?'

She nodded. She could see it now, in her mind. She needed all the details. I'd come to realise this; she needed the small details so that she could see it all, so that she could pretend that it was her eyes that saw it all. She nodded again, urging me on.

'So, I came up behind two armed men and overheard them taking bets on something. They were planning to use something for target practice. When they agreed the bets I realised they were talking about an eight-year-old boy who was playing alone on the road. I don't know what he was doing there to be honest. Why his mother would let him—'

'What was he wearing?' she said. 'The eight-year-old boy. What was he wearing?'

'A red jumper and a pair of blue shorts. They were jean shorts.'

'And what colour were his eyes?'

'I didn't see his eyes. I suppose they were brown.'

'Was it a boy I would know?'

'Maybe,' I said. 'I didn't recognise him.'

'And what was he playing?'

'He had a toy truck.'

'What colour?'

'Yellow.'

She was postponing the inevitable, holding on to the living boy for as long as possible, keeping him alive. I let her sit in silence for a few moments, while she turned it around in her mind. Perhaps she was memorising the colours, the boy's movements. She would keep them.

'Go on,' she said.

'I realised too late,' I said. 'One of them had taken the bet and shot him in the head. Everyone else ran and the street was deserted.'

'What did you do?'

'I couldn't move. The child was lying on the street. I couldn't move.'

'You could have been shot.'

'It wasn't a clean shot and he didn't die right away. His mother was inside the house on the same street and she was screaming. She wanted to go to him, but the men kept firing into the street, shouting. They were shouting, "You can't get to your child. You can't get to your child."'

I cried into my palms. I pressed my palms against my eyes. I wished I could take it away, what I saw. I wanted to take it all away.

Then I felt arms around me, and the smell of bread around me.

* * *

A bomb dropped in the darkness and the sky flashed and I helped Afra to get ready for bed. She knew her way around the house by now, feeling the walls with her hands, palms open, feet shuffling, and she could make bread, but at night she wanted me to undress her. She wanted me to fold her clothes, to place them on the chair by the bed where she used to put them. I took off her abaya as she lifted her arms over her head like a child. I removed her hijab and her hair fell onto her shoulders. Then she sat on the bed and waited for me while I got ready. It was quiet that night, no more bombs, and the room was full of peace and full of moonlight.

There was a huge crater in this room; the far wall and part of the ceiling were missing, leaving an open mouth into the garden and sky. The jasmine over the canopy caught the light and behind it the fig tree was black and hung low over the wooden swing, the one I'd made for Sami. The silence was hollow though; it lacked the echo of life. The war was always there. The houses were empty or home to the dead. Afra's eyes shone in the dim light. I wanted to hold her, to kiss the soft skin of her breasts, to lose myself in her. For one minute, just one, I forgot. Then she turned to me like she could see me, and as if she knew what I was thinking she said, 'You know, if we love something it will be taken away.'

We both lay down, and from beyond came the smell of fire and burnt things and ashes. Although she faced me, she wouldn't touch me. We hadn't made love since Sami died. But sometimes she let me hold her hand, and I circled my finger around her palm.

'We have to go, Afra,' I said.

'I've already told you. No.'

'If we stay—'

'If we stay, we'll die,' she said.

'Exactly.'

'Exactly.' Her eyes were open and blank now.

'You're waiting for a bomb to hit us. If you want it to happen, it will never happen.'

'Then I'll stop waiting. I won't leave him.'

I was about to say, 'But he's already left. Sami's gone. He's not here. He's not here in hell with us, he is somewhere else. And we're no closer to him by staying here.' And she would reply, 'I know that. I'm not stupid.'

So I remained silent. I traced my finger around her palm, while she waited for a bomb to hit us. And when I woke in the night I reached out to touch her, to make sure that she was still there, that we were still alive. And in the darkness I remembered the dogs eating human corpses in the fields where the roses used to be, and somewhere else in the distance I heard a wild screech, metal on metal, like a creature being dragged towards death. And I put my hand on her chest, between her breasts, and felt her heart beat, and I slept again.

In the morning the muezzin called to empty houses to come and pray. I went out to try to find some flour and eggs before the bread ran out. I dragged my feet in the dust. It was so thick, like walking through snow. There were burnt cars, lines of filthy washing hanging from abandoned terraces, electric wires dangling low over the streets, bombed-out shops, blocks of flats with their roofs blown off, piles of trash on the pavements. It all stank of death and burnt rubber. In the distance smoke rose, curling into the sky. I felt my mouth dry, my hands clench and shake, trapped by these distorted streets. In the land beyond, the villages were burnt, people flooding out like a river to get away, the women in terror because paramilitaries were on the loose and they feared being raped. But there, beside me, was a damask rose bush in full bloom. When I closed my eyes and breathed in the smell, I could pretend for a moment that I hadn't seen the things I'd seen.

When I looked up from the ground, I saw that I'd reached a checkpoint. Two soldiers stood in my path. They both held machine guns. One of them wore a checked keffiyeh. The other one took a gun from the back of a truck and pushed it against my chest.

'Take it,' the man said.

I tried to mimic my wife's face. I didn't want to show any emotion. They would eat me for it. The man pushed the gun harder into my chest, and I stumbled, falling back against the gravel.

He threw the gun on the ground and I looked up to see both men standing over me, and now the man with the keffiyeh was pointing his gun at my chest. I could no longer stay calm and I could hear myself begging for my life, grovelling with my knees in the dust.

'Please,' I was saying, 'it's not that I don't want to. I'd be proud, I'd be the proudest man in the world to take that gun in your name, but my wife is very ill, gravely ill, and she needs me to look after her.' Even while I was saying this I didn't think that they would care. Why would they? Children were dying every minute. Why would they care about my sick wife?

'I'm strong,' I said, 'and intelligent. I'll work hard for you. I just need a few days. That's all I'm asking for.'

The other man touched the man with the keffiyeh on the shoulder and he lowered his gun.

'The next time we see you,' the other man said, 'either you take a gun and stand beside us, or you find someone to take your body.'

I decided to go straight home. I sensed a shadow behind me as I walked and I wasn't sure if I was being followed or if it was my mind playing tricks on me: I kept imagining a cloaked figure, the type in childhood nightmares, hovering over the dust at my back. But when I turned around there was no one there.

I arrived home and Afra was sitting on the camp bed, her back against the wall, facing the window, holding the pomegranate in her hands, turning it around, feeling its flesh. Her ears pricked up when I entered the room, but before she could say anything I ran around the house, searching for a bag, cramming things into it.

'What's going on?' Her eyes searched the blankness.

'We're going.'

'No.'

'They'll kill me if we stay.' I was in the kitchen, filling

plastic water bottles from the tap. I packed an extra set of clothes for each of us. Then I searched under the bed for the passports and the stash of money. Afra didn't know about it – it was the money Mustafa and I had managed to put aside before the business collapsed, and I also had some in a private account, which I hoped I could still access once we got out of here. She was saying something from the other room. Words of protest. I packed Sami's passport too; I couldn't leave it here. Then I returned to the living room with our bags.

'I was stopped by the army. They held a gun to my chest,' I said.

'You're lying. Why has this never happened before?'

'Maybe before there were still younger men around. They didn't notice me. Had no reason to. We're the only stupid people left.'

'I won't go.'

'They'll kill me.'

'So be it.'

'I told them that I needed a few days to take care of you. They agreed to give me just a few days. If they see me again, and I don't join them, they'll kill me. They said I should find someone to take my body.'

At these last words, her eyes widened and there was sudden fear on her face, real fear. At the thought of losing me, maybe at the thought of my dead body, she came alive and stood up. She felt her way along the hallway and I followed, breathless, and then she lay on the bed and closed her eyes. I tried to reason with her, but she lay there like a dead cat, with her black abaya and her black hijab and that stone face that I now despised.

I sat on Sami's bed and stared out of the window and watched the grey sky, a metallic grey, and there were no birds. I sat there all day and all evening until the darkness swallowed me up. I remembered how the worker bees would travel to find new flowers and nectar and then come back to tell the other bees. The bee would shake her body – the angle of her dance across the comb told the other bees the direction of the flowers in relation to the sun. I wished that there was someone to guide me, to tell me what to do and which way to go, but I felt completely alone.

Just before midnight I lay down beside Afra. She hadn't moved an inch. I had the photograph and the letter beneath my pillow. And this time when I woke up in the middle of the night I saw that she was facing me and whispering my name.

'What?' I said.

'Listen.'

From the front of the house, footsteps and men's voices and then a laugh, a deep-throated laugh.

'What are they doing?' she said.

I climbed out of bed and walked quietly over to her side and took her hand, helping her up, leading her to the back door and out into the garden. She followed without question, without hesitation. I tapped my foot on the ground to find the metal roof, then slid it aside and helped her sit beside the hole with her legs over the edge so that I could climb in first and lower her in. Then I pulled the roof over us.

Our feet sank into inches of water, full of the lizards and insects that had made this space their home. I'd dug this hideout last year. Afra wrapped her arms around me and buried her face in the crook of my neck. We sat like this in the darkness, both blind now, in this grave made for two. In the deep quiet her breathing was the only sound left on earth. And maybe she was right. Maybe we should have died like this and nobody would need to take our bodies; and then some creature moved about, close to my left ear, and above us and outside things moved and broke and cracked. The men must have entered the house now. I could feel her shaking against me.

'Do you know what, Afra?' I said.

'What?'

'I need to fart.'

There was a second of silence and then she began to laugh. She laughed and laughed into my neck. It was a quiet laugh, but her whole body shook with it, and I tightened my grip around her, thinking that her laugh was the most beautiful thing left on earth. But for a while I couldn't actually tell if she was still laughing or if she'd started to cry, until I felt my neck wet with tears. And then her breathing was soft and she was asleep – as if this black hole was the only place she felt safe. Where inner darkness met outer darkness.

For a while I knew what it meant to be blind. And then memories blossomed, like dreams, so rich in colour. Life before war. Afra in a green dress, holding Sami by the hand;

he'd just started to walk and was waddling along beside her, pointing up as a plane crossed the cool blue sky. We were going somewhere. It was summer and she was walking in front with her sisters. Ola was wearing yellow. Zeinah, pink. Zeinah was flapping her arms around as she talked, in her usual way. The other two said, 'No!' in unison at something she said. There was a man beside me, my uncle. I could see his cane, hear its tap-tap-tap on concrete. He was telling me about work: he owned a café in Old Damascus, and he wanted to retire now, but his son didn't want to take over the business, the lazy, ungrateful boy; he married the monkey for its money, and the money went and the monkey stayed a monkey . . .' And in that moment Afra lifted Sami onto her hip and then turned back and smiled and her eyes caught the light and turned to water. And then it all faded. Where were these people now?

I blinked in the darkness. It was impenetrable. In her sleep, Afra sighed. I asked myself if I should break her neck, put her out of her misery, give her the peace she wanted. Sami's grave was in this garden. She would be close to him. She wouldn't need to leave him. All her self-torture would be over.

'Nuri,' she said.

'Hmmm?'

'I love you.'

I didn't reply and her words became part of the darkness, I let them sink into the soil, into the waterlogged earth.

'Will they kill us?' she asked, a slight tremor in her voice.

'You're scared.'

'No. We're so close to it now.'

Then there were footsteps close by and the voices became louder. 'I told you,' a man said. 'I told you not to let him go.'

I held my breath and I held her tight so that she couldn't move. I thought of covering her mouth with my hand. I didn't trust her not to speak, not to call out. It was her choice now: to live or to die. Above, there was movement and shuffling and mumbled words, and then, finally, the footsteps retreated. It wasn't until Afra released her breath that I realised she still had an instinct to live.

It was morning when I decided that the men must have left, there had been no sound for a few hours and light spilled through at the edges of the metal roof, illuminating the mud walls. I pushed up the roof and saw the sky, vast and unscathed: the blue of dreams. Afra was awake but silent, lost in her black world.

When we entered the house I wished I was blind too. The living room was trashed and the walls covered in graffiti. *We win or we die.*

'Nuri?'

I didn't reply.

'Nuri . . . what have they done?'

I watched her stand there among the broken things, a dark ghost of a figure, erect and unmoving and blind.

But I remained silent and she took a step forward and knelt down, searching with her hands. From the floor she picked up a broken ornament: a crystal bird with the words *99 names of Allah* inscribed in gold on an open wing. A wedding present from her grandmother.

She turned it around in her hands, as she had done with the pomegranate, feeling its lines, its curves. Then, in a soft voice, like the voice of a child resurrected from years past, she began to recite the list engraved in her mind:

'The maker of order, the subduer, the knower of all, the seer of all, the hearer of all, the giver of life, the taker of life . . .'

'Afra!' I said.

She put the ornament down and leant forward, searching the space ahead with her fingers. Now she picked up a toy car. I had put them all away in the cupboard a few weeks after Sami died. Now I couldn't bear to look at them, broken and strewn across the floor. There was even a jar of chocolate spread there, Sami's favourite treat, rolling away from Afra and stopping at the foot of the chair. It must have been mouldy by now, but I had kept it in the cupboard with all of the things that reminded me of him. When she realised that she had a toy car in her hand, Afra put it down immediately and turned her head towards me, somehow managing to catch my eye with hers.

'I'm going,' I said, 'whether you come or not.'

I left her side and searched for our bags. I found them in the bedroom, untouched, slung them over my shoulders and returned to the living room, to find her standing in the middle of the room. In her open palms she had colourful pieces of Lego: the remnants of a house that Sami had built – the house we would live in when we got to England, he had said, once he'd agreed that it would be a good thing to go.

'There'll be no bombs there,' he'd said, 'and the houses

won't break like these do.' I wasn't sure if he'd meant the Lego houses or the real houses, and then it saddened me when I realised that Sami had been born into a world where everything could break. Real houses crumbled, fell apart. Nothing was solid in Sami's world. And yet somehow he was trying to imagine a place where the buildings didn't fall down around him. I had stored the Lego house safely in the cupboard, carefully, to make sure it was exactly as Sami had left it. I'd even thought of taking it apart and reassembling it with glue, so that we could always keep it.

'Nuri,' Afra said, breaking the silence, 'I'm done. Please. Take me away from here.'

And she stood there with her eyes moving about the room, as if she could see it all.

3

I WAKE UP FLAT ON MY back in the garden. It has been raining and my clothes are damp. There is one tree in this concrete space, its roots cracking through the paving and poking into my back. I realise that I'm holding some blossoms in my fist. There is someone standing above me, blocking the sun.

'What are you doing there, *geezer?*' The Moroccan man looks down at me, a broad smile on his face. He speaks in Arabic. 'Did you sleep here in the garden, geezer?' He holds out his hand to me, unreasonably strong for such an old man and stable on his feet as he pulls me up.

'Giza?' I say, half dazed.

'Geeeeezer,' he says, and chuckles. 'The man in the shop says *geeeeezer*. It means old man.'

I follow him inside, into the warmth. He tells me that Afra

has been looking for me. 'She's been crying,' he says, which I find hard to believe, and when I see her in the kitchen she is already dressed and is sitting stiff at the table just as she was when Lucy Fisher was here. It doesn't seem to me like she's been crying, and I haven't seen or heard her cry since Aleppo. She is holding Mohammed's marble, twirling it around in her fingers. I've tried to take it from her before but she won't let it go.

'So you can dress yourself then?' I say. But I immediately regret these words when I see her face drop.

'Where did you go?' she says. 'I was up most of the night and I didn't know where you were.'

'I fell asleep downstairs.'

'Hazim told me you were sleeping in the garden!'

My body stiffens.

'He is kind,' she says. 'He said he would find you and he told me not to worry.'

I decide to go for a walk. It's my first time outside. This whole place is strange, the shops standing shabby and proud – Go Go Pizza, Chilli Tuk-Tuk, Polskie Smaki, Pavel India, Moshimo. At the end of the road there is a convenience store where someone is playing Arabic music very loudly. I make my way down to the sea. There is no sand on this beach, only pebbles and shingle, but along the promenade by the seafront there is a huge sandpit for children to play in. A boy in red shorts is making a sandcastle. It's not hot, but they think it is, so his mother has put him in shorts, and this boy is scooping up sand and placing it carefully into a blue bucket, until it is full. He evens it out with precision, using the handle of his spade.

Kids are running around with ice cream and lollies the size of their heads. The sandcastle boy has made a whole city – he's used bits of plastic, bottle tops, sweet wrappers, to add colour to his buildings. He's made a flag out of a lost sock and a candyfloss stick. He crowns the castle in the middle with a teacup.

The boy gets up and stands back to admire his creation. It's impressive, he's even used the teacup to make houses to surround the castle, and a water bottle looks like a glass skyscraper. He must sense I am staring because he turns and glances at me, for a moment pausing and holding my gaze. He has that innocent, preoccupied look, like the children before the war. For a moment I think he is going to say something to me, but a girl calls him to come and play. She entices him with a ball. He hesitates, taking one last glance at his marvellous creation, looking at me one more time, before he sprints off, abandoning it.

I sit for a while on the promenade by the sandpit and watch the sun move across the sky. In the afternoon the place is quieter, clouds have gathered, the children have gone. I take the asylum documentation out of my backpack.

To stay in the UK as a refugee you must be unable to live safely in any part of your own country because you fear persecution there.

The sky cracks and there's a flash of lightning. Thick raindrops fall onto the piece of paper in my hand.

UK.

Any part.

Persecution.

It rains harder. I put the documents into my backpack and start up the hill towards the B&B.

Afra is sitting by the double doors in the living room; there are a few other residents milling around and the TV is on full blast. The Moroccan man raises his eyebrows. 'How're you doin', geezer?' He says the whole sentence in English now, his dark eyes sparkling.

'Not too bad, geezer,' I say, and force a smile. This satisfies him. He laughs with his chest and slaps his hand on his knee. I sit at the desk again and stare at my reflection in the computer screen. I touch the keyboard but I cannot bring myself to check for emails. My eyes keep moving to the glass doors. Whenever the wind picks up and the light comes on, I expect to see the shape of Mohammed in the garden.

I go out into the courtyard and search for the bee, and eventually I find her crawling over some twigs and fallen petals beneath the tree. When I put my hand out she crawls onto my finger and makes her way to my palm, and there she tucks in her legs and nestles, so I take her inside with me.

The landlady brings us all tea on a tray, and some Kenyan sweets, yellow with turmeric. She speaks English perfectly, from what I can tell anyway. She is a tiny woman, so small, like she was meant to be a doll. She is wearing shoes with huge wooden blocks at the ends of her skinny legs and, as she clomps around the living room handing out the sweets and tea, she reminds me of a baby elephant.

The Moroccan man told me that she is an accountant; she works part time in an office in South London and the rest of the time she runs this bed and breakfast. The council gives her money to do this and to keep us here. She scrubs the walls and the floors as if she is trying to wipe away the filth of our journeys. But there is something else about her – her story is not simple, I can tell. There is a mahogany cabinet in the corner of the living room. It is lacquered with a sheen like water, and it is full of glasses for alcohol. Every day she polishes spotless glasses. She stands there with a cloth that looks like a torn-off part of a man's striped shirt – I have noticed there is even a button on it. She can't get rid of the green mould on the walls though, or the grease in the kitchen that's as thick as my skin, but I can see she takes pride in caring for us. She remembers all of our names, which is a great feat considering how many of us come and go. She spends some time talking to the woman from Afghanistan, asking her where she got her hijab, which is handwoven with gold thread.

'The bee is still alive!' the Moroccan man says.

I look at him and smile. 'She's a fighter,' I say, 'and it was raining last night. She won't survive out there though, not for long, if she can't fly.'

I take the bee back outside, put her on a flower and I go to bed with Afra. I help her get undressed and I lie down to sleep beside her.

'Where is Mustafa?' she says. 'Have you heard from him?'

'Not for a long time,' I say.

'Have you checked your emails? Maybe he is trying to get hold of you? Does he know we are here?'

There is a strange sound now, a whistle deep in the sky. 'Can you hear that?' I say.

'It's the rain on the window,' she says.

'Not that. The whistling. There is a whistle. It doesn't stop. Like a dust storm is coming.'

'There's no dust storm here,' she says. 'Only rain or no rain.'

'You can't hear it then?'

She looks concerned now and rests her head on her palm. She is about to say something and I laugh, stopping her. 'It was cold but sunny today! Now it's raining! This English weather is like a madman! Maybe you should come out tomorrow? We can go for a walk along the seafront.'

'No,' she says. 'I can't. I don't want to be out in this world.'

'But you're free now, you can go outside. You don't have to be afraid anymore.'

She doesn't say anything in response.

'A boy made the most amazing sandcastle, a whole city, with houses and a skyscraper!'

'That's nice,' she says.

There was a time when she wanted to know, when she would ask me what I saw. Now she doesn't want to know anything at all.

'We have to contact Mustafa,' she says.

* * *

The darkness gets to me, and the way my wife smells gets to me, that mixture of rose perfume and sweat. She puts the perfume on before she goes to bed, takes the glass bottle out of her pocket and dabs it on her wrists and neck. The other residents are still talking in the living room downstairs, that strange combination of tongues. Someone laughs, and there are footsteps on the stairs. The floorboards creak, and I know it is the Moroccan man; I've come to recognise the sound of his walk. He has a particular way of pausing. It seems random at first, but there is a specific rhythm to it. He walks past our room, and at that moment I hear a marble rolling over the planks of wood. I know the sound. I jump up and turn on the light. I find Mohammed's marble moving towards the rug, pick it up and look at the glass under the light, the red vein running through the middle.

'What is it?' Afra says.

'It's just the marble. It's nothing. Go to sleep.'

'Put it on the dressing table next to me,' she says.

I do as she says and get back into bed, this time lying with my back to her. She puts her hand on my back, presses her palm against my spine as if she is feeling for my breath. My eyes stay open in the dark because I am afraid of the

night

fell and we were in Bab al-Faraj, in the old city. We were waiting beneath a narenj tree for a Toyota. The corpse of a man was waiting with us. The Toyota was going to be a pickup, no headlights, with metal bars on the sides, the type that usually transports livestock like cows and goats. The dead man was lying on his back with one arm bent over his head. The man was probably in his mid-twenties, wearing a black jumper and black jeans. I didn't tell Afra that he was there.

This was where the smuggler had told us to wait.

The dead man's face suddenly lit up. A glow of white light. On and off. There was a phone in his hand, the hand that was bent over his head. His eyes were brown, thick eyebrows. An old scar on his left cheek. The glint of a silver chain, a calligraphy name necklace: Abbas.

'It's beautiful here,' she said. 'I know exactly where we are.'

There were once vines across this street and at the bottom a set of steps that led to the gated terrace of a school.

'We're by that clock,' she said, 'and there's that café around the corner with the rosewater ice cream, where we took Sami that time, remember?'

* * *

Just behind the buildings, the time on the Bab al-Faraj Clock Tower glowed green. Eleven fifty-five. Five minutes. I stood there helpless, watching her, her expression warm with memory. Since she had laughed and cried she had come back to life, in fragments. A little of her showed through a crack and then she was gone again. Now, standing there with her face so close to mine, I could see the desire, the determination to hold on to an illusion, a vision of life, of Aleppo. The old Afra would have been disgusted by this. I felt suddenly afraid of her. The phone stopped flashing. It was darker now.

In the distance I could see the citadel on its elliptical mound, like the tip of a volcano.

The wind blew and brought with it the smell of roses.

'Can you smell roses?' I said.

'I'm wearing the perfume,' she said.

She rummaged in her pocket and pulled out a glass bottle. She held it in her palm. I had it made it for her the year we got married. A friend of mine owned a rose distillery and I'd selected the roses myself.

She was whispering now. She wanted to come back in spring when the flowers were in bloom. She would wear the perfume and her yellow dress, and we would walk together. We would start at our house and move through the city and up the hill to the souq. Then we would wander through the covered lanes of the old market, the alleyways of spices and soaps and teas and bronze and gold and silver and dried lemons and honey and herbs, and I would buy her a silk scarf.

I suddenly felt sick. I'd already told her that the souq was empty, some of the alleys bombed and burnt, only soldiers and rats and cats wandered through the lanes where all those traders and tourists once walked. All the stalls had been abandoned, apart from one where an old man sold coffee to the soldiers. The citadel was now a military base, occupied by soldiers and surrounded by tanks.

The al-Madina Souq was one of the oldest markets in the world, a key post on the Silk Road, where traders would travel from Egypt and Europe and China. Afra was talking about Aleppo like it was a magical land out of a story. It was like she'd forgotten everything else, the years leading up to the war, the riots, the dust storms, the droughts, the way we had struggled even then, even before the bombs, to stay alive.

The dead man's phone flashed again. Someone was desperate to speak to him. A hoopoe bird was sitting in the narenj tree, its inky eyes shimmering. The bird opened its wings, and black and white stripes caught the phone's light. I became afraid of the light. I knelt down and peeled the phone from the man's stiff fingers and stuffed it into my rucksack.

The clock struck twelve. From the distance, the soft rumble of an engine. Afra straightened up, her face full of fear. A Toyota took the bend, lights off, wheels churning the ash. The driver got out, rough features, bearded, bald head, black T-shirt, army boots, army trousers, bumbag, handgun at his waist. He was a replica of a regime fighter: he'd shaved his head, his beard too. A trick in case he got caught by Assad's Shabiha.

He stood there for a moment, inspecting me. Afra moved her feet in the dust, but the man didn't look at her.

'You can call me Ali,' he said finally, and he smiled, a broad smile, so wide that his whole face creased into folds. But something about his smile made me uncomfortable; it reminded me of another smile, a windup clown that Sami's grandmother had bought him from the market. The smile suddenly faded and Ali's eyes now darted around in the darkness.

'What is it?' I said.

'I was told three people.'

I gestured to the man on the ground.

'Too bad.' There was an unexpected tone of sadness in Ali's voice and he stood for a moment over the man's body, head bent, before he knelt down and took a gold wedding band from the dead man's finger, placing it neatly on his own. He sighed and looked up at the clock tower, then at the sky. I followed his gaze.

'It's a clear night. We are in a dome of stars. We have four hours before sunrise. We have to make it to Armanaz by three if you're going to get across the border by four.'

'How long does the journey take?' Afra said.

Ali looked at her now as if he was seeing her for the first time, but he replied with his eyes fixed on me, 'Just under two hours. And you're not going to sit with me. Get in the back.'

There was a cow in the back of the pickup, the floor scattered with its faeces. I helped Afra in and the driver instructed us to sit low so we wouldn't be seen. If we were caught, the snipers would shoot the cow instead. The cow stared at us. The engine started and the Toyota moved as quietly as possible through the ash streets, bumping over rubble.

'There's a phone ringing,' Afra said.

'What do you mean?'

'I can feel it vibrating on my leg, in your bag. Who's calling us?'

'It's not my phone,' I said. 'I switched mine off.'

'Whose phone is it then?'

I took the phone from the rucksack. Fifty missed calls. It rang again.

Zujet Abbas: *the Wife of Abbas*.

'Who is it?' Afra said. 'Answer it.'

'Give me your hijab,' I said.

Afra unwrapped the hijab from her head and handed it to me. I covered my head with it and answered the phone.

'Abbas!'

'No.'

'Where are you now, Abbas?'

'No, I'm sorry, I'm not Abbas.'

'Where is he? Can I talk to him? Did he get picked up? Did they pick him up?'

'Abbas isn't here.'

'But I was talking to him. We got cut off.'

'When?'

'Not long. About an hour. Please let me speak to him.'

Just then the pickup stopped, the engine was turned off, footsteps approached. The driver pulled the hijab off me, threw it in the back, and I felt metallic cold between my eyebrows.

'Are you stupid?' Ali said. 'Do you have a death wish?' He pushed the gun into my forehead, his eyes gleaming. From the phone the wife of Abbas was saying, 'Abbas, Abbas . . .' again and again and again.

'Give me that!' the smuggler said, and so I handed him the phone and we set off again.

We were heading to Urum al-Kubra, about twenty kilometres west of Aleppo. We meandered through the ruins of the old city; the western neighbourhoods were held by government forces, the rebels had the east. The river could see it all, running now through the no-man's-land between the opposing front lines. If something was tossed in the Queiq on the government side, eventually it made its way to the rebels. As we reached the edge of the city we passed an enormous billboard of Bashar al-Assad, his blue eyes bright, like jewels, even in the darkness. The poster was intact, completely untouched.

We reached the dual carriageway and the world suddenly opened up, black fields all around us, mulberry trees and olive trees blue under the moon. I knew that battles had been fought between rebels and Syrian troops amid the Dead Cities, the hundreds of long-abandoned Greco-Roman towns that littered the countryside outside Aleppo. In this blue emptiness, I tried to forget the things I knew, the things I'd heard. I would try to imagine that it was all untouched. Just like Bashar al-Assad's blue eyes. What was lost would be lost forever. The Crusader castles, mosques and churches, Roman mosaics, ancient markets, houses, homes, hearts, husbands, wives, daughters, sons. Sons. I remembered Sami's eyes, the moment the light fell away and they turned to glass.

Afra was silent. Her hair loose now, the colour of the sky. I watched her as she sat there, picking at her skin, her white face paler than usual. My eyes began to close, and when I opened them I saw that we had arrived in Urum al-Kubra and in front of us was the skeleton of a bombed-out lorry. Our driver was pacing around. He said we were waiting for a mother and child.

The place was empty. Unrecognisable. Ali was agitated. 'We have to make it before sunrise,' he said. 'If we don't make it before the sun, we will never make it.'

From the darkness, between the buildings, a man appeared on a bicycle.

'Let me do all the talking,' Ali said. 'He could be anyone. He might be a spy.'

When the man came close I could see that he was as grey as concrete, it didn't seem possible that this man could be a spy, but Ali wasn't taking any chances.

'I was wondering if you had any water,' the man said.

'It's OK, my friend,' Ali said. 'We have some.' He took a bottle from the passenger seat and gave it to this man, who drank it as if he'd been thirsty for a hundred years.

'We have some food too.' From a bag Ali took a tomato.

The man held out his hand, palm open, as if he was receiving gold. Then he stood there like that, unmoving, with the tomato on his palm, inspecting each of us, one by one.

'Where are you off to?' he said.

'We're going to visit our aunt,' Ali said. 'She is very sick.'

He pointed at the road ahead to indicate which way we were heading. Then, without saying another word, the man put the tomato into a basket on his bike, climbed on and headed off, but instead of riding away, he made a big circle in the road and came back to us.

'I'm sorry,' the man said, 'I forgot, I need to tell you something.' He dragged his hand over his face, wiping away some of the dust so there were now finger tracks across his cheeks, revealing white skin.

'I would not feel like a good man if I took your water and tomato and left without telling you. I would go to sleep tonight and wonder if you were dead or alive. If you take the road you said, you will find a sniper on top of a water tank about five kilometres away. He will see you. I would advise you strongly to take this road instead.' He pointed to a dust road that led to a country lane, and he explained which way to go from there so that we would eventually get back on the right route.

Ali would not wait for the mother and child any longer, and we decided to trust this man and take the detour, a right turn onto the country road that would take us between the towns of Zardana and Maarat Misrin.

'Where are we?' Afra said as we rattled along the country lanes. 'What do you see?'

'There are vines and olive trees for many miles around. It's dark but very beautiful.'

'Like it used to be?'

'Like it has never been touched.'

She nodded and I imagined that there was no war, that we were really going to see our sick aunt and that when we arrived the houses and the streets and the people would be as they always were. This is what I wanted: to be with Afra in a world that was still unbroken.

As the pickup bumped almost soundlessly along the

country track, I forced myself to stay awake, to breathe in the Syrian night with its untouched stars and untouched vines. I caught the smell of night jasmine and from further away the scent of roses. I imagined a great field of them, flashes of red in the moonlight in the sleeping fields, and at dawn the workers would arrive and the thick petals would be packed into crates. And then I could see my apiaries in the adjoining field, inside the hives rows of honeycomb, each tray containing delicate golden hexagons. On top were the roofs and from the holes in the sides the workers hummed, in and out, secreting wax from their glands, chewing it up and creating row after row of symmetrical polygons, five millimetres in diameter, as though they were laying down crystals. The queen bee in the queen cage, along with her few attendants, her royal scent acting like a magnet to the swarm. And the humming, that quiet musical humming that went on forever, and how the bees flew around me, past my face, getting caught in my hair, pulling themselves free, and off again.

Then I remembered Mustafa, on the days that he arrived at the apiaries from the university in his suit, holding a flask of coffee and a rucksack full of books and papers. He would change and put on his protective gear and join me, checking the honey combs, the consistency and smell and taste of the honey, dipping his finger in and tasting it. 'Nuri!' he would call. 'Nuri! You know, I think our bees make the best honey in the world!' And later, when the sun set, we would leave the bees and head home through the traffic of the city. Sami would be waiting by the window, with a look on his face like he'd done something wrong, and Afra would open the front door.

'Nuri. Nuri. Nuri.'

I opened my eyes. 'What is it?'

Afra's face was close to mine. 'You were crying,' she said. 'I heard you crying.' And with both of her hands she wiped away my tears. She looked into my eyes, as if she could see me. In that moment I could see her too, the woman inside, the woman I'd lost. She was there with me, her soul open and present and clear as light. For those few seconds I was no longer afraid of the journey, of the road ahead. But in the next moment her eyes darkened, they died, and she sank down and away from me. I knew that I couldn't force her to stay with me, there was nothing I could say to bring her back once she had disappeared. I had to let her go and wait for her to come back.

We skirted around Maarat Misrin and then rejoined the dual carriageway, we crossed a mountain and then the valley between Haranbush and Kafar Nabi and eventually we approached Armanaz, and there, ahead, were the great spotlights of the Turkish border, shining across the flat land like a white sun.

Between Armanaz and the border is the Asi River. It separates Turkey from Syria and I knew that we would need to get across. The driver stopped the pickup in a dark place beneath some trees and he led us along a path through a wood. Afra was holding my hand so tight, sometimes tripping and falling, and I had to keep lifting her and holding her around the waist. But I could barely see in that darkness and things moved in the leaves and branches. Not too far away I could hear voices and then, as we came out of the woods, I saw thirty or forty people standing like ghosts on the riverbank. A man was lowering a young girl into a large saucepan – the kind that we normally used to boil couscous. There was a long cable attached to it so that men on the other side of the river could pull it across. This man was trying to help the girl into the saucepan, but she was crying and had both arms wrapped around his neck and wouldn't let go.

'Please, get in,' the man said. 'Go ahead with these nice people and I will see you on the other side.'

'But why won't you come with me?' she said.

'I promise I will see you on the other side. Please stop crying. They will hear us.' But the girl wouldn't listen. So he pushed her in and slapped her hard around the face. She sat back shocked, her hand on her cheek, the men pulling at the cable as she floated away. When she was out of sight completely, the man sat on the ground, like there was no life left in him, and he began to sob. I knew he wouldn't see her again. And that's when I looked back. I shouldn't have, but I turned away from the crowd of people and looked back into the darkness at the land I was leaving. I saw the opening between the trees, the path that could take me back the way I came.

4

THERE IS A NEW RESIDENT at the B&B. His shoulders are so sharp and his back so bent that when he sits in the chair, hunched over, it looks like he has wings under his T-shirt. He is talking to the Moroccan man and they are both trying to communicate in a language they don't know very well. The Moroccan man seems to like this young man. His name is Diomande and he is from the Ivory Coast. He glances at me from time to time while he is speaking, but I don't show him that I am paying any attention.

The bee is still alive. I located her in the garden perched on the same flower where I left her. Once again, I coaxed her onto my hand and brought her into the sitting room with me and now she is crawling up my arm. Most of the time my eyes are fixed on the patio doors. I focus on

Diomande's reflection and on the dappled shadows of the trees behind it.

'I was working in Gabon,' Diomande is saying, 'and I heard I should go to Libya, that there are many opportunities there. My friend say there was war there but now it is safe, so I decide to go and get a good job. I pay fifteen thousand CFA francs to drive eight days through the desert but I was captured and put in prison.' He has his elbows on his knees as he talks, and as he moves his shoulder blades rise up, and I think maybe his wings will open. He is very tall and very lanky, his knees coming up high so that he is folded over himself.

'We would go three days no food,' he continues, 'just maybe some bread and water, many of us to share. They beat us, they beat us all the time. I don't know who they were, but then they want two hundred thousand CFA for my freedom. I called my family but money never came.'

He adjusts his position now and places long brown fingers over his knees. I turn away from his reflection and take a good look at him, at the way his knuckles bulge and his eyes pop. There is no meat on this boy. It's like birds have eaten him. He's like a corpse or a bombed-out building. He catches my eye, holds my gaze for a moment and then looks up to the ceiling at the naked light bulb.

'So, how did you get out, geezer?' the Moroccan man says, impatient to hear the rest.

'After three month rival militia broke into the prison and release all the hostages. I was free. I walk to Tripoli, where I find my friend and get job.'

'I am pleased for you!' the Moroccan man says.

'But new employer no pay me and when I demand money he say he will kill me. I want to go back to Gabon but there is no way back, so I board smuggler boat to cross the Mediterranean.'

The Moroccan man leans back in the armchair now and follows the boy's gaze to the light bulb on the ceiling.

'You made it here. How?'

'This is long story,' Diomande says. But he doesn't say more. He seems tired now and, probably noticing this, the Moroccan man taps the young man's knee and changes the subject, telling him about the strange customs of the people here.

'They wear trainers with suits. Who wears this together? And they wear sleeping clothes outdoors! Why?'

'This is tracksuit,' Diomande says, pointing at his own.

The old man is usually in his pyjamas at this time of night, but during the day he dresses in an old grey-blue suit with a tie.

I wait until they have gone to bed and step out into the garden where I put the bee back onto the flower. The sound of traffic is soft and a breeze blows, moving the leaves. The sensor hasn't caught me and the darkness is soothing, the moon is full and high up in the sky, and that's when I sense someone standing behind me. When I turn, Mohammed is sitting on the ground playing with the marble, rolling it in the cracks of the concrete. Beside him there is a worm slithering into a puddle. He glances up at me.

'Uncle Nuri,' he says, 'I'm winning against the worm! His name is Habib. Do you want to say hello to Habib?'

He picks up the worm and holds it high for me to see.

'What are you doing here?' I say.

'I came looking for the key because I want to get out.'

'What key?' I say.

'I think it's in that tree. It's hanging there but I didn't know which one.'

I turn and see that there are more than a hundred golden keys hanging from the tree. They twirl in the breeze and sparkle in the light of the moon.

'Will you get it for me, Uncle Nuri?' he says. 'Because I can't reach and Habib is getting tired.'

I look at Habib, dangling from his fingers.

'Sure,' I say. 'But how do I know which key you want?'

'Just get all of them and then we will try until we find one that fits.'

I go into the kitchen and find a mixing bowl. Mohammed sits patiently waiting for me to return and then I start picking the keys off the tree – there is a stepladder in the garden and I use this to get to the ones on the higher branches. Soon the bowl is nearly full and I check and double-check to make sure there are no keys left. When I turn, holding the bowl, Mohammed is no longer there. The worm is making its way into the puddle.

I take the bowl inside and upstairs into the bedroom, where I put it on the bedside cabinet on Afra's side, next to the marble. I am very careful not to wake her. I lie down beside her. She is facing me with her eyes closed and both hands tucked under her cheek and I can tell she is fast asleep because her breathing is slow and deep. I turn the other way and stare into the darkness because I can't close my eyes. I think back to our time in

Istanbul

was where I met Mohammed.

On the other side of the Asi River there was a barbed-wire fence with a hole about two metres in diameter, like an open mouth. People threw their belongings over the fence and passed infants through the hole. It was still dark and we were told by the smugglers to lie on our bellies and crawl on our hands and knees across the flat land of dusty soil and bracken.

Once in Turkey, we walked for what felt like a hundred miles, through fields of wheat and barley. It was quiet. Afra was holding onto my arm and she was shivering because the cold was unbearable. We were about half an hour into our journey when in the distance we saw a child run into the road, a silhouette against the sun. He was waving at someone and then he sprinted off in the direction of some houses.

We approached a village, small bungalows with terraces and open shutters, people looking through windows, others coming out of their homes, standing at the side of the road, their eyes wide with wonder as if they were seeing a travelling circus. There was a long table with plastic cups and jugs of water. We stopped and drank and women from the village brought out blankets. They gave us bread and cherries and small bags of nuts, then they stood back and watched us leave. I realised afterwards that the look I had mistaken for wonder was actually fear, and I imagined swapping places with them, seeing hundreds of people battered by war heading to an unknown future.

We walked for another hour at least, and the wind became stronger, pushing us back. Then there was the sudden smell of sewage and we were in an open field. There were tents everywhere and people sleeping on blankets amid rubbish.

I found a space beneath some trees. There was a sense of quiet here that was unfamiliar to me; in Syria, silence held danger, it could be shattered at any moment by a shell bomb or the sound of gunfire or the heavy footsteps of the soldiers. Somewhere in the distance, towards Syria, the earth rumbled.

The wind blew down from the mountains, bringing the smell of snow. I had an image in my mind – the white glow of Jabal al-Shaykh, the first snow I had ever seen, many years ago, Syria to the left and Lebanon to the right, the borders defined by the ridge, and the sea far below. We had placed a melon in the river and it had cracked from the cold. My mother was biting into the iced green fruit. What were we doing there at the top of the world?

A man next to me said, 'When you belong to someone and they are gone, who are you?' The man looked haggard, dirty face, dishevelled hair. He had stains on his trousers and reeked of urine. There were sounds in the darkness, like the cries of animals, and I thought I could smell the rot of death. This man gave us a bottle of water and told me to sit on it for a while to warm it up before we drank it. The night came and went and the sun came up. There was food on the ground and a new blanket. Someone had brought hard bread and bananas and cheese. Afra ate and then fell asleep again with her head on my shoulder.

'Where are you from?' the man said.

'Aleppo. And you?'

'Northern Syria.' But he didn't say where.

He took the last cigarette out of a box and lit it. He smoked it slowly, looking out across the arid land. He might have been a strong man once, but there was no flesh on him now.

'What's your name?' I asked.

'I lost my daughter and my wife,' he said, letting the stub of his cigarette drop to the ground. And that was all he said about it, in a flat toneless voice. But then he seemed to be thinking about something. 'Some people . . .' he said, finally, after a long pause, 'some people have already been here a month. It would be best to bypass the authorities and find a smuggler. I have some money.' He glanced at me, hopeful, to see what I would say.

'Do you know how?' I said.

'I've spoken to a few people, and there is a bus that can take us to the next town, and from there we can find a smuggler. I've seen people go and not return. I didn't want to try alone.'

When I agreed to go with him he told me his name was Elias.

For the rest of that day, Elias was on a mission; he spoke to a few people, making calls from my phone, which had just a tiny bit of battery left. By the afternoon he had arranged for the three of us to meet a smuggler in the nearby town and from there we would go to Istanbul. It was strange to think how easy it had been to set up, that there existed an organised system for those of us who were lucky enough to be able to afford it.

The next day we walked to the bus station and took the bus to the nearest town, and there we met the smuggler, a short asthmatic man with eyes that buzzed around like flies. He drove us to Istanbul in his car. When we arrived, Elias was never far behind me. The buildings in the city were tall and bright, old and new, gathered around the Bosporus, where the Sea of Marmara meets the Black Sea. I had forgotten that buildings could still stand, that there was a whole world out there that was not destroyed like Aleppo.

At night, we slept on the floor of the smuggler's apartment. There were two rooms, one for the women and the other for the men. In my room, there was a picture on the wall of a family who had lived there before. The photograph was nearly white from the sun and I wondered who they were and where they had gone. The night was cold and a wind blew in from the seas. It whistled beneath the wooden door frames and windowsills and brought with it the howls of dogs and cars. It was so much warmer than the open land, and at least here there was a toilet and a roof over our heads.

Early in the morning, when the birds had started to sing, the people unfolded themselves from their sleeping positions and prayed. There was nothing to do but wait. Each day the smuggler returned from wherever he'd been hiding and informed us about the conditions of the weather and the sea. We couldn't risk crossing while the wind was so strong. When he left, people talked for a while, telling stories of the ones who never made it across to Greece, of whole families, men and women and children, lost at sea. I didn't join these conversations; I listened and waited for silence to return. Afra sat on a wicker chair by the window, her head twitching slightly to the left or to the right, listening to everything.

When I went over to her she said, 'Nuri, I don't want to go.'

'We can't stay here.'

'Why not?'

'Because if we do we'll live in the camps forever. Is that what you want?'

'I don't want anything anymore.'

'Our life will be stuck. How will I work?'

She didn't reply.

'We've started the journey – there's no point giving up now.'

She grunted.

'And Mustafa is waiting for us. Don't you want to see Dahab? Don't you want to be settled and safe? I'm tired of living like this.'

'I'm scared of the water,' she said finally.

'You're scared of everything.'

'That's not true.'

That's when I noticed the little boy, about seven or eight, sitting cross-legged on the floor, rolling a marble across the tiles. There was something odd about him, as if he was far away, lost in his own world. He seemed to be there alone.

Later, when I went outside to stand on the balcony, the boy followed me. He stood beside me for a while, shifting from foot to foot, picking his nose, wiping it on the back of his jeans.

'Will we fall into the water?' he said, and he looked up at me with wide eyes, just like Sami would have done.

'No.'

'Like the other people?'

'No.'

'Will the wind take the boat? Will the boat turn over into the water?'

'No. But if it does we'll have life jackets. We'll be all right.'

'And Allah – have mercy on us – will he help us?'

'Yes. Allah will help us.'

'My name is Mohammed,' the boy said.

I held out my hand and he shook it like a little man.

'Nice to meet you, Mohammed. I am Nuri.'

The boy looked up at me again, this time his eyes wider, full of fear. 'But why didn't he help the boys when they took off their heads?'

'Who took their heads off?'

'When they stood in a line and waited. They weren't wearing black. That's why. My dad said it was because they weren't wearing black. I was wearing black. See?'

He tugged at his black, stained T-shirt.

'What are you talking about?'

'Then my dad gave me a key and said go to a house, and he told me where it was, and he said to go inside and lock the door. But when I got there the house didn't have a door.' He took a key out of his back pocket and showed it to me, as if he was still expecting to find the door that the key would fit. Then he tucked it again into his pocket.

'But Allah will help us in the water? Because in the water they can't find us.'

'Yes, he will help us cross the sea.'

Mohammed's shoulders softened and he stayed beside me for a while with his black jeans and black top and black fingernails and black eyes. As the days passed I realised that nobody else spoke to Mohammed and after our conversation on the balcony, he always glanced over at me, constantly checking to see where I was. I think I made him feel safe.

On the third day, I went for a walk. There was a concrete pathway that led deep into a wood, and if you kept walking eventually the path opened out to the big buildings. There were not many clouds, the weather was very similar to Syria, maybe slightly cooler. The sky was full of fog from the pollution, especially in the morning, a thick grey mist that lurked above the water and above the streets and the mist was not clean like a winter frost, it was full of the smells of the city and its people.

On the fourth day, Elias decided to join me on my walk. He rarely spoke unless he was going to say something about the weather, which was more or less the same every day anyway, but he commented on the tiny changes, like, 'The mist is thicker this morning,' or, 'There is a bitter wind this evening.' He always said the most obvious things, but the weather became important to us as we waited and watched for signs that the sea would be calm, so that we could continue our journey.

As we walked, I became aware of other things too, like the cats, which reminded me of Aleppo; how they woke up from their sleepy state and waited all day in the shadows for food. And the street dogs too, unpredictable and unkempt, with their old scars and new wounds, from injuries or disease or accidents. They all looked similar with light or sometimes dark brown coats. They were everywhere: wandering into alleys and side streets behind the restaurants, waiting for food, or walking through traffic. In the night, the wild dogs of Istanbul would call to one another across the city. And in the morning they rested under chairs and tables in front of the coffee shops on Taksim Square. Often they just lay dozing, recovering from the night's activities. Most people didn't seem to notice them, but the dogs watched everyone, with half-moon eyes and heads resting on paws: they watched the children darting through traffic tapping on car windows, trying to sell bottles of water to passers-by.

There were whole families wandering through the streets, some barefoot, sometimes sitting by the sidewalk when they became tired of walking, and other refugees on the market stalls, trying to make enough money to move on from here, selling things that people couldn't live without: phone chargers, life jackets, cigarettes.

Sometimes I forgot that I was one of these people. Like the dogs, I sat everyday on the same bench and watched the yellow cabs circling the red poppies on the roundabout. I took in the smells from the grill houses and kebab shops, with their spits and wood fires, and the wonderful smells of the dough rings, fresh from the ovens, or from the vendors who circled the square each day. There were raw burgers in glass display cases and in the storefront windows women in traditional dress made hand-rolled crêpes. I watched how the refugee children learnt to adjust, how they mastered the art of survival – these little entrepreneurs, the lucky ones. What would Sami have thought of these streets? Of the market stalls and restaurants and streetlights on Istiklal Avenue, just down the road from the slums and ghettos. He would have dragged me by the hand into the chocolatiers, and Afra would have loved the boutiques, bookstores and patisseries.

From the day we arrived at the smuggler's apartment, Afra again refused to go outside. When I returned to her after walking the streets, I would tell her about the Ottoman buildings, about the cars and the noise and the chaos and the food and the dogs. If I had some change, I would buy her a dough ring with sesame seeds. She loved them, especially when they were still warm, and she would break it in half to share with me. Afra would never eat anything without sharing it – that was her way. I didn't tell her about the children on the streets. I didn't want her to see them in her mind's eye, to become trapped with them in the inescapable tunnels of her mind.

In the night, when the street dogs woke up, Afra was restless. She slept in the adjoining bedroom with the other women. Every night she dabbed the rose perfume on the soft skin of her wrists and neck as if she was going somewhere in the dark. I had to share a room with ten other men. I missed Afra. It was the first time in years that I hadn't slept beside her. I missed her silent breathing. I missed resting my hand on her chest to feel her heartbeat. I didn't sleep much. I thought about my wife. I knew that there were times in the night when she would forget that she wasn't in Aleppo. Her mind would play tricks on her, and she would walk out into the corridor. I would recognise the sound of her footsteps on the tiles and I'd get up to greet her in the high-ceilinged hallway with the long window.

'Nuri, is that you? I can't sleep. Are you awake?'

'I am now.'

'I can't sleep. I want to go for a walk.'

'It's late. It's not safe now. We'll go tomorrow.'

'I want to go to see Khamid with his big pants hanging on the washing line.'

Khamid was her great-uncle. He lived down the road opposite a dry field with a metal swing and slide. In the evenings Afra used to take Sami to the swing and they would laugh about Khamid's giant pants.

I would hold her face in my palms, kiss one eyelid, then the other. Part of me wished I could kill her with those kisses, put her to sleep forever. Her mind terrified me. What she could see, what she could remember, locked up behind her eyes.

After a few days I tried to find some work. There were so many refugees selling life jackets and cigarettes on the streets, everyone working illegally because they had no permits to be there. It wasn't too difficult to find a job washing cars. Elias joined me. We worked together, scrubbing away the soot and grit of the city. Sometimes we stole small things from the boot or the glove compartment, things that the customers were unlikely to notice or care too much about – packets of chewing gum, half-drunk bottles of water, some loose change. Elias took cigarette butts from the ashtrays. The boss was a sixty-year-old Turkish man who smoked sixty cigarettes a day and paid us very little, but it had already been three weeks since we arrived in Istanbul and the weather was still bad so a bit of extra money and something to pass the time did us both some good.

One afternoon, after finishing work at the car wash, I walked around Taksim Square until I found an Internet café. My phone wasn't working and I wanted to see if Mustafa had tried to get hold of me. I knew that if he was alive and well he would have sent a message, and sure enough, when I logged into my account, there were three emails from him.

* * *

22/11/2015

My dear Nuri,

I hope you found the letter I left for you. I have been thinking of you and Afra every day. I am sorry that I had to leave without saying goodbye. If I stayed they would have found me and killed me. I hope you understand and can forgive me.

Each and every day I wonder how we got here, how life can be so cruel. Much of the time I can't stand to be alive. The thoughts I have poison me and I am alone with them. I know that every other person here is trapped in their own hell – there is one man who holds his knees and rocks himself all through the night, and he sings, Nuri. He sings a lullaby that freezes my heart. I want to ask him who he once sang it to, or who it was that sang it to him. But I am afraid of his answer, and so I offer him cigarettes instead, it's all I can do, because he stops singing for a few minutes while he smokes. I wish I could escape my mind, that I could be free of this world and everything I have known and seen in the last few years. And the children who have survived – what will become of them? How will they be able to live in this world?

The journey did not go as planned. I travelled through Turkey and Greece and then crossed the border into Macedonia, but things became complicated there – I was caught and deported and put on a train to Bulgaria, which is where I find myself now, in a camp in the woods. I am sending this from the phone of a young man I have met here. There are big tents and we sleep on bunk beds, all stacked next to each other. I think when the wind blows everything will fall over. There is a train station. They are old-fashioned trains that come to this station and people try to jump on and they hang off them because they want to get to Serbia. So far I have not tried to jump onto one of these trains.

The food cart has just arrived and we will wait to be served, sardines and bread. This is what we eat every day. If I make it out of here I will never eat another sardine again.

I hope to hear from you. I am praying for your safety.

Your cousin,

Mustafa

* * *

29/12/2015

My dear Nuri,

I am now in Serbia in a camp near a factory. It is an industrial place at the end of a train track that goes no further. So here I am at the end of the track. I hope this isn't a sign that my journey will end here. From Bulgaria I boarded a train that took one day and one night and I was brought to this barbed-wired camp just outside a village. I cannot get out of here – the camp is locked and there is a queue to leave. The train has no platform. From the coach coming here I saw people walking across a ladder to get onto it, but at least they are leaving. There is one girl here who has lost her voice – she must be about eighteen, and every day her mother pleads with her to speak, and the girl opens her mouth, but not a sound comes out. I wonder what words are trapped inside her that can't come out. She is the opposite of the boy by the river who was crying for his father. But who knows what this girl has been through, what she has seen?

There is so much silence here, but the silence is filled with chaos and madness. I try to remember the sound of the bees. I try to find some light by closing my eyes and imagining the field and our beehives. But then I remember the fire, and I remember Firas and Sami. Our sons have gone to where the bees are, Nuri, to where the flowers and the bees are. Allah is keeping them safe for us there, until we see them again once this life is over.

I am tired, Nuri. I am tired of this life, but I miss my wife and daughter. They are waiting for me and I don't know if I will ever get to them. They are both well in England, waiting to see if they will be granted asylum. If they are it will be easier for me to get there.

I must keep going, and if you are reading this then I urge you to do the same. Spend your money wisely – the smugglers will try to get as much out of you as they can, but keep in mind that there is a longer journey ahead. You must learn to haggle. People are not like bees. We do not work together, we have no real sense of a greater good – I've come to realise this now.

The good news is that I haven't eaten sardines for one week. Here they give us cheese and bread, some days also a banana.
Mustafa

The last email was written in English:

20/01/2016

Dear Nuri,
I spent one day in Austria in a military compound near the German border where they scanned us and took our fingerprints and then we were deported to a German youth hostel in the mountains. The winter here is very cold — we are surrounded by snow in an old house so high up that we are near the clouds. It reminds me of the Anti-Lebanon mountains and of my father and grandfather, of the days I spent with them at the apiaries, learning about the bees. But those mountains were full of sunlight and they looked down on the sea. These mountains are white and silent, and I do not know where they end and where they begin.

I would like to make it to France. One of the guards has kindly offered to send an email from his phone and he is typing this for me. I have also sent an email to my wife, who is waiting for me still, and praying. I pray for her and I pray for you and Afra too. I haven't heard from you but I will not imagine anything.

Your dear friend,
Mustafa

I sat for a while and imagined what might have happened after Germany. It was now the beginning of February. Did he make it to France? Was he still alive and well? I thought about the first time I had visited the apiaries in the mountains. Yes, it was full of light and you could see the shimmer of the water far below. Mustafa had given me a tour; he was young then, in his late twenties, and I was only eighteen. He walked around in his shorts and flip-flops, unafraid of the bees.

'Aren't you scared?' I'd said, hypervigilant and flinching.

'I know them,' he'd replied. 'I know when they will get angry.'

'How do you know?'

'They release pheromones that smell like bananas.'

'Bananas?!'

He nodded, pleased at my excitement. 'The other bees smell it and know to attack.'

'But what will you do if they do get angry?'

'I will stand very, very still and not move an inch. Pretend to be a tree.'

Then he stood there, like a giant statue, with his hands shielding his eyes, smiling. I copied him, standing as still as I could, holding my breath while the bees flew around me in hundreds, or what felt like thousands, their humming surrounding me, enveloping me, winding itself around me like an invisible web. Not one bee landed on me.

'You see,' he whispered. 'You see, you have to relax and turn into nature. Then you will be fine.'

1/02/2016

My dearest Mustafa,

Your last email was sent in January and there are no more messages after this so I wonder if you made it to France. More than anything I wish that you are in England with your wife and daughter. I just remembered the first time I visited the beehives in the mountains. It is like a moving picture in my mind. We were so young. If only we knew then what life would bring. But if we had known, what would we have done? We would have been too afraid to live, too afraid to be free and to make plans. I wish I could go back to that moment and stand there surrounded by the bees, learning with every second that passed that they were not my enemy.

    I am in Istanbul now. Afra and I are staying in a smuggler's flat with twenty other people and we are waiting to leave for Greece but the wind is too strong at the moment. There is a young boy here, the same age as Sami. He is alone and I'm not sure what has happened to his family. I dread to think. But he trusts me, and I am looking after him.

    I know that I have a long journey ahead. Some days I think I cannot take another step, but I have a dream in my mind of meeting you in England. This is what keeps me moving forward. I have money and passports. I feel lucky to have these as I see that some people have nothing. I will be waiting for your response.

    Nuri

When I returned to the smuggler's flat in the evening, I gave the things I had found to Mohammed: chewing gum, mints, a penknife, a pen, a key ring, a glue stick and a road map.

The map was Mohammed's favourite item; he opened it out on the floor and traced his finger along the lines of roads and mountains. He found stones in the plant pots on the balcony and, using the pen, he drew faces on them. He made a whole family of stones, gliding them across the map as if they were on a journey: father, mother, grandmother, a brother and two sisters. That night I found him fast asleep on the map, so I picked him up, draped him over my shoulder, and then carried him to the bedroom and laid him down gently on the blanket. Mohammed didn't even stir; he was lost in his dreams.

'We'll be leaving soon,' I said to Elias the following night. He stood like a great ancient statue on the balcony, opening a fresh packet of cigarettes. He put one to his mouth and lit it, looking out into the woods. Now that he'd been eating more and working hard his frame had fleshed out and it was easier to see the natural physical strength of this man.

'The smuggler says two more days.'

Elias considered until he finished his cigarette and lit another. 'I don't want to go. I'll stay here.'

'Haven't you already paid the smuggler? Where will you stay?'

'I'll find somewhere. Don't worry about me. I don't want to go on – I've travelled too far already. I'm done.' His eyes were sad but his smile was different now; there was life in his face and an internal strength. We both stood there, silent, for a long time, listening to the night sounds of the wind and the cars and the dogs.

5

When Afra wakes up in the morning she asks me why she can smell flowers.

'It's probably your perfume,' I say.

'But these aren't roses. They smell faint, like blossoms.' She reaches over to the bedside cabinet and I remember the bowl of keys. She feels around until she is touching the bowl and then she sits up and rests it on her lap, leaning over it, inhaling deeply, putting both of her hands in, and that's when I realise that the bowl is filled not with keys but with handfuls of white blossoms.

'Did you pick these for me?' she says.

'Yes.'

'Another gift!' Her eyes are full of the morning light. I don't want to see this. I hate to see her like this and I'm not sure why. I get up and close the gap in the curtains and watch their shadow move across her face. 'You haven't brought me one for a while,' she says, and she brings the flowers up to her face, breathing in their scent, and in that moment a small smile appears on her lips, as faint as the smell of the flowers.

'Thank you,' she says. 'Where did you find them?'

'There's a tree in the garden.'

'Is it a big garden?'

'No, it's small like a courtyard and mostly concrete, but there's this one tree in it.'

'I thought you'd never bring me a gift again.'

She puts the bowl back onto the bedside cabinet and checks to make sure that the marble is there. I take her to the bathroom and sit on the toilet while she brushes her teeth, then I help her to get dressed. Taking the abaya off the hanger, slipping it down over her arms, over her body, over the bulge of her stomach, over her scar from the caesarean section – a permanent smile across her abdomen – over the fine hairs on her thighs. I smell her. Roses and sweat. The scar and the crinkling of her skin around her stomach are constant reminders to me that she carried our child, brought him into this world, and I don't want to touch her. I tie up her hair and wrap the hijab around her head, securing the hairpins where she wants me to. I try not to be abrupt, not to push her fingers away. The smile still seems to be lingering on her lips and I don't want to spoil it. It horrifies me that a gift from me can have the power to make her smile now, even if it is so slight as to be almost non-existent. All those times I wanted to be able to affect her, to bring some light to her eyes, and now I hate it that I can, because it means that she loves me and that she has been hoping for me to love her. But I am no longer worthy of her, or her forgiveness.

We have another meeting with Lucy Fisher later that afternoon, so find ourselves back where we were before, sitting opposite her at the kitchen table. Afra still won't turn to face her, and clasps her hands on the table, looking like she's staring out of the window.

Lucy Fisher seems happier today. She has brought with her the paperwork to prove that we are claiming asylum. She is very efficient – she ticks boxes and makes quick notes in a ring binder.

'I'm glad we don't need a translator for you,' she says, preoccupied, glancing up at me quickly with her big blue eyes. Her hair is down today. She has very soft fine hair which reminds me of feathers, unlike Afra's, which is thick and heavy and was once as black as tar.

There is a lightness about Lucy Fisher that I like. She is proud of herself for keeping things in order. And when things do not go as she wishes, her face fires up and she becomes beautiful. I wonder if she knows this. Right now though, she is calm and her face is ordinary. She reminds me of a newsreader. Her voice does too. Remembering her reaction the other day, I try to imagine how many people she has worked with, how many she has seen sent back, how many questions people have asked her, how everyone must hold on to her as if she is a lifeboat on a stormy sea.

'Will you be sending the Moroccan man away?' I say.

'Which one?' she says.

'The old man.'

'Hazim?' she says.

'Yes.'

'I'm afraid that's confidential information. I'm not permitted to discuss any of the clients' cases. And not yours either.' She smiles at me again and closes the file before continuing. 'So what you need to do is take this letter to the GP's office, the address is on this piece of paper.' She points at it. 'You'll have no problem,' she says, 'and when you're there you can make an appointment for your wife, and also for yourself. It might be a good idea to have a quick check-up.' She glances at Afra, and I can see that my wife is uncomfortable.

'When will we have the interview?' I say so that her eyes return to me.

'I'll be in contact again soon with a date for the asylum interview. I suggest you start preparing. Think about your story, how you got here, what happened along the way. They will ask you all sorts of questions and you need to be ready, because they will be emotionally difficult to answer.'

I don't say anything.

'Have you been thinking about it?'

'Yes,' I say. 'Of course. I think about it all the time.' And again I see something more real in her than the straight-talking newsreader.

She rubs the back of her right hand over her eye, smudging

the make-up a bit, in the way a young girl might. 'It's just they'll pounce on anything,' she says, 'especially if your story's a mess.'

I nod, feeling worried but she doesn't seem to notice my concern. She glances at her watch to let me know that the meeting is over. Afra and I get up to leave.

Next to see her is Diomande. We swap places at the door and he goes in and sits down, with his folded-up wings poking under his T-shirt. He is much more talkative than I am. He greets her warmly in his broken English and starts immediately to talk about where he's from, how he got here. Before she's even asked him anything, he's jabbering away. And I can still hear his voice even from the end of the corridor, a charging energetic ramble, and something about it reminds me of a galloping horse.

Afra tells me she is tired, so I take her to the bedroom and she sits on the edge of the bed, facing the window, just like she used to in our house in Aleppo. I watch her for a while, wanting to say something to her, but no words come to my mind, so I head downstairs.

The Moroccan man isn't in the living room. I think he heads out during the day and wanders around the shops, speaking to people, picking up new words, observing and learning things along the way. There are a few others in here: the Afghan woman with the handwoven hijab. She is making something with some blue string. There is nothing much to do but sit in the living room and watch the TV. A politician with a face like a frog is speaking.

We literally have opened up the door unconditionally, without being able to secure-check anybody . . . the Dusseldorf bomb plot had been uncovered, all right – a very, very worrying plan for mass attacks along the style of Paris or Brussels. All of those people came into Germany last year posing as refugees.

My face heats up. I change the channel.

This guy's admitted cheating six times! But it's only on breaks! And you want him gone! Ashley's on The Jeremy Kyle Show, *ladies and gentlemen!*

I turn off the TV and the room plunges into silence. Nobody seems to care.

I wander over to the computer desk and sit down. I think of the field in Aleppo before the fire, when the bees hovered above the land like clouds, humming their song. I can see Mustafa taking a comb out of a hive, inspecting it closely, dipping a finger into the honey, tasting it. That was our paradise, at the edge of the desert and the edge of the city.

I look at my face on the dark screen, thinking of what to write – *Mustafa, I believe I am unwell. I have no dreams left.*

The landlady comes in and begins to clean the living room with a bright yellow duster. She tries to reach the cobwebs in the corners, tiptoeing with her platform shoes and skinny elephant legs, and so I get up and offer to do it for her. I spend the afternoon dusting the walls and tables and cabinets in the living room and any of the rooms upstairs that have been left open. I get a glimpse into some of the other residents' lives. Some have made their beds, while others have left their rooms in a mess. Some have trinkets on their bedside cabinets, precious things from a past life, photographs on the dresser. Propped up without frames. I don't touch anything.

The Moroccan man's room is tidy, everything folded neatly, a bottle of shaving foam on the dresser, razors lined up. There is a black and white photograph of a woman in a garden. The photo is faded and white at the edges, and there is a small gold wedding band on the dressing table next to it. The photo next to that is of the same woman, some years later. She has the same eyes and smile; she is sitting on a wicker chair holding a baby, a toddler standing beside her. Another photo, glossy, many years later, is of a family: a man, a woman and two teenage children. The last one is of a woman standing on the shore with the sea behind her. I turn it over and read the words in Arabic:

Dad, my favourite place. I love you x

I head downstairs feeling heavier than before and decide to go for a walk. I make my way to the convenience store; the Arabic music reaches me as I walk along the street. Although I'm not familiar with the song that is playing, the music transports me home, its tones and rhythms, the sound of my language surrounding me and soothing me as I enter the little shop.

'Good morning,' the man says in English. His accent is good and he is standing very upright, as if he is guarding the place, middle-aged, cleanly shaven. He turns the volume down and follows me with his eyes while I walk around. I stand by the counter staring at the unfamiliar newspapers: *The Times*, the *Telegraph*, the *Guardian*, the *Daily Mail*.

'It is a beautiful day,' he says.

I am about to reply in Arabic, but I don't want to have a conversation with this man. I don't want him to ask me where I am from and how I got here.

'Yes,' I say finally, and he smiles.

Just beneath the magazines, on the last row of shelves, I notice a sketch pad and colouring pencils. I have some change in my pocket so I buy them for Afra. The man glances at me a few times and opens his mouth to say something, but a woman calls him from the back of the shop and I leave.

In the late afternoon the Moroccan man returns, calling my name as soon as he walks through the door.

'Nuri! Mr Nuri Ibrahim! Please come here – there is a gift for you!'

I go out into the hallway and he is standing there, a huge smile on his face, holding a wooden tray with five plants it.

'What's this?' I say.

'I had a bit of money saved and I went to the vendor on the street and got this for the bee!' He shoves the tray into my arms and nudges me through the living room, toward the patio doors. He picks up an overturned plastic table in the corner of the courtyard, wiping the muck and dried leaves off with his hand.

'Right,' he says, 'put it on here!' Then he stands there for a while admiring the flowers – sweet clover, thistle and dandelions. 'The man told me which flowers to get, which ones the bee would like.' He goes into the kitchen and comes back with a saucer of water. He rearranges the plant pots into a line, so the bee will be able to get from one to the other without flying, and he puts the saucer in the tray.

'I think she will be thirsty,' he says.

For a while I can't move. I can see him staring at me, waiting for me to put the bee into her new home, and there is a shadow of disappointment in his eyes at my lack of enthusiasm. In this moment, standing beneath the tree with the flowers beside us and the sun beaming down, I remember my father. I remember the look on his face when I told him I didn't want to take over the family business, that I wasn't interested in selling fabric. I wanted to be a beekeeper with Mustafa, I wanted to work outdoors in nature, I wanted to feel the land beneath my feet and the sun on my face, to hear the song of the bees.

For so many years I'd watched my father work hard in that little dark shop, with his scissors and needles and tape-measure and swollen knuckles, the colours of the world, of deserts and rivers and forests, printed on the silks and linens around him. 'You can make blinds with this silk. Doesn't it remind you of the colours of Hamad when the sun is setting?' This is what he would say to the customers, and to me he would say, 'Close the blinds, Nuri! Close the blinds so the light won't get to the fabric.' How I remember his eyes when I told him I didn't want to work in that tiny dark cave for the rest of my life.

'You don't like it?' the Moroccan man says. His expression is different now, a deep frown.

'I like it,' I say. 'Thank you.'

I put my hand out to the bee and she crawls onto my finger and I transport her to her new home. She inspects the flowers, making her way from one plant pot to the next.

'Why did you come here?' I say to the Moroccan man. 'What are you doing here in the UK?'

His shoulders stiffen and he takes a step away from the wooden box. 'Why don't we go in and maybe you can come and see it again tomorrow.'

In the living room he sits in the armchair and opens his book. 'I think queuing is very important here,' he says to me, with the usual tone of laughter back in his voice.

'But where is your family?' I say. 'You bring the plants and remind me of Syria, and when I ask you about why you are here you ignore me.'

He closes the book now and looks at me straight in the eyes.

'As soon as I was on that boat to Spain I knew I had sold my life, whatever life I have left. But my children wanted to leave; they were in search of a better life. I didn't want to be alone there without them. They had dreams. Young people still have dreams. They couldn't get visas and life was becoming too difficult at home – there were problems, too many . . . so they went underground, and this is dangerous.

We all decided to leave together, but my son and daughter were taken to another hostel where children are allowed. They are waiting, too, and my daughter . . . my daughter. . . .'
He stops talking and I see that his small eyes, almost hidden in the creases, are shimmering. He is far away. I don't ask any more questions.

Diomande is up in his room. He went upstairs after Lucy Fisher left, closed the door and hasn't come out since. When the Moroccan man and everyone else go up to bed, I head out into the courtyard. I go close to the sensor for the light so that it will come on and I watch the bee crawling over the dandelions, settling into her new home.

Then the flowers on the tree catch my eye. There are still thousands of blossoms on it. I turn around expecting to see Mohammed in one of the dark corners of the garden. I kneel down and look through the hole in the fence, trying to see the green of the leaves on the bushes and trees. Then I sit with my back against the tree and my legs straight out in front of me and close my eyes. It is quiet, apart from the sound of the cars. I squeeze my eyes shut, concentrating, and I can hear the waves. Loud they rise, a big long breath, and fall back again. I feel the water beside me, right here, a dark monster, lapping at my feet. I lie back and my body and mind are taken by

the sea

was dark and wild. Mohammed was standing by the shore, in his black clothes, almost invisible against the night sky and inky water. He stood back when the waves lapped at his feet and slipped his hand into mine. Afra was a short distance away, facing the land instead of the water. We were brought here by coach, a three-hour journey across mainland Turkey, all of us clutching onto our life jackets and our few belongings. Although there were only twenty people in the smuggler's house, the number of travellers had increased to forty. The smuggler was standing with the man who had been appointed captain of the dinghy.

The boat that left last night had toppled over and the people were lost at sea. Only four survivors were pulled from the water, and eight bodies were found. These were the conversations I could hear around me.

'At least this isn't as bad as the crossing between Libya and Italy. That's the deadliest sea crossing in the world!' one woman standing nearby said to a man. 'And some of the bodies washed up on the shore in Spain.'

Mohammed tightened his grip on my hand.

'I told you,' he said. 'Didn't I tell you this?'

'Yes, you did, but—'

'So it's true. We might fall into the water?'

'We won't.'

'How do you know?'

'Because Allah will protect us.'

'Why didn't he protect the other people? Are we special?'

The boy was sharp. I looked down at him.

'Yes.'

He raised his eyebrows. There was a strong wind and the waves rose.

'It's like a monster,' Mohammed said.

'Stop thinking about it.'

'How can I stop thinking about it when it's right in front of me? It would be like if you held a cockroach right up to my face with all its legs wriggling and told me to stop thinking about it!'

'Well then, go on thinking until you crap your pants.'

'I'm not doing it on purpose.'

'Pretend we're getting on a ship.'

'But we're not. We're getting on a rubber boat. If we fall in the water, maybe the fishermen will catch us in their net. They'll think they've caught a big fish, but then they will get the biggest shock of their whole lives.'

Afra was listening to our conversation, but she didn't join in and she kept her back to us.

We waited there for an hour at least. People were becoming restless.

'This could be our last time on this earth,' Mohammed said. 'It would be good if we had some ice cream. Or maybe a cigarette.'

'A cigarette? You're seven.'

'I know how old I am. My dad told me never to try one because it might kill me. I thought I would try one when I was seventy. But seeing as we might die tonight, now might also be a good time. What would you like to have if you were going to die tonight?'

'We're not going to die tonight. Stop thinking about it.'

'But what would you like to have?'

'I would like very much to have some camel's wee.'

'Why?!'

'Because it's good for the hair.'

The boy laughed and laughed.

I noticed that a woman standing nearby had been looking at me, her eyes flashing towards me then away, then back again to where Mohammed was standing. She was a young woman, probably in her early thirties, and her hair was long and black like Afra's and sweeping across her face in the wind. She pushed it back with her hand and looked at me again.

'Are you OK?' I said.

'Me?' she said.

I nodded, and she glanced again at Mohammed and took a step closer to me. 'It's just that . . .' She hesitated. 'It's just that I lost my son too. It's just that . . . I know. I know what it's like. The void. It's black like the sea.'

Then she turned away from me and said nothing more, but the wind from the sea and the echo of her words got beneath my skin and froze my heart.

The appointed captain had climbed into the dinghy and the smuggler was showing him something on his phone and pointing out to sea; people were moving closer to the water, sensing that it would soon be time to go. Everyone had started to put on the orange life jackets, and I was busy adjusting the straps of Mohammed's jacket and then helping Afra with hers.

The smuggler waved us over and everyone edged closer to the water, and one by one we slowly climbed onto the rocking boat. Mohammed sat safely next to me. Afra had still not said anything, not a single word had come out of her mouth, but I could feel her fear; her soul was as dark as the sky now, as restless as the sea.

The smuggler told us to turn off our torches and our phones. There must be no noise and no light until we got to international waters.

'And how will we know,' a man said, 'when we have reached international waters?'

'Because the water will change. It will become foreign,' the smuggler said.

'What does that mean?'

'It will change colour – you'll see, it will look unfamiliar.'

Only the captain had his phone on, for the GPS. The smuggler reminded him to follow the coordinates, and if something should happen to the phone, then look out for lights in the distance and follow them.

The engine turned on and we headed out into the darkness, the rubber creaking over the waves.

'It's not that bad,' I heard a child say. 'It's not bad at all!' There was triumph in the girl's voice as if we had just overcome a great danger.

'Shh!' her mother hissed. 'Shh! They told us no noise!'

A man started to recite a verse from the Qur'an, and as we went further out to sea, other people joined in, their voices merging with the sounds of the waves and the wind.

I had one hand in the water. I kept it there, feeling the movement, the rush of sea, the aliveness of it, the way it got colder as we moved away from the land. I placed my other hand on Afra's arm but she didn't respond; her lips were pursed, like a closed shell.

Mohammed's teeth were chattering. 'We haven't fallen in yet,' he said.

I laughed. 'No,' I said. 'Not yet.'

The boy's eyes widened, full of genuine fear. It seemed that he'd been relying on my ignorant optimism.

'Don't worry,' I said, 'we won't fall in. People are praying. Allah will hear.'

'Why didn't he hear the other people?'

'We've been through this already.'

'I know, because we're special. My feet are wet.'

'Mine too.'

'My feet are cold.'

'Mine too.'

Mohammed glanced over at Afra. 'Are your wife's feet cold?'

'I suppose so.'

'Why doesn't she say anything?'

The boy stared at her for a while, looking at her face, her scarf, her clothes, her hands, her legs, her feet. I followed his eyes, wondering what he was thinking, what he was trying to figure out, where his mother was.

'How long will it take?'

'Six hours.'

'How long has it been already?'

'Six minutes.'

'No! It's been longer than that!'

'Then why do you ask?'

'Sixteen minutes!'

'OK, sixteen.'

'We have five hours and forty-four minutes left. I will count.'

'Go ahead.'

He started to count, but by the time he got to the fifth minute he was fast asleep with his head on my shoulder.

I still had one hand on Afra's arm and one hand in the water. I looked out into the darkness, all this sea and sky, and I couldn't tell where one ended and the other began. Is this what Afra saw every day? This absence of form.

A girl started to cry. 'Shh!' the mother said. 'Shh! We have been told no noise!'

'But we are in international waters!' the girl cried. 'I'm allowed now!'

At this the mother started to laugh. She laughed from her stomach and the girl switched suddenly from crying to laughing too. Finally, the mother caught her breath and said, 'No, we aren't yet in international waters.'

'How do you know?'

'I know.'

'OK. When we get to that place, will you let me know?'

'So that you can cry?'

'Yes. I need to cry loudly,' the girl said.

'Why?'

'Because that's how scared I am.'

'Go to sleep now,' the mother said.

And then there was silence. There were no more prayers, no chanting, no whispers.

And maybe I fell asleep too, because I saw in front of me a series of images:

Colourful Lego pieces scattered about the floor
Blue tiles with black flowers
Afra wearing a yellow dress
Sami playing with the Lego in the living room,
   building a house
The apiaries in the field beneath the midday sun
The burned hives and the dead bees
Mustafa sitting in the middle of the field
Bodies floating in the river
Firas lying on the table at the morgue
Mustafa holding his hand
Afra at the souq with Sami on her knee
Sami's eyes

Then there was darkness

I startled awake because there was panic.

The waves were bigger.

One man was shouting, 'Get the water out! There is too much water!'

There were torches flashing, and hands scooping out the water, and children crying. Mohammed was wide-eyed and helping to empty out the water. I watched as men leapt into the sea, the boat immediately buoyant once again.

'Nuri!' Afra said. 'Are you on the boat?'

'Don't worry,' I said. 'We are.'

'Stay on the boat. Don't go into the water.'

Mohammed was still scooping the water with his hands; everyone else on the boat was doing the same. The girl began to cry now. She was calling out to the men in the sea, calling them to come back onto the boat.

The water continued to rise and more men jumped out of the boat. Every child was crying except Mohammed. I could see his face, serious and determined, between the flashes of light.

There was a moment of complete darkness, and when the light of the torch flashed again, he was gone. Mohammed was not on the boat. I scanned the water, the black waves, as far as I could see, and then, without thinking, I jumped in. It was freezing but the waves weren't as big as I'd thought, and I swam around, flashing the torch across the surface.

'Mohammed!' I called. 'Mohammed!' But there was no answer.

I could hear Afra's voice from the boat. She was calling, but I couldn't hear what she was saying. I continued to search the water, which was as black as ink. How would I see Mohammed with his black clothes and black hair?

'Mohammed!' I called. 'Mohammed!'

The torch flashed over the men's faces. I plunged into the

black silence, but even with the torch I could barely see anything. I stayed under for as long as I could, feeling with my hands in case I should catch onto something, an arm or a leg; when there was no air left in my lungs, when the pressure of death was pushing down on me, I came back up gasping into the darkness and the wind.

I was about to take a deep breath and go back under when I saw a man holding Mohammed, lifting him up into the boat. The women took the coughing and spluttering boy into their arms, removing their headscarves and wrapping them around him.

We were deep into international waters now; the smuggler was right, the water did change, the waves were different, their rhythms foreign. Then everyone flashed their torches, hoping a coastguard would see, hoping we were close enough to Greece that somebody would save us. These lights in the darkness were like prayers, because there was no sign of anyone coming. The men couldn't get back onto the boat – there was still too much water inside. I could feel my body becoming numb. I wanted to sleep, wanted to rest my head upon the moving waves and sleep.

'Nuri!' someone was calling. 'Nuri!'

I saw the stars above, and Afra's face.

'Nuri, Nuri, there is a boat!' There was a hand on my arm. 'Uncle Nuri, a boat is coming!'

Mohammed was staring down at me, pulling me. My life jacket had started to deflate but I began to kick my legs to stay afloat, to get the blood moving in my body again.

In the distance there was a bright light moving towards us.

6

THIS TIME WHEN I WAKE up on the concrete floor of the garden, the Moroccan man is already standing over me holding out his hand.

'How're you doin', man?' he says in English as he pulls me to my feet. Then he tells me in Arabic that Afra is inside waiting for me, that she seems even more upset than last time. When I go upstairs, I find her sitting on the bed, with her back to the door and the bowl of blossoms on her lap.

'Where were you?' she says, before I've even had a chance to speak.

'I fell asleep downstairs.'

'In the garden again?'

I don't reply.

'You don't want to sleep next to me.'

I ignore her comment. I give her the sketch-pad and colouring pencils, placing them on her lap, bringing her hands to them so that she can feel what they are.

'Another gift?' she says.

'Remember what you did in Athens?' I say, and although she smiles, she puts them down on the floor beside her.

'You're already dressed, so I'm going to go for a walk. Would you like to come with me?'

I wait for a while, standing there listening to her silent response, and when I can see that she's not going to reply, I head downstairs and out into the light. I go to the place where the sandcastle city was. The sand is lumpy, with colourful bits and pieces embedded in it. I pick up a piece of transparent pink plastic, probably part of a broken cup, and toss it into the sea. The waves swallow it up.

Just behind me, there is an old woman sitting in a deck-chair reading a book. She is under an umbrella with a sun hat on, a bottle of sunscreen by her side. She doesn't seem to notice that the sun has gone and it might even rain.

A few people are walking their dogs, an attendant picks up rubbish. The aftermath of sunshine. The aftermath of war is something else. There is a sense of calm here, of life continuing. Hope for another sunny day. In the distance, to the left, the faint sound of music comes from the fairground on the pier. It never stops.

The sun pushes through the clouds and the sea suddenly shimmers.

'Excuse me,' a voice says behind me. I turn around and see that the woman is frowning, her skin so leathery and brown she looks as if she's been sunbathing on Syria's dust plains.

'Yes?' I say.

'Would you mind kindly moving out of my light, please? Thank you.' She's thanked me for moving before I've even moved. It's difficult getting used to British manners – I can understand the Moroccan man's confusion. Apparently queuing is important here. *People actually form a single line in a shop. It's advisable to take your place in the queue and not try to push your way to the front, as this usually pisses people off!* This is what the woman in Tesco told me last week. But I don't like their queues, their order, their neat little gardens and neat little porches and their bay windows that glow at night with the flickering of their TVs. It all reminds me that these people have never seen war. It reminds me that back home there is no one watching TV in their living room or on their veranda and it makes me think of everything that's been destroyed.

I ask for directions to the GP surgery and find it on a hill on one of the side streets leading up from the sea. The place is full of children with colds. A mother is holding a tissue to her son's face and telling him to blow his nose. Some children play with toys on a mat in the corner of the room. The adults read magazines or watch the monitor, waiting for their names to come up.

I stand in the queue at the receptionist's desk. There are five people in front of me. There is a yellow line on the floor with the words: 'Queue behind this line.'

The woman at the front is handing the receptionist a urine

sample. The receptionist pulls a pair of red-framed glasses out of a mass of tiny curls. She inspects the container, types something in the system, seals the jar of urine into a cellophane bag and calls out, 'Next!'

It takes about fifteen minutes for me to get to the front and I have the asylum letter ready. When I put it on the desk, she lowers her glasses onto her nose and reads it through.

'We can't register you,' she says.

'Why not?'

'Because the asylum letter doesn't have an address.'

'Why do you need an address?'

'In order to register you, we need to see an address.'

'I can tell you the address.'

'It needs to be on your letter. Please come back when you have all the correct documentation.'

'But my wife needs to see a doctor.'

'I'm sorry, sir.' she says. 'That's our policy.'

'But the NHS guidelines clearly say that a practice cannot refuse a patient because they do not have identification or proof of address.'

'I'm sorry, sir,' she says, putting her glasses back into her curls, her mouth a tight line, 'that's our policy.'

The woman behind me tuts politely. The receptionist pushes the papers apologetically towards me. I stand there looking at them, and in that moment something crushes me. It's just a piece of paper. It's just a receptionist in a doctor's surgery. But the sounds of chattering, people moving around me, phones ringing from the cubicles behind the desk, children laughing . . . I hear the sound of a bomb ripping through the sky, glass shattering . . .

'Are you OK, sir?'

I look up. There is a flash and a crashing sound. I kneel down and cover my ears. I feel a hand on my back, then there is water.

'I really am sorry, sir.' the receptionist says, once I've stood up and drunk the water, 'There's nothing I can do. Could you get the correct paperwork together and come back?'

I follow the road that twists away from the sea, with its row of identical brown-bricked houses side by side, and I head back to the B&B.

I find Afra on our bed again, now with some of the blossoms in her hands. I kneel down in front of her and look into her eyes.

'I want to lie down with you,' she says, and what she means is, 'I love you. Please hold me.' There is an expression on her face I recognise from years ago, and it makes my sadness feel like something palpable, like a pulse, but it makes me afraid too, afraid of fate and chance, and hurt and harm, of the randomness of pain, how life can take everything from you all at once. Although it's only early afternoon I lie down next to her on the bed and I let her put her arm around me and press her palm onto my chest, but I won't touch her. She tries to hold my hand and I edge it away. My hands belong to another time, when loving my wife was a simple thing.

When I wake up it is dark, and the darkness pulsates. I've had a dream about something vague, not of murder this time;

in my mind there is a glimpse of corridors and staircases and footpaths that make a grid, somewhere far away from here, and a picture of the sky in the morning and a red fire

flickered on the beach at dawn. Like driftwood washed ashore, we were left on the tiny military island of Farmakonisi. We were wet and shivering and the sun had just begun to rise. Mohammed's face was white and blue, he still had the women's headscarves wrapped around his body and for some reason he was now holding Afra's hand. They did not speak to each other though; not a word passed between them. They just stood there on the shore with the sea behind them and the sun rising up to greet them. One of the men had collected the life jackets and made a huge fire with them. The flames warmed us and we gathered around.

'I fell into the water,' Mohammed said, holding onto my hand now.

'I know.'

'I died a little bit.'

'It was close.'

'But I died a little bit.'

'How do you know?'

'I saw my mum. She was holding my hand in the water and pulling me and pulling me, and she was telling me not to go to sleep, because if I fell asleep I would sleep forever and I wouldn't be able to wake up again and play. So I think I died a little bit but she told me not to.'

I wondered what had happened to his mother, but I didn't want to ask. Apparently another NGO vessel would be coming to pick us up, to take us to another island; in the meantime we had to wait here on the shore. There was a large shipping container, but this was already full of people; the story going around was that they'd arrived earlier that night from another part of Turkey, further along the coast. They were meant to go to another island but the engine had stopped working and their boat had drifted towards Farmakonisi. The coastguard had found them, and brought them back here. Some of the men and children came outside to talk to us and to warm themselves by the fire.

'Uncle Nuri!' Mohammed said, a huge smile revealing a missing tooth. 'This place is called Biscuit Island! The girl from the container told me!'

It was a cold morning and gulls and pelicans dipped down to the sea. On the safety of this land and in the warmth of the fire and the sun, people began to fall asleep. Mohammed was lying flat on his back. He was not asleep; he was looking up at the vast blue sky, squinting his eyes against the brightening light. In his hand he held his tiny marble, rolling it around in his fingers. Afra was sitting on the other side of me. She had her head on my shoulder and her hand grasping my arm as if I might slip away. She was holding on to me so tight that even when she fell asleep her grip didn't loosen, and I remembered Sami when he was a baby, the way he used to fall asleep with Afra's nipple in his mouth, his little hand still clutching the material of her scarf. It's amazing, the way we love people from the day we are born, the way we hold on, as if we are holding on to life itself.

'Uncle Nuri?' Mohammed said.

'Yes.'

'Can you tell me a story so that I can fall asleep? My mum used to tell me a story when I couldn't sleep.'

I remembered a tale my own mother used to tell me when I was a little boy in the room with the blue tiles. I remembered her with her head in the book, a red fan flickering in her right hand; eating kol w Shkor, her beloved Aleppo sweet.

'Come on, Uncle Nuri!' Mohammed said. 'Come on, or I will fall asleep by myself and not hear a story!'

I was suddenly irritated with the boy. I wanted to stay in my own mind, with my mother's voice, with the fan flickering in the lamplight.

'If you can fall asleep, why do you want a story?'

'So that I can fall asleep better.'

'OK,' I said. 'The story goes like this: a wise caliph sends his servants – I can't remember exactly how many there were – on a quest to find the mysterious City of Brass in the far desert wastes, which no one has ever entered. The journey takes two years and a few months and it is full of hardship. The servants take one thousand camels and two thousand cavalry. This I remember.'

'That's a lot! What would anybody do with a thousand camels?'

'I know, but that is how the story goes. They pass an inhabited land and ruins and a desert with a hot wind and no water and no sound.'

'How can there be no sound?'

'There just isn't.'

'What – no birds or wind or talking?'

'Nothing.'

Mohammed sat up. He was more awake than before. Perhaps I'd chosen the wrong story to tell him.

'Come on!'

'OK,' I continued. 'One day, they come to a wide plain. They see something on the horizon, tall and black with smoke rising to the sky. When they come closer they see that it is a castle, built of black stone with a door of steel.'

'Wow!' Mohammed's eyes had widened now, full of curiosity and wonder.

'I don't suppose you're getting sleepy now?'

'No,' he said, shaking my arm so I would go on.

'OK. So beyond is the City of Brass, protected by a towering wall. Behind the wall is a shiny paradise of mosques and domes and minarets and high towers and bazaars. Can you imagine it?'

'I can. It's beautiful!'

'It *is* very beautiful and gleaming with brass and jewels and precious stones and yellow marble. But . . . but . . .'

'But?'

'But the whole place is empty. There is no movement, no sound. The men find no people. In the shops, in the homes, on the streets . . . only emptiness. There is no life in this place. Life is as useless as dust. Nothing can grow here. Nothing can change.'

'Why?'

'Listen. In its midst is a very big pavilion with a dome rising high in the air. They come to a place with a long table which has words etched onto the surface. It says, "At this table have eaten a thousand kings blind in their right eye, and a thousand kings blind in their left eye, and a thousand kings blind in both eyes, all of whom have departed the world and have gone to tomb and catacomb." Every king who ever ruled this place was blind, in one way or another, so that they left it full of riches and devoid of life.'

I watched Mohammed's face, saw the thoughts moving behind his eyes. There was a pause, as if he was holding his breath. Then he exhaled.

'That's a very sad story.'

'Yes, it is a sad story.'

'Is it true?'

'It's always true, don't you think?'

'Like back home?'

'Yes, just like home.'

Mohammed lay back and turned towards the glowing fire and closed his eyes.

Seeing the smoke rising into the morning sky, I remembered Mustafa smoking the colonies during harvesting season; we used the smoke to protect ourselves while we harvested the honey. That way the bees would not smell each other's pheromones and would be less likely to sting in self-defence.

We filled a can with wood chips and shavings and started a fire, and once we got the fire going a bit, we snuffed out the open flame and stuffed more fuel on top of it. You don't want an open flame, because if it hits the bellows they can become like a flamethrower and burn the wings of the bees.

When we had so many colonies we couldn't manage them on our own we hired workers who would help us build new hives, raise queen bees, check the colonies for infestations and also collect the honey. In the field where Mustafa stood, our employees were also smoking the colonies, and puffs of smoke rose from their cans and into the blue sky where the sun blazed down upon us all. Mustafa prepared lunch for everyone – usually lentils or bulgur with salad or pasta and egg stew, followed by baladi soft cheese with honey. We had a small hut with a kitchen and outside a canopy with fans to provide some relief from the heat. We sat together to eat, Mustafa at the head of the wooden table, stuffing food into his mouth after the morning's hard work, dipping bread into the tomato sauce. He would be so proud, proud and grateful for what we had achieved together, but a part of me always wondered if this gratitude also came from fear, a fear of the unknown, of some future disaster.

Mustafa lost his mother when he was five years old. She and his unborn brother died during labour, and I think he lived forever on the edge of imminent catastrophe, and so he came to appreciate everything with the joy and terror of a child. 'Nuri,' he would say as he wiped the sauce from his chin, 'look what we have created! Isn't it marvellous? Isn't it just so marvellous?' But there in his eyes was a glint of something else, a darkness I had come to recognise as belonging to his childhood heart.

7

I N THE MORNING, WHEN I get up to use the bathroom, I see that Diomande's door is wide open and he is collecting scattered sheets of paper from the floor. The Qur'an is open on his unmade bed. He puts the pile of paper in a drawer, opens the curtains so that the sunlight floods into the room and sits down on the edge of the bed. He is wearing only tracksuit bottoms, his body is hunched over and he is holding a T-shirt in his hands.

He hasn't noticed me standing in the doorway. His mind is elsewhere, and he turns slightly towards the window so that I see a strange deformity jutting out of the skin of his back where his shoulder blades should be. As if he's just hatched out of an egg, there are small white wings, tight and muscular, like scrunched-up fists. It takes a moment for my mind to catch up with my eyes. He quickly pulls the

T-shirt over his head. I shift my feet and he turns to face me.

'Nuri – this is your name?' The sudden sound of his voice startles me. 'I met Lucy Fisher,' he says. 'She is very nice lady. I think maybe she is worried for me. I tell her not to worry, *Mrs Fisher, don't worry! There are opportunities in this country. I will find job! My friend told me if I want to be safe and if I want to stay living I should come to UK.* But she look more worry than before and now I am worrying too.'

I stand there staring at him. I can't find my voice to reply.

'When my dad died, we had very difficult time, there was no work, money was very little, and not much food for two sisters, and my mother she told me, "Diomande, I will find some money and you will go, you will go from here and find a way to help us!"'

He hunches over further now so that the bulges rise up, and he puts his long fingers on his knees and pushes himself to stand.

'On the night before I left, she make me best food in the world: kedjenou!' He licks his fingers and rolls his eyes. 'I no have kedjenou for many months, but on this night she make special for me.'

I watch his back, the movement of the wings beneath his T-shirt as he leans down to line up a pair of sandals, which he slips on over his socks. He seems to be in pain.

'What is wrong with your back?' I say.

'I have bent spine from when I was a baby,' he says.

I must be staring at him in an odd way because he pauses for a moment and looks at me. He's so tall that even when he's standing he is hunched over, and when he meets my gaze I notice that he has the eyes of an old man.

'Will you be coming to have the tea with milk?' he says. 'I like it very much.'

'Yes,' I say, and my voice comes out in a rasp. 'I will see you downstairs soon.'

I lock the door of the bathroom so that the Moroccan man will not come in again. I wash my face and hands as far as the elbows and wipe my head and my feet to the ankles. I am sweating and I can't draw my mind away from the wings to think about the words of the prayer. As I stand on the mat to say 'Allahu abkar' I catch sight of my face in the mirror above the sink and I pause with my hands by my ears. I look so different now, but I can't quite put my finger on how. Yes, there are deep lines that were not there before, and even my eyes seem to have changed – they are darker and wider, always on the alert, like Mohammed's eyes, but it's not that; something else has changed, something unfathomable.

The door handle rattles. 'Geezer!'

I don't reply but let the water run so that the bathroom steams up, hoping to see Mohammed, but he is not here.

I take my time dressing Afra. I'm not sure why she won't do it herself, but she stands there, sometimes with her eyes closed, as I pull her dress down over her body, as I wrap her hijab around her head. This time she does not guide my fingers when I put in the hairpins, she just stays silent, and I can see in the mirror that her eyes are still closed, and I wonder why they are shut, if she can't see anyway. But I don't ask her. She is holding the marble so tightly that her knuckles are white. Then she lies down on the bed, reaching for the sketch-pad on the bedside cabinet, and she places it on her chest and stays there in silence, in her own world, breathing slowly.

When we go downstairs, the Moroccan man and Diomande are not there. The landlady tells me they have gone out to get some sun. She is cleaning again. She is wearing a lot of make-up, long black lashes that look too big to be real and bright red lipstick the colour of new blood. But no matter how much of that sheen she sprays and no matter how much she scrubs, she can't get rid of the dampness and the mould and the smell of terrible journeys filled with fear. I wonder how she came to be in this country. I guess that she was born here because of her excellent British accent, and I know she has a lot of family members because in the evenings I can hear so much noise from her place next door, children and other relatives coming and going. And she always smells of spices and bleach, as if she is always either cleaning or cooking.

I contact Lucy Fisher and tell her about the problem at the GP surgery and she apologises and says that she will bring the new documents tomorrow. She is calm and business-like, and I like that Lucy Fisher is looking out for us. But her error, however small, reminds me that she is human, that she has limitations and this makes me afraid.

Afra is sitting on the sofa listening to the TV. Apart from meetings with Lucy Fisher, this is the first time that she has agreed to venture out of our bedroom, to allow herself in some small way to be part of the world. I sit with her for a while, but eventually I drift outside into the concrete courtyard and look through the fence at the landlady's garden. Mohammed was right! It is so green, full of shrubs and trees and flowers, with a hanging basket and a bird feeder and some children's toys – a small blue bicycle and a sandpit. There is also a pond with a water feature of a boy angel holding a conch, but no water is coming out of it. The courtyard is bare and grey compared to the landlady's garden, but the bee is nestled on one of the flowers, sleeping. The wooden tray suddenly reminds me of the apiaries and how the hives were like the nests of wild bees. I remember removing the individual trays to inspect the honeycomb. It was my job to ensure that the honeybee populations coincided with the nectar flows. I had to know where they occurred, where the crops were located, and then make plans so that I could manage the colonies and achieve my objectives, because it wasn't just honey we were producing, but pollen and propolis and royal jelly.

'You should bring your bed out here.' I turn and the Moroccan man is standing there with a huge smile on his face. 'What a beautiful day,' he says looking up at the sky, 'and they say this country is all rain.'

In the living room, in the evening, the Moroccan man and Diomande play hangman using English words. It's a total disaster, but I don't say anything, and I don't correct their spellings, and soon the other residents have joined in. The Afghan woman is very competitive and claps loudly when she wins. The man she always speaks to, who I understand now to be her brother, is a bit younger than she is and wears a lot of gel in his hair and has a wonky goatee. They are both very intelligent. In the nights when I've sat here listening to them talk, I've heard them speak Arabic, Farsi, English and even a bit of Greek.

I watch Diomande's back, the wings that I mistook for shoulder blades, the way they move beneath his T-shirt, the way he brings his hand to his spine now and then, a habit he has probably had all his life. He is always in pain, this boy. But his smile and his laugh are full of light. He is arguing with the Moroccan man about how to spell 'mouse'. The Moroccan man thinks there is a 'w' in it. Diomande is whacking his hand on his forehead.

My eyes close and the voices begin to merge together and when I open them again I can hear the bees, thousands of them working like they used to. The noise is coming from outside. The room is quiet now, apart from the sound of the marble rolling on the floorboards. Mohammed is sitting on the floor.

'Uncle Nuri!' he says when he hears me moving. 'You've been sleeping for such a long time.'

The clock on the wall says 3 a.m.

'Did you find the key?' he says.

'There was no key. They were flowers.'

'You went to the wrong place,' he says. 'It's not that tree – it's in the other garden. The green garden. It's one of the small trees. The key is on there. I can see it through the hole.'

'What do you need the key for?' I say.

'I need to get out,' is all he says. 'Will you fetch it for me?'

I unlock the patio doors, and the sound of the bees hits me. The air is thick and full, but I see not even one bee. The darkness is empty. Mohammed follows me out into the courtyard.

'Do you hear that?' I say. 'Where is it coming from?'

'Just look in the other garden, Uncle Nuri, and you will find the key.'

I look through the hole, but it's so dark that I can barely see the trees, let alone a key.

'You have to go over the fence,' he says above the noise, this constant buzzing coming from the deepest place of the atmosphere, like waves or memory. I get the stepladder and climb over into the landlady's garden. I am suddenly surrounded by the softness of the black trees and flowers, blurred shapes rustling in the breeze. The small bicycle is leaning against the wall, and I recognise the outline of the sandpit and walk around it. I can hear Mohammed guiding me now, he is telling me to turn left, and eventually I see what he is talking about, a small shrub, and this time there is one key hanging from a branch. It catches the light of the moon. I have to pull hard to take it off, it's tangled in the foliage, and then I put the bicycle next to the fence so that I can step on it to climb back over.

When I'm back in the courtyard, Mohammed has gone. I close the patio doors against the noise and head upstairs and climb into bed. Afra is asleep with both hands resting beneath her cheek. She is breathing slowly and deeply. I lie on my back this time and hold the key close to my chest. The buzzing is distant now. I think I can hear

the waves

of the Aegean were calm in the late afternoon. The fire had been extinguished, and we were aboard a marine vessel heading to the island of Leros.

'This is the second time I have been on a boat,' Mohammed said. 'The first time was a bit scary, don't you think?'

'Just a bit.' I immediately thought of Sami. Sami had been on a boat once when we'd taken him to visit his grandparents on the Syrian coast, a small town in the shadow of the Lebanon mountains. He was afraid of the water – he cried and I held him in my arms and soothed him by pointing out the fish in the water. Then he stared at the streaks of silver fish beneath the surface with tears in his eyes and a smile on his face. He was always afraid of water; even when we washed his hair, he didn't want it in his ears or in his eyes. He was a boy of the desert. He only knew the water in the evaporating streams and irrigation ponds. He and Mohammed were the same age – if he was here they would have been friends. Mohammed would have looked after Sami because Sami was a more sensitive, more fearful boy, and Sami would have told Mohammed stories. How he loved to tell stories!

'I wish my mum was here,' Mohammed said, and I placed a hand on his shoulder and watched him as his eyes flickered, following the fish in the sea. Afra was sitting behind us on one of the chairs; an NGO worker had given her a white stick to hold, but she didn't like it and so left it on the floor beside her.

When we disembarked, volunteers were already waiting. There was structure here, I could tell. Many people had passed through already, and the NGOs were well prepared. We were led away from the port, up a small hill, to the registration centre for new arrivals: a large tent. The place was brimming with refugees and soldiers and police officers who were wearing blue-mirrored sunglasses. From what I could see, there were people from Syria, Afghanistan, other Arab countries and parts of Africa. Men in uniform and straight faces divided us into groups: single females, unaccompanied minors, single men with passports, single men without passports, families. Luckily the three of us got to stay together. We were shown to one of the long queues and given some bread rolls with cheese. People were restless as they waited to be identified. They wanted their papers so that they could exist in the eyes of the European Union. And the ones who were the wrong nationality would get no papers – except for a ticket back to wherever.

Finally, after hours of standing in line, we reached the front of the queue. Mohammed had fallen asleep on one of the benches on the far side of the tent and Afra and I took a seat facing a man who was leafing through some notes on the desk. Afra was still holding the bread roll in her hand. The man looked at her and leant back in his chair, his stomach big enough to balance a plate on. Although it was cold in the tent, he had beads of sweat on his forehead and there were shadows under his eyes as wide as smiles. The man lowered the sunglasses from his head onto his nose.

'Where are you from?' he said.

'Syria,' I said.

'Do you have passports?'

'Yes.'

I took all three passports out of my rucksack and placed them open on the table. He lifted his glasses, scanning them.

'What part of Syria?'

'Aleppo.'

'Is this your son?' He pointed at the picture of Sami.

'Yes.'

'How old is he?'

'Seven.'

'Where is he?'

'Asleep on the bench. He's very tired after the long journey.'

The man nodded and stood up, and for a moment I thought that he would go and find Mohammed to check his face against the picture, but he walked across the tent to a row of photocopiers, then he returned, stinking of cigarettes, puffed out his cheeks and asked for our fingerprints. We were being transformed into verifiable, printable entities.

'Do you need Sami's fingerprints?' I asked.

'No, not if he's under ten. Can I see your phone?'

I got my phone out of my bag. The battery was dead.

'What's your PIN?' the man said. I wrote it down and he went away, again in the direction of the photocopiers.

'Why did you tell him we have a son?' Afra said.

'It's easier that way. They won't ask so many questions.'

She didn't say anything, but I could see from the way she was scratching her skin, pressing so hard that there were red streaks on her wrists, that she was uncomfortable. After a long time the man returned, out of breath, stinking of more cigarettes and coffee.

'What was your occupation in Syria?' he said, sitting down again, his stomach bulging over his trousers.

'I was a beekeeper.'

'And you, Mrs Ibrahim?' He looked at Afra now.

'I was an artist,' she said.

'The pictures on the phone, are they your paintings?'

Afra nodded.

The man leant back in his chair again. With his glasses on it was difficult to know what he was looking at, but he seemed to be staring at Afra. I could see a reflection of her in each lens. Although there was so much noise in the tent, the place seemed to fall into silence.

'They are very special, your paintings,' the man said. Then he leant forward, his huge stomach pressing against the table – pushing it slightly towards us.

'What happened to her?' he said to me, and there was an unmistakable note of curiosity in his voice. I could suddenly imagine him collecting horror stories – real-life tales of loss and destruction. His glasses were fixed on me now.

'A bomb,' I said.

The man's glasses moved back to focus on Afra.

'Where do you hope to get to?'

'The United Kingdom,' she said.

'Ha!'

'We have friends there,' I said, trying to ignore his mocking laugh.

'Most people are more realistic,' the man said, handing me the passports and my phone, explaining that we would have to wait on the island until the authorities gave us clearance to leave for Athens.

We were led away from there, with two or three other families, to a gated camp near the port. Mohammed held onto my hand, asking me where we were going.

We found ourselves enclosed in barbed wire, and before us was a grim village with immaculate concrete walkways, wire mesh fences and white gravel. There were rows and rows of square boxes for people to stay in until they got their papers. An empire of identification.

The pebbles were meant to soak up water, but the ground was saturated, probably from rain earlier. In the alleys between the cabins there were clothes hanging on lines and, at the entrance of every cabin, a gas heater, and on top of these heaters people had placed shoes and socks and hats to dry. In the distance, beyond the cabins and across the sea, I could see the faint outline of Turkey and, on the other side, the dark hills of the island.

As I stood there with Afra and Mohammed and the other families, I felt lost, as if I was out alone in a dark cold sea with nothing to hold on to. This was the first time in a long time that I had felt any safety, any security, and yet in this moment the sky felt too big, the rising dusk held an unknown darkness. I stared at the orange glow of the gas heaters, felt the certainty of my feet on the pebbles. But somewhere nearby there was shouting in a language I didn't understand, followed by a long cry – the voice was desperate and came from a deep and hollow place and it sent the birds flying into an orange sky.

Each cabin was already divided, partitioned with blankets and sheets to make room for more families. We were given a section of one of these cabins and told that there was food in the old asylum next to the registration centre, and that the gates would be locked at 9 p.m., so if we wanted to eat we should go soon. But Mohammed was rocking from foot to foot, as if he was on a boat, and as soon as he got the chance, he lay down. I covered him with a blanket.

'Uncle Nuri,' he said, opening his eyes a little bit, 'can I have chocolate tomorrow?'

'If I can find some.'

'The type you can spread. I want to spread it on bread.'

'I'll try to find some for you.'

It was evening and cold. Afra and I lay down too, and I rested my palm on her chest and felt the beating of her heart and the rhythm of her breathing. 'Nuri,' she said as we lay there.

'Yes?'

'Are you OK?'

'Why?'

'I think you're not all right.'

She was close to me and I could feel the tension in her body.

'None of us are OK,' I said.

'It's . . .' She hesitated.

'What is it?'

She sighed. 'It's the boy . . .'

'We're all so tired,' I said. 'Let's sleep now, talk tomorrow.'

She sighed again and closed her eyes.

She fell asleep quickly and I tried to mirror her breath, slow and steady, so that I could shut off my mind, but her tone had been so dark, as if she knew something that I didn't, and I couldn't sleep. Her unspoken words had opened a chasm, and from that place images came and went like dreams – Mohammed's black eyes, Sami's eyes the colour of Afra's. Even as I drifted off, my body jolted from a sudden noise in my head, like a door creaking open, and there, on the other side, the shadow of a boy. 'Will we fall into the water?' I heard. 'Will the waves take us? The houses won't break like these do.' Sami's voice. Mohammed's voice.

Then my mind plunged into darkness and silence. I turned away from Afra and focused on patterns on the bedsheet partition. I was kept awake by the mutterings and whisperings on the other side, a young girl talking to her father. As she became more distressed their voices rose.

'But when will she come?' the little girl was saying.

'When you're asleep she will stroke your hair. Just like she used to, remember?'

'But I want to see her.'

'You won't see her, but you'll feel her. You'll feel that she is near you, I promise.' I could hear a crack in the man's voice.

'But when those men took her . . .'

'Let's not talk about that.'

The little girl let out a sob. 'But when they took her she was crying. Why did those men take her? Where did they take her? Why was she crying?'

'Let's not talk about this now. Go to sleep.'

'You said they would bring her back. I want to go back home and get her. I want to go home.'

'We can't go home.'

'Never?'

The man didn't reply.

Then there was a shout outside, a man's voice, and a deep thumping. The sound of beating? A body being beaten? I wanted to get up to see what was happening, but I was afraid. There were footsteps outside the cabin, and people running, and then there was quiet and eventually the distant sounds of the waves drew me in, took my mind away from where I was, far away into open water.

I woke up to the sound of the birds. There were voices and footsteps and I noticed that Mohammed was not in the cabin, and Afra was still asleep.

I went out to find him. People had ventured out of their cabins to catch the warmth of the sun, others were hanging clothes on the lines in the alley. Children were jumping over the puddles or punching balloons onto the barbed wire with their fists, like volleyballs, laughing as they popped. I couldn't see Mohammed among them.

I noticed soldiers walking around, guns in their belts. I made my way to the old asylum building; I'd been told there were services and a children's centre. There was something haunting about the island – half-finished crumbling properties, empty storefronts – as if the residents themselves had suddenly run out of there in a hurry, leaving the place to fall apart. Windows like eyes opened into dark uninhabitable buildings. Shutters hung off their hinges. The old asylum was like some place from a nightmare. In the hallway there was a huge unlit fireplace behind cast-iron bars; a staircase led up and around towards voices that were echoing from other rooms on other floors.

'What do you need?' a voice behind me said.

I turned around: a girl in her early twenties, sun-kissed cheeks, a dozen silver hoops in one ear and one in her nose. She was smiling but she looked tired, the skin beneath her eyes purple. Her lips were cracked.

'I was told there were resources here. I wanted to get a few things for my wife.'

'Third floor, to the left,' she said.

I hesitated. 'And I'm looking for my son.' I looked over my shoulder as if Mohammed might just appear behind me.

'What does he look like?' the girl said, yawning. She covered her mouth. Her eyes swam. 'Sorry,' she said, 'I didn't sleep well. There was trouble last night.'

'Trouble?'

She shook her head, holding back another yawn. 'The camps are getting too full, some people have been here so long, it's hard to . . .' She stopped there. 'What does your son look like?'

'My son?'

'You just said you were looking for your son.'

'He's seven. Black hair, black eyes.'

'You've just described most of the boys here.'

'But they have brown hair and eyes. This boy's eyes are black. As black as the night. You can't ignore them.'

She seemed preoccupied now, taking a phone out of her back pocket, checking it so the screen lit up the shadows on her face.

'Where are you staying?' she said.

'In the cabins by the port.'

'You're lucky you're not in the other place.'

'The other place?'

'Does your wife need clothes? There's a boutique upstairs. I'll take you.' The hallway started to get busier, people from so many parts of the world. I could hear variations of Arabic, mixed in with the unfamiliar rhythms and sounds of other languages.

'Your English is very good,' she said as we climbed the stairs.

'My father taught me when I was a child. And I was a businessman, in Syria.'

'What kind of business?'

'A beekeeper. I had hives and I sold honey.'

I watched her flip-flops as they slapped against the soles of her feet.

'This island was a leper colony once,' she said. 'This asylum was like a Nazi concentration camp. People were caged and chained without names or identities. The children here were abandoned, tied to their beds all day.'

She suddenly stopped talking as we passed a policeman who was coming down the stairs. He was not wearing glasses, too dark in here, and he nodded and smiled at her with warm eyes.

'The second and fourth floors are camps,' she continued, once he was out of sight. 'In the courtyard at night they light a big campfire and make food, because otherwise all you will eat are bread rolls with cheese, and maybe a banana. Sometimes old women bring vegetables from their gardens for the stew. On this floor there are two boutiques, one for women and children, and one for men. You might want to get something for your son too. There's quite a lot of stuff today and you've come early, which is good.'

She led me to the women's boutique and left me there, and as I entered I heard a man in the hallway say to her, 'You know the rules. Just ask them what they need. Don't talk to them.'

I hovered in the doorway for a few seconds to hear her response. I expected her to apologise, but instead I heard a throaty laugh, full of defiance. There was a confidence in her that she had brought with her from another place. There were only footsteps after this, fading away as I entered the boutique. The walls were damp and green, light coming in through a long barred window, shining onto a rack. A woman stood alert with both hands behind her back.

'Can I help you?' she said. 'What do you need?'

'I need some clothes for my wife and my son.'

She asked me questions about their sizes and body shapes, pushing the hangers along the rail until she pulled out a few suitable items.

I left the place with three toothbrushes, a couple of razors, a bar of soap, a bag full of clothes and underwear, and an extra pair of shoes for Mohammed; I imagined he would want to run around a lot here with the other children. Perhaps he had heard them playing in the morning and got up to join them? Maybe some of them went down to the sea to greet the new arrivals? Along the harbour there were shops – Vodafone, Western Union, a bakery, a café and a newsagent – all with signs outside in Arabic: *SIM cards, Wi-Fi connection, Charge your phones.*

I went into the café. The place was full of refugees drinking tea or water or coffee, a break from the camps. There were people speaking Kurdish and Farsi. Ahead, a man and boy were having a conversation in Syrian Arabic. A waitress came out of the kitchen in the back holding a notepad, asking me what I would like. She was followed by an older woman, who was holding a tray full of glasses of water. She placed the drinks on the tables, speaking to the customers, greeting them by name. She had learnt a bit of all three languages.

I ordered a coffee, which I was told was free, and I took a seat at one of the tables, and when my coffee was brought out I savoured it, sip by sip. I never thought I would be sitting down somewhere, next to other families, drinking coffee, without the sound of bombs, without the fear of snipers. It was at this time, when the chaos stopped, that I thought of Sami. Then there was guilt, for being able to taste the coffee.

'Here by the self?'

I looked up. The older woman was looking at me and smiling.

'Speak English?' she asked.

'Yes, I do. No, I'm not here alone, I'm with my wife, and my son. I'm looking for him. He's about this tall, black hair, black eyes.'

'Sound like all boy!'

'Do you know where I can buy chocolate?' I said.

She explained to me that there was a convenience store down the road. I noticed that some people had ordered food. The refugees had brought business to this place; usually in March the island would have been almost deserted.

When I left I headed to the convenience store down the road, and there I bought a jar of Nutella and a loaf of fresh bread. The boy was going to love it! I couldn't wait to see the excitement in his eyes.

I found an Internet café because I wanted to see if Mustafa had replied to my email. I was nervous as I typed in my username and password – there was a part of me that didn't want to know, because if there was no email from him then I would find it even harder to keep going, but I was happy when I saw a stream of messages waiting for me:

* * *

04/02/2016

Dear Nuri,

Mustafa has not been able to get to his emails. I spoke to him today, he has made it to France and has asked me to check his messages and respond. He was hoping there would be a message from you, he has been hoping every day. I cannot even begin to explain how pleased I am to hear from you. Mustafa and I were both very worried. He tried not to imagine bad things but he found it hard not to, as you must know.

When I speak to him again I will tell him the good news. He will be very happy. Aya and I are in England. We are living at the moment in a shared house in Yorkshire and waiting to find out if we have been granted asylum.

I am glad you made it to Istanbul, Nuri, and I hope that you make it safely to Greece and further.

With love,
Dahab

* * *

28/02/2016

Dear Nuri,

I finally made it to my daughter and wife in England. It was a horrible journey through France and I do not want to write about it here, but I will tell you when you arrive. I know that you will make it to us. We are waiting for you. I cannot rest until you get here. You are like my brother, Nuri. My family is not complete without you and Afra.

Dahab is very unhappy, Nuri. She was trying to stay strong for Aya, but since I arrived here she has been lying down all day with the lights switched off, holding on to a photograph of Firas. Sometimes she cries, but most of the time she is silent. She will not talk about him. All she says is that she is happy that I am by her side now.

I see from your last email that you were in Istanbul. I hope that you have made it to Greece by now. I have heard that Macedonia has closed their borders so it will be difficult from there, as it was for me, but you must keep going. By the time I hear from you again I hope that you will have moved closer to where we are.

So many times I wish I had not stayed behind, that I had left Aleppo with my wife and daughter because then my son would still be with us. This thought brings me close to death. We cannot go back, cannot change the decisions we made in the past. I did not kill my son. I try to remember these things because if I don't I will be lost in the darkness.

The day that I hear that you have made it to England will bring light to my soul.

Mustafa

I sat there and read and reread the email. *You are like my brother, Nuri.* And the memory came back to me of Mustafa's father's house in the mountains. The house was surrounded by pines and fir trees and it was dark and cool inside, old mahogany furniture and handwoven rugs, and on a console table at the far end, beneath a window, a shrine to the mother and wife who had left them. There were photographs of her as a young girl and then as a young woman, tall and beautiful with glittering eyes. There were wedding photographs and pictures of her holding Mustafa in her arms, and others when she was pregnant with the child she would die with. Mustafa grew up under the care and protection of his father and grandfather, no women to soften the place or bring light to it, no siblings to play with, so he found solace in the brilliant light and beautiful sounds and smells of the apiaries.

He got to know the bees like they were his siblings, he watched them and learnt how they spoke to one another, he followed paths deep into the mountains to find the source of their journey and sat in the shade of the trees and watched as they collected nectar from eucalyptus and cotton and rosemary.

Mustafa's grandfather was a strong man, with huge hands like Mustafa, a sharp eye and a sense of humour – he encouraged Mustafa to be curious, to have adventures with nature. He liked it when I came to visit and would cut up tomatoes and cucumbers for us, as if we were children, as if I had become the missing link in their family. On soft bread he would spread butter and honey fresh from the hives, then he would sit with us and tell us stories about his own childhood, or about his beloved daughter-in-law.

'She was such a kind woman,' he would say. 'She looked

after me well, and she would never tell me to shut up when I babbled on.' And even after all these years he would wipe his eyes with his liver-spotted hand. Sitting in that cool living room, we seemed to be surrounded by his mother's never-faltering smile, a smile that engulfed us and weaved itself around us, a bit like the sweet sound of the bees.

Then he would become brisk. 'Right, you two do something useful now. Go and show Nuri how to extract the honey. And give him some royal jelly to eat – he needs it after being cooped up in the city like he is.'

And Mustafa would take me to the place where the bees sang.

'We will build things together, I can tell,' he said. 'We balance each other you and me. Together we will do great things.'

* * *

03/03/2016

Dear Mustafa,

You have always been like a brother to me. I remember the days when I visited your father's house in the mountains, I remember the photographs of your mother, and your grandfather . . . What a man he was! Without you, my life would have been very different. We created great things together, just as you said we would. But this war snatched it away from us, everything we dreamed about and worked for. It's left us without our home, without our work and without our sons. I am not sure how I can live like this. I fear that I am dead inside. The only thing that is keeping me going is the wish to reach you and Dahab and Aya.

I am so happy to hear that you have finally reached your wife and daughter. This thought alone, knowing that you are with them, brings joy during these dark times.

Afra and I have reached Leros and hope we will be leaving for Athens soon. If the Macedonian border is closed, then I will find another way. Don't worry, Mustafa, I will not stop until I get there.

Nuri

I returned to the camp, back to the shining metal and white gravel and concrete and rows and rows of square box containers, all surrounded by wire mesh. Afra was standing in the doorway of our cabin holding the white stick like a weapon.

'What are you doing?' I said.

'Where did you go?'

'To get some things.'

'There was noise. Too much. I told them to go away.'

'Who?' I said.

'The children.'

'Did the boy come back?'

'What boy?'

'Mohammed.'

'Nobody came,' she said.

I put the bag down and told her that I was heading out again to find some food for dinner, and this time I searched the streets for Mohammed. I followed the laughter of children around every corner, in the open fields, beneath the trees. I went back to the asylum, checked in every room, including the children's centre and the mother-and-baby room and the prayer room. I took the road down to another shore, on a quiet beach with children's footprints in the sand, but whoever was there had already left and the sun was setting. I stood there for a while, inhaling the fresh air, feeling the orange sunlight on my face.

When I opened my eyes I saw the strangest thing: about thirty or forty octopuses hanging on a line to dry, their silhouettes against the setting sun making them look like something from a dream. I rubbed my eyes, thinking I might have fallen asleep, but the octopuses still hung there, their arms pulled down by gravity, taking on an odd shape, like the faces of men with long beards. I touched the rubbery flesh, smelt them to see if they were fresh, and took one to cook on a fire. I held it in my arms as if I was holding a child and headed back to the cabins, buying a lighter from the sweet shop and collecting some twigs and branches along the way.

When I got back to the camp, Afra was sitting on the floor, twirling something in her fingers. I saw that it was Mohammed's clear marble with the red vein.

I was about to ask about Mohammed, but I noticed that her face had suddenly dropped and her eyes were no longer blank; they were alive and full of sadness.

'What's wrong?' I said. 'You have sad eyes.'

'I do?'

'Yes,' I said.

'It's because I just realised that I lost my platinum bracelet – you know, the one my mum gave me?'

'Yes,' I said, 'I remember.'

'The one with the little stars.'

'I remember.'

'I put it on before we left. I must have lost it on the boat. It's in the sea now.'

Sitting down on the floor beside her, I wrapped my arms around her and she rested her head on my shoulder, just like she did in the hole in the garden before we left Aleppo. She didn't cry this time; I could feel her breath on my neck and the flutter of her eyelashes on my skin, and we stayed like this for a long while, as the cabin darkened and only the glow of the gas fire could be seen. There was noise around us: people shouting, children running, a strong wind in the trees from the sea, coming to us in waves. I wondered if Mohammed was still playing, or if he was on his way back to the cabin.

Then I went outside to cook the octopus. I put the twigs and branches in a pile on the ground; I held the octopus on a branch above the fire. It took a lot longer than I thought, even though the octopus was already slightly cooked from hanging in the sun.

When it was soft enough and cool enough, I tore it into pieces and took it in to Afra. She devoured it, licking her fingers, thanking me for making it, asking me where I found such a thing.

'Did you get it from the sea yourself?'

'No!' I laughed.

'But you couldn't have bought it – it's far too expensive!'

'I found it,' I said.

'What, you were walking along, minding your own business, and you just found an octopus?'

'Yes,' I said, and she laughed from her stomach, her eyes laughing too.

I looked through the doorway, anxious, waiting for Mohammed.

Afra lay her head on some of the blankets and closed her eyes without saying another word. I lay down beside her, and after a while I heard gates opening and closing, distant doors locking. On the other side of the partition the child was crying, her father muttering words of reassurance. 'No, the men with the guns won't kill us. Don't worry at all! No, they won't. I promise.'

'But they might shoot us.'

The man laughed now. 'No. They're here to help us. Just close your eyes now. Close your eyes and think of all the things you love.'

'Like my bicycle at home?'

'Yes, that's good. Keep thinking about your bicycle.'

There was silence for a long time and after a while I heard the girl speak again, but this time her voice was softer, calmer.

'Daddy,' she said.

'Yes?'

'I felt it.'

'What did you feel?'

'I felt Mummy stroking my hair.'

And then neither of them spoke again, but I could almost

feel this man's heart drop in the silence. Further away there was banter, people talking and laughing. There was no shouting tonight.

I looked at the octopus and the Nutella and the bread, all placed on the floor in case Mohammed came back in the night – he would see the food and know it was for him. But the camp was closed now. I was locked in and Mohammed locked out. I got up and made my way through the grid of boxes in the dark, to the edge of the camp until I found the entrance. There were two soldiers standing at the gate, holding guns.

'Can I help you?' one said.

'I need to go out.'

'It's too late now. You can go in the morning.'

'So I'm locked in? Like a prisoner?'

The man said nothing in response and didn't avert his eyes either.

'I need to find my son!'

'You can find him in the morning.'

'But I have no idea where he is.'

'How far do you think he went? This is an island!'

'But he might be alone and scared.'

The soldiers were having none of it. They sent me away and I tried to go back to the cabin, but it was difficult in the dark, every corner was the same, and I hadn't counted the grids so that I could find my way. Maybe this was what happened to Mohammed? Maybe he ventured out without counting and couldn't find his way back? Maybe another family had taken him in? I decided to lie down on the ground, by the doorway of another cabin, so that I was close to the warmth of their gas fire.

I woke up in the morning to the sound of rain on the metal roofs of the cabins. I was drenched and I got up and somehow managed to find my way back to Afra. I recognised a pink bedsheet hanging out on one of the lines. The rain was pounding down. Flies had gotten in and were all over the octopus.

Afra was already awake. She was lying on her back, staring up at the ceiling as if she was looking at the stars, and twirling the marble in her fingers, just as Mohammed had done.

'Where did you go?' she said.

'I went out and got lost.'

'I didn't sleep last night. The rain started, and all I could hear and see in my head was rain.'

I swept my hand over the octopus and the flies dispersed, buzzing around our section of the cabin, making rings around one another and then returning to the octopus like magnets.

'Are you hungry?' I said.

'You want me to share the octopus with the flies?'

'No,' I laughed. 'We have bread and chocolate spread.'

I took the bread out of the paper bag and tore it into pieces, leaving some for Mohammed. Then I opened the Nutella, considering how I would spread it onto the bread without a knife. Afra said we could dip the bread into the chocolate.

Later that morning, when the rain finally stopped, I headed

out again to look for Mohammed. At first I wandered around the enclosure, making my way through the people-containers, the rows and rows of the compound, the walkways, beneath the hanging clothes, calling out Mohammed's name. The ground was saturated with water – even the shoes outside the doorways were full of water. The white gravel had been able to soak up only a certain amount. But this rain felt like it was coming out of the sea. The wire mesh, and everything now, was covered in a sheen of silver, like shining liquid metal, making the place seem even more like a prison than before, and now that the sun had come out, there were reflections and splashes of light.

I made my way to the old asylum. A teenage boy was sitting on the steps with headphones on, his head against the wall, eyes closed. I nudged him awake to ask him if he'd seen anyone who could be Mohammed. But the boy's head rocked on his shoulders, and his eyes opened only ever so slightly. I could hear children playing on one of the upper floors, faint echoes of laughter, and I followed the laughter through the corridors to the fourth-floor camps, looking into each room; inside there were blankets hanging as partitions, shoes in neat rows, here and there I glimpsed someone's hair, or a leg or an arm. I called out, 'Mohammed!' and an old man with a gruff voice replied, 'Yes!' and then, 'What do you want? I am here! Have you come to take me?'

I could still hear him as I made my way down the corridor. The children were in the last room, which was full of toys and board games and balloons. A few NGO workers were kneeling next to the younger ones. One of them held a baby in her arms. She caught my eye and came to greet me.

'This is the children's centre,' she said, pronouncing the words very slowly.

'Clearly,' I said. 'I'm looking for my son.'

'Name?'

'Mohammed.'

'How old?'

'Seven.'

'What does he look like?'

'He has black hair and black eyes. Not brown. Black like the sky at night.'

I could see that she was searching her mind for a moment, but then she shook her head. 'Try not to worry – he'll turn up, they always do, and when he does you can give him these.' With her free hand she rummaged through a plastic container and retrieved a box of coloured pencils attached to a notepad. I thanked her and left, and this time as I headed back down the corridor and down the stairs, I could almost see the ghosts of those people, not so long ago, gagged and chained to their beds. I heard echoes now, not of the children's laughter, but other sounds, at the edges of the imagination, where humans cease to be human.

I made my way out of there quickly, down the stairs and out into the silver light and down to the port. The café was full of people, and I sat for a while to charge my phone and have a coffee, watching the two women, who I realised were mother and daughter, bringing out glasses of water and tea and coffee, interacting with the refugees, trying to communicate as best they could in the little Arabic or Farsi they had picked up. On this day, the father and son were also there, the son a smaller version of his dad, minus the moustache. I allowed myself to relax a bit, and lean back in the chair and close my eyes, listening to the conversations going on around me and to the distant thunder over the sea.

I waited there until the afternoon, but there was no sign of Mohammed. At four o'clock I went to the registration centre to find out if the authorities had checked the papers and granted clearance. There were hundreds of people gathered around a flustered man who was standing on a stool, holding up cards and calling out names. He didn't call ours, but I was pleased because I didn't want to leave without Mohammed.

The next day passed in a similar way – the sun dried up the rain and the wind was much warmer. It was as if the darkness had been washed away, and even though there were more people streaming onto the island, tossed in by the waves, and fewer people leaving, the place somehow seemed more peaceful. Maybe there was just so much noise that it all blended together and became like the drumming of rain or the sound of waves or the buzzing of the flies around the octopus, and away from the campsite the soil smelt fresh and sweet, and the trees were beginning to blossom and bear fruit.

And there was still no sign of Mohammed.

By the evening of the next day I started to lose hope. I took the coloured pencils out of their packaging.

'What is that?' Afra said, her ear tuned into the sound. 'What are you opening?'

'Pencils.'
'Coloured ones?'
'Yes.'
'Is there paper?'
'Yes, a notepad.'
'Can I have it?'

I placed all the pencils in front of her in a row and led her hand to them. I opened the notepad and placed it on her lap.

'Thank you,' she said.

I lay back and stared up at the ceiling of the cabin, at the spiders and insects and cobwebs that had gathered in the corners. I listened to the soft conversations through the sheets and out in the alleys, and the pencils swishing over paper.

Hours later, when it was almost dark, Afra finally spoke. 'I made this for you,' she said.

The picture she had drawn was so different from her usual artwork – a flower-filled field overlooked by a single tree.

'But how did you draw this?' I said.

'I can feel the pencil marks on the paper.'

I looked at the picture again. The colours were wild – the tree blue, the sky red. The lines were broken, leaves and flowers out of place, and yet it held a beauty that was mesmerising and indescribable, like an image in a dream, like a picture of a world that is beyond our imagination.

The following afternoon my name was called out at the registration centre. I was given the cards and permission to leave the island for Athens: Nuri Ibrahim, Afra Ibrahim, and Sami Ibrahim. My stomach turned when I looked at Sami's name, printed so clearly on the piece of paper in my hand. Sami. Sami Ibrahim. As if he was still among us.

I didn't tell Afra that we'd been granted clearance. I didn't even go to the travel agency to buy the ferry tickets. The days and nights passed and Afra was feeling restless.

'I'm having nightmares,' she said. 'I am dead and there are flies all over me and I can't move to shake them off!'

'Don't worry,' I said. 'We'll be off this island soon.'

'I don't like it here,' she said. 'This place is full of ghosts.'

'What kind of ghosts?'

'I don't know,' she said. 'Something not human.'

I knew that she was right. I knew that we had to go, but I didn't want to leave without Mohammed. What if the boy returned and wondered where I was? I knew he was coming back, he must be. As the police officer said – this is an island, he couldn't have gone far.

The following night it was raining again and Afra had a terrible fever. Her head was hot, her hands and feet as cold as the sea. I dabbed her forehead and chest with a damp cloth – my T-shirt dunked in water.

'He's playing,' she said.

'Who?'

'Sami, I can hear him. Tell him to be careful.'

'He's not here,' I said.

'He's lost,' she said.

'Who?'

'Sami. The houses are all gone and he's lost.'

I didn't say anything. I rubbed her hands between my

palms to warm them up, watching her beautiful face. I could see she was frightened.

'I want to leave here,' she said.

'We will.'

'When? Why is it taking so long?'

'We need to get the papers.'

The following day her fever was worse. She was shivering and complaining about pain in her back and her legs.

'Tell him to come in and have his dinner,' she said as I wrapped one of the blankets around her.

'I will.'

'He's been off playing all day.'

'I'll tell him,' I said. I found some lemons to make her a soothing drink to sip, but Afra was becoming more unwell as the days passed. I thought she was losing hope. I knew we had to leave this place, so I told her that we'd been given the papers. I waited several days for her to get a bit stronger, until at least she could stand on her own and go outside to feel the sun on her face. Then I bought the tickets and wrote a note.

Mohammed,
I have waited for you now for one month. I have no idea what happened to you, where you are and whether you will even come back to find this note, but I have been looking for you every day, and I pray that Allah will protect you and look after you. Take this money and the card. You must use the name Sami (this was my son's name) and go to the

travel agent (you will find it next to the Seven Gates café) and buy yourself a ferry ticket to Athens. Don't miss the boat, because there will be no more money to buy another ticket. You will have one chance, so make sure you get the times right.

This will be your third time on a boat! When you make it to Athens, try to find us. Here is my phone number: 0928-----. Keep in mind that the phone might not work. My full name is Nuri Ibrahim. I am planning to go from Athens to the UK. If you get to Athens and you do not find us, please continue to search. Please try to make your way to England, and if you meet any person who seems kind, give them my name and hopefully they will help you to find me.

I hope to see you soon. In the meantime be very careful, make sure you eat well and don't give up. It is easy sometimes to give up. I will be thinking about you and praying for you even across seas and mountains. If you do need to cross any more water, try not to be afraid. I will pray for you every day.

Uncle Nuri

I folded the letter and money into an envelope and placed it on the floor, in the corner of the cabin, beneath the jar of Nutella.

* * *

The cargo ferry was so big, and painted with yellow stars; there were lorries and cars parked on the bottom level. At the port people were saying goodbye to the NGO workers. The ferry was due to depart for Athens at 9 p.m. and the journey was going to take roughly eight hours. There were chairs for women and older people. The air was warm and the sea that night was calm. Until the last moment I was on the lookout for Mohammed, but it wasn't long before all the passengers had boarded and the horn for departure sounded loud and clear. Then the ferry edged out into the open sea, leaving the island of ghosts behind. Afra breathed deeply, inhaling the sea air. The darkness now entered my mind from the sea and the sky, and I felt it again, that sense of being lost: the sky and the sea and the world seemed too big. I closed my eyes and prayed for Mohammed, the lost boy who was never mine.

8

I WAKE UP WITH AFRA'S HAND resting on my chest. I can feel her fingers on mine, but there is also something else. I remember Mohammed and the key I found in the landlady's garden. But when I move my hands I see that I am holding a chrysanthemum.

'You got me another gift?' she says. There is a question in her voice.

'Yes,' I say.

She runs her fingers over the petals and the stem.

'What colour is it?' she says.

'Orange.'

'I like orange . . . I thought you would stay downstairs all night. You fell asleep and Hazim helped me up – he didn't want to wake you.'

There is something desperate in her voice, questions that

she is not asking, and I can't bear the smell of the rose perfume on her body.

'I'm glad you like it,' I say, and I remove her hand from my chest, allowing the flower to drop onto the bed.

Later, after I have prayed and dressed Afra, Lucy Fisher arrives. She is in a hurry today, holding two rucksacks as if she is going away somewhere. This time there is another woman with her who I think is a translator; she is dark-skinned and round and holds an old-fashioned handbag.

We sit in the kitchen for just ten minutes. She gives me the new letter with the B&B address printed clearly on it and tells me the date and time of the asylum interview.

'You have five days,' she says, 'to prepare.'

'As if I am taking an exam,' I say, and smile. But her face is very serious. She explains that Afra and Diomande will each have their own translators, and there will be one on hand for me too.

'Diomande's interview is on the same day?' I say.

'Yes, you can travel there together. It's in South London.' She continues to talk, opening a map, pointing out the location, opening another train map, explaining things to me, but I'm not really listening. I want to tell her about Diomande's wings. I want to tell her about Mohammed and the keys, but I'm afraid of her reaction. And then, from the window, something catches my eye. White planes searing through the sky. Too many to count. I hear a whistle followed by a rumbling, as though the world has ripped open. I rush to the window: bombs are falling, planes are circling. The light is too strong, I shield my eyes. The sound is too loud, I cover my ears.

I feel a hand on my shoulder.

'Mr Ibrahim?' I hear.

I turn and Lucy Fisher is standing behind me.

'Are you OK?'

'The planes,' I say.

'The planes?'

I point at the white planes in the sky.

There is a pause and I hear Lucy Fisher exhale. 'Look,' she says, very gently. 'Look, Mr Ibrahim. Look carefully. They are birds.'

I look again and I see seagulls. Lucy Fisher is right. There are no planes circling, only a passenger plane far away, appearing through a wisp of clouds, and above us only seagulls.

'You see?' she says.

I nod and she leads me back to my chair.

Lucy Fisher is a very practical woman and gets back to what she was saying almost immediately, after only a slight hesitation and a sip of water. She wants to make sure that everything is in place. And as she runs the tip of a pencil along one of the train lines, I feel grounded, calmer. She says names of places that I've never heard of before, and she consults the other map and I imagine the roads and the houses and the side streets and the parks and the people. I imagine what it will feel like to go deeper into the country, away from the sea.

* * *

In the evening we sit in the living room. The Moroccan man is helping Diomande prepare for the asylum interview. They are sitting opposite each other at the dining table, and Diomande has a piece of paper and a pen in front of him so that he can make notes.

'I want you to explain why you leave your country,' the Moroccan man says. And Diomande begins to talk, the same story he told us before, but this time with added detail. He mentions the names of his mother and sisters, he describes his job in Gabon and their financial situation and then he is talking about history and politics, about French colonisation, independence in 1960, civil unrest and civil war, increasing poverty. He talks about how Côte d'Ivoire was once a place of economic prosperity and stability, and how things changed after the death of the nation's first president. He goes on and I stop listening, until the Moroccan man interrupts him.

'I think, Diomande, that they will want to hear *your* story.'

'This my story!' Diomande insists. 'How else will they understand if I don't tell it?'

'Maybe they know these things.'

'Maybe they not know. If they not know, how they will understand why I need to be here?'

'You tell your story. Why you leave.'

'I am explaining these things!' Diomande is angry now, and I see that he is sitting more upright. His anger has somehow straightened his spine.

The Moroccan man shakes his head. 'This anger will not help your case,' he says. 'You must make your story. What was your life? How was life there for you and sisters and mother? Only this, Diomande! This is not a history lesson!'

They start the mock interview again. Afra is sitting on the armchair, with the sketch-pad and colouring pencils on her lap, rolling the marble around in her fingers; I watch the vein of the marble, twisting and brightening in the lamplight, and their voices fade into the background. I drift away from the conversation and I begin to think about the bees. I can see them in the summer sky, heading up and out to find the plants and flowers. I almost hear their song. I can smell the honey and see the glimmer of the combs in the sunlight. My eyes begin to close but I see Afra opening the sketch-pad, running her fingers over white paper, taking a purple pencil out of the box.

I wake up to the sound of the marble again, rolling along the floorboards. I know immediately that Mohammed is here and I take a moment to open my eyes, and when I do he is sitting on the floor cross-legged and there is a key beside him.

'You found the key, Mohammed?' I say to him.

'You dropped it when you were climbing over the fence.' He stands up now, beside me. He has different clothes on today, a red T-shirt and denim shorts, and he seems preoccupied with something. He is looking over his shoulder through the open door of the living room and into the corridor.

'You'll get cold dressed like that,' I say.

He begins to walk away from me and I get up and follow him. We climb the stairs and follow the hallway, past all the bedrooms and the bathroom, until we reach a door at the end of the corridor that I previously did not know existed.

'Why have you brought me here?' I say to him, and he hands me the key.

I put the key in the lock, turn it and open the door. An intense light dazzles me, and when my eyes adjust I see that I am high up on the top of a hill, looking down over Aleppo. There is a full moon, close to the horizon, full of the colours of the desert. A blood moon.

I can see far across the city, the ruins and hilltops, the fountains and balconies. In a field to the east there are apiaries, thorn bushes and wildflowers. The bees are silent at this time. Only the nurse bees work by moonlight. Bees become blind before humans. The air is warm and sweet with the smells of heat and soil. There is a path to the left of me, leading down into the city; I follow it until I reach the river. It is trickling out of the city park and struggling across the ravine, and the light of the moon glows and the water shimmers beneath it.

Ahead, someone is running, a flash of red. I follow the sound into the alleyways. It is darker now and the lanterns are on, but in the market stalls there are golden pyramids of baklava. Tables are set up outside cafés, menus and glasses and cutlery, a single flower in a slim vase on each. Shoes are displayed in shop windows, fake designer handbags, rugs and boxes and coffee urns and perfume and leather, and at the end of the row a stall full of headscarves of the finest material, like smoke streaming in the lamplight, blue and ochre and green.

A sign hanging from an arch high above me reads: *The Museum*. Just beneath the arch, I see that I've reached my father's old shop. The door is closed and I press my face against the glass. Rolls of fabric are piled high in the back, silks and linens of all shades and colours. In the front is the till and his pots of scissors and needles and hammers.

At the end of the alley a purple glow. When I look again, I see Mohammed, turning a corner. I call him, ask him to wait for me, to stop running away from me, ask him where he is going, but he doesn't slow down, so I walk faster to catch up with him, but when I reach the end of the alley, the world opens, and I am back at the river and the moon is higher in the sky. Mohammed is nowhere to be seen, so I sit down on the ground, close to the water, and wait for

sunrise

revealed Piraeus, the sky filled with seagulls. We disembarked at the port in Athens and were taken to a concrete yard by the harbour overflowing with tents and overlooked by construction cranes. The people who did not have tents were wrapped in blankets, sitting on the ground. Birds were scavenging on rubbish among them and there was the strong smell of sewage.

We were in the shadow of a rectangular building, heavily graffitied to show a rugged port with huge white waves and an ancient ship with billowing sails. On the rocks of the painted harbour there was a picture of a crane and beneath it people from a distant time. Sami would have loved this painting. He would have made up stories about the people; the ship probably would have been a time-travelling device, or, knowing Sami's sense of humour, the crane would have been the time-travelling device – it would have lifted people up by their collars and dropped them into another time.

I wished that I didn't have to move from here, that I could become part of the painting and sit forever on the rocks of the harbour and watch the sea.

Afra and I found some space on one of the blankets on the groud. A woman opposite me had three children hanging off her: one in a sling at the front, one strapped to her back and a toddler holding onto her arm. She had almond-shaped eyes and a hijab draped loosely over her hair. Either the babies were twins or one of them was not hers. She was talking now, saying something to the boy in Farsi, and the boy was shaking his head, pressing his nose against her sleeve. There was a girl nearby with burn marks across her face. I noticed that three of her fingers were missing. She caught my eye, and I looked away. I watched Afra instead, sitting there so silent, safe in her darkness.

Suddenly there was a flash and for a moment my mind was full of light.

When my vision adjusted, I saw a round black object pointed straight at me. A gun. A gun? My breath caught in my throat, I struggled to inhale, my vision blurred, my neck and face felt hot, my fingers numb. A camera.

'Are you OK?' I heard the man say. The camera dropped to his side and he seemed suddenly embarrassed, as if it hadn't occurred to him that he was taking a picture of a real human. He averted his eyes, apologised quickly and moved on.

People came by to check our papers, and we were taken that night by coach to the city centre, downtown Athens, to a crumbling building, an old school where long windows looked down on a courtyard. The courtyard was full of people, some sitting on a raised platform, others in school chairs, or standing beneath lines of washing. Intermingled with all these people were the NGO workers. One of them, a white man with dreadlocks, came to greet us and led us into the building and up two flights of stairs to an abandoned classroom. Afra climbed slowly, careful with each step.

'It's nice to be able to speak English to you,' the man said, 'but I'm trying to learn Arabic, and a bit of Farsi too. Bloody difficult.' He shook his head, keeping an eye on Afra. 'The classrooms downstairs are used for activities. Does your wife speak English too?'

'Not much.'

'Will she be all right climbing the stairs?'

'She'll be fine,' I said. 'We've had worse.'

'You're lucky. If you'd come two months ago you would have been out on the streets for weeks on end, and in the middle of winter. But the military came and moved a lot of people, so these camps were set up. There's a huge one at Ellinikon – the old airport – and at the park . . .' His voice trailed off as if he had suddenly become distracted, and I got the impression that he didn't want to say more about it.

He showed us into one of the classrooms, presenting it with an extended arm and open palm and a hint of irony. Inside the classroom were three tents made of bedsheets. I liked him already. There was a glint in his eyes, and he didn't seem afraid or tired like the others on Leros.

'I'm Neil, by the way.' He flashed his name tag. 'Choose one of the tents. Dinner is in the courtyard later. Check the schedule on the wall on the right as soon as you come in – there's lessons and stuff in the afternoons for the kids. Where's your child?' These last words reached me, quickly, abruptly, like bullets.

'Where's my child?'

Neil nodded and smiled. 'This place is only for families . . . I assumed . . . Your exit card . . . This school is for families *with* children.'

'I lost my child,' I said.

Neil hovered in front of me without moving, and his forehead creased into deep lines. Then he glanced down at the floor, puffed out his cheeks and said, 'Listen. This is what I can do. You can stay tonight, and I'll see what we can do about tomorrow night too, so your wife can have a good rest.' And with that he left us in this old classroom in this abandoned school, returning a few minutes later with another family, a husband, wife and two young children.

I didn't want to look at these children, a boy and a girl, holding on to their parents' hands. I didn't want to acknowledge their presence, and so I didn't greet them like I normally would. Instead I turned around, and Afra and I climbed into one of the tents, put our bags down, and without saying anything, we both lay on the blankets, facing each other. Before we fell asleep she said, 'Nuri, can you get me some more paper and pencils tomorrow?'

'Of course,' I said.

The other family soon settled themselves as well and the classroom fell into a welcome silence. I could almost believe that I was staying in a grand hotel and the faint creaking and noises above me were the sounds of the other guests. I remembered my mother and father's old house in Aleppo, how as a child I had been afraid to fall asleep until I could hear my mother's reassuring footsteps on the landing outside my door. She would peek in, and when I saw the crack of light coming into the dark room, I would feel safe and drift off. In the morning, my mother would help my dad in the fabric shop, and she spent the afternoon hours reading the newspapers, holding the red fan her grandmother had given her. It was made of silk and had a picture of a cherry tree and a bird and there was a Chinese word on it which my mother thought meant fate. She said it was a word that was hard to translate; Yuanfen was a mysterious force that causes two lives to cross paths in a meaningful way.

This always reminded me of how I had met Mustafa. After his mother, my aunt, had died, the families lost touch and at least fifteen years passed without communication. Mustafa's father lived a solitary life in the mountains, while my mother and father were city people, working in the heat and chaos of the markets, where trade bustled from all over the world. In fact it was an old Chinese merchant who had given my great-grandmother the red fan. He was a fabric maker from Beijing and had made the silk and hand-painted it himself. One day my father had sent me on an errand to get some fruit and I had taken a detour and stopped by the river to rest beneath a tree. I was tired of being locked up in the shop, and my father was eager for me to learn as much as possible, to serve the customers, to speak English well, so even when the shop was quiet I would be sitting there with an English grammar book on my lap because, according to my father, that was the way forward.

I was hot and exhausted and, as it was the middle of August, it felt like we were breathing in the desert. It was a relief to sit by the river, beneath the cool shade of the narenj tree. I must have been there for about fifteen minutes when a young man approached me, about ten years older than I was and much darker, as if he lived and worked beneath the sun.

'Do you know the way to this shop?' He pointed at the piece of paper in his hand where there was a sketch of a road and a shop with an arrow and the words: *Aleppo Honey*.

'The Aleppo Honey Shop?' I said.

He nodded, then shook his head very quickly, a tic I was to become so familiar with.

'No?' I said.

'Yes,' he said, smiling, shaking his head again.

'I'm going that way. Why don't you follow me? I'll show you the way.' And as we walked we began to talk. He immediately told me about the apiaries in the mountains and that his grandfather had sent him to the city to sample different types of honey. He told me he had recently applied to the University of Damascus to study agriculture, and that he wanted to learn more about the composition of honey. I told him a bit about my father's shop, though not too much, because I wasn't as talkative as he was, and also because the work didn't interest me that much. I showed him the shop as we walked past and I took him on to the front door of the honey shop, where we said goodbye.

A week later he came to find me at my father's shop. He brought a huge jar of honey with him. He had just found out that he had been accepted at the university and so would be visiting Aleppo more often, and he had wanted to say thank you to me for taking him to the shop that day. The moment my mother saw him, standing in the doorway of the shop with the jar of honey in his hand, she dropped her fan and stood up. She walked over and stared at him for a while, then she began to sob.

'Mustafa,' she said, 'it is you, isn't it? How old were you when I last saw you? You were just a little boy. But that face, it hasn't changed!' She said later that it was as if she had seen the reincarnation of her sister. And there our friendship began, by the river and later with a pot of honey. A mysterious force that I could never understand had brought my cousin into my life, had led him to find me sitting by the river with no hope in my heart for my future career, and from that moment on my life was changed forever. Yuanfen. Yuanfen, flickering in the red heat, beneath my mother's eyes.

I ran through the memory three times in my mind, repeating it as if I was rewinding and replaying a videotape, until I slipped off to sleep.

But I woke up in the middle of the night to the sound of screaming, and a whistling in the sky, a bomb tearing through the darkness. I sat upright, my body wet, my head pounding, the darkness around me pulsating. I saw the faint outline of a window through a bedsheet, the light of the moon streaming in. I saw Afra's face fuzzy in the darkness and slowly remembered where I was. I reached out to hold her hand. There were no bombs. We were not in Aleppo. We were safe in Athens, in an old school. The heartbeat in my head subsided, but the screaming continued, and when it stopped abruptly a few moments later, there were other sounds, echoes from other rooms on other floors, desperate adult sobs, creaking floorboards, footsteps and whispers and laughter. The laughter seemed to be coming from outside, from the courtyard below – the laughter of a woman.

I stepped out of the tent, out of the classroom and into the long corridor. At the far end, by the window, a woman was pacing up and down, her flip-flops slapping against the marble, her eyes to the floor. Her body paused, jerked, started up again, like a mechanical toy. I approached her, hesitant for a moment, and put my hand on her arm, hoping to calm her movements, to ask her if she needed any help, but when she glanced up at me I saw that she was asleep. She looked straight through me with wide fearful eyes, shimmering with tears. 'When did you come back?' she said.

I didn't answer. I knew that you should never wake a person who is sleepwalking, in case they should die from shock. I left her there to walk around in her nightmare.

I heard the laughter again, shrill and abrupt, cutting through the sleep sounds. In one of the classrooms above, someone was snoring; in another a child was crying. I followed the laughter down the stairs and out into the courtyard, and was shocked to find so many people still awake. It must have been 2 o'clock in the morning. The first thing I saw was a huddle of boys and girls in a corner on wooden chairs beneath a climbing-wall. They were passing around a paper bag, inhaling some substance from it.

One of the girls glanced at me, held my gaze for a moment.

Something was wrong with her, her pupils dilated so that her eyes were almost black. Nearby, two men were sitting on the ground with their backs against the wall, smoking. On the platform, which must have once been used as a stage, two boys were kicking a ball beneath the only floodlight. At the entrance of the courtyard, three men were having a heated discussion; they were speaking a different type of Arabic and had much darker skin. One of them pushed the other's shoulder, and another man came over and separated them, raised his voice and then slid the bolts of the entrance, pushing open the heavy door, and the three left.

When the door was closed again – its metallic sound which reverberated around the courtyard had died – I was left facing a huge blue heart painted across the double panels, outlined on both sides with red wings. The top of the heart was flat, and there was an island and a palm tree and a yellow sun rising out of it. On the cool green background of the old school walls, the heart almost pulsated in the flickering floodlight.

And from behind me, again, the sound of laughter. I turned away from the heart. At the far end of the courtyard, on the only deckchair, beneath a line of washing, was the laughing woman.

She was a young black woman with cornrows gathered into a high ponytail. As I walked towards her I noticed that her breasts were leaking milk into her white top. She caught my eye and self-consciously folded her arms across her chest.

'Is because they took her,' she said in English.

'They took who?'

She didn't answer at first. Her eyes darted around.

'I no live here. I come here at night sometimes to be safe.'

I sat down on the ground beside her. She turned to me and showed me her arm. There were dozens of tiny round wounds.

'It's my blood,' she said. 'They poisoned it.'

'Who did?'

'I was staying in a room, and then he try to kill me. He got my head and bash it on the floor. And I lost my breath. My breath it stop then, and I didn't get it back. I have no breath in me now. I am dead.'

And yet her eyes were full of life.

'I want to go to Germany mostly. Or to Denmark,' she went on. 'I need to leave here. Is not easy because Macedonia has shut border. Athens is the heart. Everyone comes here on the way to wherever. Peoples are get stuck here.' She seemed more troubled now, a deep frown between her brows. 'This the place where people die slowly, inside. One by one, people die.'

I was beginning to feel nauseated. I wished I had never approached this woman with the leaking breasts and poisoned blood.

The boys who were playing football had gone now so the place was quieter and the floodlight shone down onto an empty stage. The two men were still smoking, but the kids on the chairs had dispersed. There were only two boys left and they were both looking at their phones, their faces lit up.

'They tell me I need to drink a lot of water, for my blood,

but I'm a dead.' She pinched her skin now. 'I am like meat. You know, raw meat? Like a dead meat. I am being eaten.' She pinched her arm and showed me the scars again. I had no idea what to say to any of this. I was glad that her laughter had stopped, for a while at least. But soon the silence was worse.

'Where do you live?' I said.

'At the park. But sometimes I come here, safer here, and there is less wind, because at the park we are high up, next to the gods.'

'How come you know English so well?'

'My mother taught me.'

'Where are you from?'

Instead of answering, she got up suddenly, saying, 'Is time to go. I need to go now,' and I watched her as she unbolted the door and pushed it open, breaking the blue heart. And when the door closed, there was so much quiet. The two boys had gone now and only the two men remained, leaning against the wall, still smoking, and through the classroom windows I could hear the sounds of children crying: a baby and an older child.

I made my way back up the stairs and along the corridor, the sleepwalking woman had gone, and there was a stillness to the whole place now that was soothing to my mind.

I woke up to glowing white sheets and the confused sounds of engines and people shouting in Arabic or Greek or Farsi, or all three in one sentence. Afra was still asleep.

When I went downstairs the courtyard was full of crates of almost black bananas and boxes of nappies. Two men were holding sacks of potatoes, and another three carried in boxes labelled *razors, toothbrushes, notepads, pens*. Beyond the broken heart of the open door there were a couple of white vans with charity logos on their sides. I made my way inside to the children's area, where a woman was putting out toys and board games, notepads and colouring pencils.

'Excuse me,' I said.

'Can I help you?' the woman said. She spoke English with a different accent.

'Do you have any paper and colouring pencils?'

'They're really for the children,' she said.

'My son is upstairs. He's not well – I thought he might like to draw.'

The woman dug through a bag and produced a notepad and a box of pencils. She handed them to me, reluctantly, but with a smile.

'I hope he can join us when he's better,' she said.

Afra was still asleep, but I slipped them under her hand so that she would feel them there when she woke up. Then I sat for a long time beside her, staring into the whiteness of the sun-filled sheet of the tent, and for a while my mind was blank. Then images began to emerge. There, to my left, was the Queiq River; to my right a grey street with a narenj tree; ahead the famous Baron Hotel; over there was the Umayyad Mosque of Aleppo in the Al-Jalloum district of the ancient city, with the sun setting, painting the domes orange; over that way were the walls of the citadel, and here were crumbling buildings; and there was a broken archway in the al-Madina Souq, and over there a street in the western neighbourhood, the Baby al-Faraj Clock Tower, the abandoned terraces and balconies, the minarets. Then the wind blew through the window and the bedsheet moved and the images faded away. I rubbed my eyes, turned to Afra. She seemed frightened in her sleep – she was restless, her breathing was fast and she was saying something, but I couldn't make out the words. I put my hand on her head, stroked her hair, and slowly her breathing calmed and the muttering stopped.

She woke up an hour later, but her eyes stayed shut. She was moving; her fingers running over the notepad and then over the pencils.

'Nuri?' she said.

'Yes.'

'Did you get these for me?'

'Yes.'

There was a tiny smile on her face.

She sat up and put them on her lap and ran her hands through her hair with her eyes still closed. Her skin was so clear, and when she opened her eyes they were a metallic grey, her irises so small, as if they were trying to keep out the light.

'What shall I draw?' she said.

'Anything you like.'

'Tell me. I want it to be for you.'

'The view from our house.'

I watched her as she sketched, her fingers tracing the pencil marks, following each line as if it were a path. Her eyes flickered onto the paper and away again, blinking a lot now, as if there was a light flashing too close.

'Can you see anything, Afra?'

'No,' she said. 'Be quiet. I'm thinking.'

I watched the picture take shape, I saw the domes emerge and the flat rooftops. In the foreground of the sketch she began to add the leaves and flowers that spiralled the railing of the balcony. Then she shaded in the sky with purple and brown and green – she had no idea what colours she was using, she just seemed to know that she wanted three for the sky. I watched her following the lines of the landscape with the tips of her fingers so that the colour didn't bleed into the buildings.

'How do you do that?' I said.

'I don't know,' she said, her eyes smiling for a moment. 'Is it nice?'

'It's so beautiful.'

For some reason, when I said this she stopped drawing, so that the right side of the picture was left without colour. Strangely this reminded me of the white crumbling streets once the war came. The way the colour was washed out of everything. The way the flowers died. She handed it to me.

'It's not finished,' I said.

'It is.' She pushed it towards me. Then she lay back down and, resting her head on her hands, she remained silent. I didn't move for a long time. I just lay there looking at the picture, until Neil popped his head around the door to tell us that we had to leave.

9

I AM SURROUNDED BY MATERIAL, WHAT seem to be coats, and there are shoes on the floor and a vacuum cleaner squashed up in the corner. It is warm in here and there is a boiler above me. To my left, at the end of the corridor, the Moroccan man is standing, staring at me. He walks towards me and silently offers me his hand. He doesn't say anything, but there is a sombre look on his face, and he leads me into my bedroom. Afra is not there, the bed has been made and her abaya is not on the hanger. But on the cabinet, on my side of the bed, there is a beautiful sketch of the apiaries – the field stretching far and wide, the beehives dotted around, the sun rising. She has even drawn in the kitchen and the tent where we would all sit to have lunch. The colours are wrong, the lines rough and broken, but the picture moves. It breathes: I can almost hear the buzzing of the bees. There are black roses in the field beyond, their colour leaking into the sky.

The Moroccan man sits me down on the bed, unties my laces, takes off my shoes, and lifts up my legs. I hold the picture to my chest.

'Where is Afra?' I say.

'Don't worry, she's OK, she's downstairs. Farida is keeping her company.'

'Who is Farida?' I say.

'The woman from Afghanistan.'

He is gone for a while, and he returns with a glass of water. He holds it to my mouth and I drink it all. Then he adjusts the pillows behind my head, closes the curtains and tells me to get some rest. He shuts the door and leaves me here in the dark.

I remember the alleyways and the sound of running and Mohammed's red T-shirt, but my body is heavy, my legs and arms like rocks, and I feel burning in my eyes and I close them.

It's even darker when I wake up. I can hear the sound of laughter – it spreads out across the darkness like the ringing of bells. I head downstairs to the living room, where some of the residents are playing dominoes. Afra is among them and she is leaning over the dining table, there are six dominoes balanced in front of her in a row, and with steady fingers and a look of pure concentration she is trying to place the seventh one next to them. Everyone around the table is holding their breath and watching. She stops and shakes her hands and laughs again. 'OK, I do it! I do it! You see!'

It is the first time I've heard her speak to anyone in weeks, the first time there has been light and laughter in her voice for months.

The Moroccan man spots me standing in the doorway.

'Geezer!' he says in English, his eyes alight. 'Come sit, play. I make you tea.' He pulls up a chair for me and leads me to it with his hand on my shoulder, and then he goes off into the kitchen.

The other residents glance up at me for a second and nod or say hello, but their attention is back on Afra and the domino. She is sitting up straighter, her hands shaking a little bit now, and I see that she has turned her head slightly towards me. She places the domino too close to the previous one and they all tumble down.

Everyone laughs and cheers and groans and the Afghan woman collects the dominoes and pulls them towards her. She is good at this game. By the time the Moroccan man comes back with the tea she already has fifteen tiles in a row, she is numbering for Afra, who is sitting right beside her.

I drink my tea, which is too sweet, and then I call the GP surgery to inform them that I have the correct information now and want to make an appointment for Afra about her vision.

When night comes I make sure to go to bed with Afra. I follow her up the stairs, trying not to look at the door at the end of the corridor. Diomande's bedroom door is open again and he is standing with his back to us, looking out of his window, the shape of the wings visible through his T-shirt. As if he can tell that I am looking, he turns to face me.

'Goodnight,' he says, and smiles, and I see that he is holding a photograph in his hands. He brings it over to show me. 'This my mum, these my sisters.' They are all smiling women with big teeth.

In the bedroom I help Afra to get undressed and I lie down beside her.

'Did you have a nice day?' I say.

'It would have been nicer with you.'

'I know.'

I can hear a boy's voice calling something in Arabic. It seems to be coming from one of the other bedrooms, but I know there are no children here, unless new people arrived today. But the voice seems to be coming from the garden below.

'What are you doing?' Afra says. I am standing by the window now, looking down into the dark courtyard.

'Did you not hear that?' I say.

'It's just the TV,' she says, 'downstairs. Someone is watching TV.'

'Not that. Someone was calling in Arabic.'

'What did they say?'

'Over here! Over here!'

I press my face on the window. From what I can see, the courtyard is empty; apart from the cherry tree and the rubbish bins and the stepladder, there is no one and nothing there.

'Just come and lie down,' Afra says. 'Lie down and close your eyes and try not to think about anything.'

So I do as she says. I lie down beside her and feel the

warmth of her body and I can smell the roses. I shut my eyes against her and the darkness but I hear it again, a child's voice, it is Mohammed's voice, I know it, he begins to sing a lullaby, I recognise it, it reminds me of Sami. I put my hands over my ears, but it doesn't block out

the song

of the crickets greeted us as we arrived at Pedion tou Areos. Wrought-iron railings stretched along the length of the high street that led to downtown Athens.

I couldn't stop thinking about Mohammed. I thought I could hear him calling me, but I realised it was just the sounds of the city. Neil was leading the way. He'd insisted, maybe out of guilt, on holding all the bags, so he had my rucksack on one shoulder and Afra's on the other. Before we left the school, Neil had thrown away all our old bags and given us new rucksacks and thermal blankets.

'They built this place to celebrate the revolt against Ottoman rule in 1821!' Neil called back to us. We passed some open wooden boxes on the pathway, but he continued deeper into the woods. Then, beneath the ferns and palm trees we saw a small village of tents and people sprawled on blankets. The place was dirty, even in the open air there were horrible smells: rot and urine. But Neil walked on. As we made our way deeper into the park, gaping potholes scarred the footpaths and the weeds grew wild and brittle. A few people walked their dogs, pensioners sat talking on the benches and, deeper still, drug addicts prepared their fixes.

Eventually we came to another area of tents and Neil

found us some space on a couple of blankets between two palm trees. Opposite was a statue of an ancient warrior, and on the step of this statue sat an emaciated man. His eyes reminded me of the kids at the school the previous night.

It was much later, after Neil had left and the darkness had closed in around us, that I began to notice what was wrong with this place. First, men gathered in gangs like wolves; Bulgarians and Greeks and Albanians. They were watching and waiting for something; I could see it in their eyes. They were the eyes of intelligent predators.

The night was cold. Afra was shivering and saying nothing. She was frightened here. I wrapped as many blankets around her as I could. We did not have a tent, just a large umbrella that blocked the wind from the north. A campfire close by gave out a little warmth, but not enough to be comfortable.

There was noise and laughter and movement all around. Some children played football in an open space between the trees, boys and girls kicking up the soil. Others played cards, or chatted outside their tents. A group of teenagers sat in a circle on a blanket. They were telling one another stories, tales they remembered from childhood. One girl was speaking, the rest listening attentively, legs folded, eyes catching the light of the dwindling fire.

As I watched, an NGO worker approached them, a small blond man holding two white plastic bags, one in each hand. The girl stopped talking and they all turned to face him, the whole group erupting with excitement, talking over one another. The NGO worker put down the bags and they all waited with anticipation as he pulled out cans of Coca-Cola which the teenagers grabbed, one by one. Once they each had a can, they opened them, laughing with excitement at the *tssssk* and *pshhhhhhhh*.

Then they all drank, at the same time.

'That's my first sip of Coke in three years!' one of them said.

I knew that Daesh had banned Coca-Cola because it was an American multinational brand.

'It's even better than I remember!' said another.

The NGO worker saw me watching them. He took out one last can from the bag and came over. He was younger than I thought, with blond spikey hair and small dark eyes. He brought the laughter and the joy with him as he handed me the can, a beaming smile on his face.

'Amazing, eh?' he said.

'Thank you.' I opened the can and took a small sip, savouring the sweetness. Then I handed it to Afra, who was still shivering, wrapped up in the blanket. She took a huge gulp.

'Wow, Coca-Cola?' she said. It seemed to bring some colour to her face. So we passed the can between us and listened to the stories the youngsters told.

Later, past midnight, when Afra was finally asleep and her body had stopped shaking, I noticed some older men hanging around, watching the boys and the girls. One of them was leaning on crutches, the stump of his leg bare and visible even in the darkness. The emaciated man on the step of the statue was now playing a guitar. A sad and beautiful song as soft as a lullaby.

'They bring you here too?'

I looked up and saw the black woman from the night before. She had a blanket around her shoulders and a piece of bread in her hand.

'Make sure you get food in the morning,' she said. 'They bring food from the church but is finish quickly. They bring medicines too.'

She spread the blanket out on the ground and sat down beside me. She was wearing a headwrap the green of an emerald.

Suddenly, from nowhere, a violent wind swept through the camp, as if the gods of the place had awoken. Leaves and dry soil streaked past us, but she just waited for it to settle, which suggested to me she was used to these unexpected and short-lived blasts of weather. Then she plunged her hand into a small linen bag and pulled out a container of talcum powder, shook a perfumed cloud into her palm and smeared it all over her face and hands. This had the strange effect of making her look grey, the life and light in her cheeks suddenly extinguished. She was watching me the whole time.

'They steal children here,' she said. 'They snatch them.'

From among the foliage, men's eyes gleamed in the moonlight.

'Why would they do that?'

'To sell their organs. Or for sex.' Again she said this casually, as if she had become immune to such things. I didn't want to listen to this woman, and I wished I couldn't see the shadows moving in the woods. I noticed again that her breasts were leaking, fresh wet patches on her white top.

'My mind is ill,' she said, tapping her forehead. Then, pinching the skin on her inner arm, 'I am a dead. I'm turn black inside. Do you know what that means?'

Her dark eyes glimmered in the firelight, the whites slightly yellow. There was a roundness to her features, a wholeness, a softness, a transparency; it was in her expressions and her hand movements, and yet I wanted to get away from her, because I didn't want to know. There was too much in my head now; there was no room for more. The wet stains on her top kept catching my eye, it was worse on the left, as if her heart was leaking, and I tried not to look.

'You cannot leave this place. Do you know that?' she said.

I said nothing in response. I was thinking about Mohammed now. Seeing these men in the woods brought new questions to my mind. Did someone take him? Did they tempt him away or snatch him in the night while he was sleeping?

'The borders have been closed, you know.' she continued. 'Everyone is coming and not many is leaving, and I can't go back. I am a dead. I want to leave from here. I want to find work. But nobody want me.'

Beneath a tree one of the older men was talking to a young girl. She was probably about eleven or twelve, but the way she was standing made her look much older; there was something overtly sexual in the way she was leaning against the tree.

'Do you know why Odysseus make his journey?' the woman said now, nudging me, and I wished she would be quiet. I turned to her for a second, and when I looked back the man and the girl had disappeared. I felt sick.

'He went from Ithaca to Calypso to god knows where – all of this journey, to find what?'

There was an intensity to her – the way she leant into me, the way she pushed my leg if I took my eyes off her.

'I don't know,' I said to her.

'To find his home again,' she said. And then she remained silent for a long time, perhaps she had sensed that I didn't really want to talk, and she sat there with her hands folded in her lap. She had a fierce presence, her eyes wide, fully alert. As much as I tried to shut her out and pretend that she was not there, I couldn't.

'What's your name?' I said.

'Angeliki.'

'That's a Greek name.'

'Yes. It means "Angel".'

'Where are you from?'

And again this question seemed to disturb her. She gathered up her blanket, wrapped it around her shoulders and wandered off into the night, picking up something from the ground along the way.

I lay down beside Afra but I couldn't sleep. Deep in the woods I could hear strange cries – of foxes or cats or people. The man who was sitting on the step of the statue was still there. In the light of the dying fire, I noticed that he had scratches on his arms. Red raw wounds as if an animal had got to him.

And although my mind was restless, I closed my eyes tight. I didn't want to see or know anything more.

In the morning there was prayer and later Pedion tou

Areos was like a playground. The sun glowed through the leaves of the trees, a canopy of emerald so that I was reminded of Angeliki sitting here the night before in her green headscarf. There were locals among the refugees, old women with bags of food; they walked around handing out packages.

I noticed one young mother sitting on a blanket, a sky-blue hijab draped loosely over her head. In her arms she held a tiny baby, probably just a few weeks old – its hands and legs like twigs, sticking out of the blanket. It was like she was holding a dead thing, rocking a dead thing in her arms, as if her eyes knew this but her body didn't. An old Greek woman knelt down on the ground beside them, helping the mother give bottled milk-formula to the baby, but the baby would not feed. The old woman gave up, and instead she poured a big glass of condensed milk and filled a paper plate with chocolate biscuits and gave it to the mother, encouraging her to eat and drink, pushing the cup up to her mouth whenever she stopped.

'*Pies to olo* – all of it,' the old woman said, in Greek and English, and the young mother seemed to understand one of them and she gulped it down now and held the cup out for more. The old woman gave her another glass, then, when she was done, the old woman took the mother's hands in hers and cleaned them with baby wipes and massaged them with cream. The mother's eyes were sad, blue as the sea and far away.

'Beautiful Mahsa,' the old lady said, and kissed the baby's forehead.

Mahsa. The baby was a girl. I watched the ease between

the women, the way they interacted with such few words. They knew each other – the old lady had probably been here many times before.

'*Den echies gala?*' the old woman said, and in response the mother pressed her breast with her palm and shook her head. '*Ochi*,' she said.

I noticed again the man on the step of the statue. He had his guitar on his lap: a beautiful instrument, almost a lute, but not exactly. He plucked the strings and then played a short melody. It produced a wash of sound, a sudden harmony like a rain shower on a sunny day, echoing softly from its wooden chamber.

There was a frown on the man's face as he abruptly stopped playing and continued to fine-tune. After a while he put the instrument down by his feet and rolled a cigarette. I got up and sat beside him in the shadow of the statue. There was something warm about this man's face, inviting, even in its silence.

'Good morning,' he said in Farsi, in a voice as deep and melodic as his music, and he offered me the cigarette he had just rolled.

'No, thank you,' I said, in Arabic. 'I don't smoke.' And in that moment we both started to laugh at the strangeness of our situations. Here we found ourselves in Greece, one man speaking Arabic, the other Farsi.

'Do you speak English?' I said.

The man's eyes lit up. 'Yes! Not very, very good, but yes! Thanks gods, we have found same language!' There was real humour in this man – he sang as he talked.

'Where are you from?' I said.

'Afghanistan, outside Kabul. You are from Syria?'

'Yes,' I said.

His fingernails were long, and although he was not a bulky man, there was a suggestion of strength in his movements.

'I like your guitar,' I said.

'This instrument is rebab. It means "door of the soul".' Then he told me his name was Nadim.

I remained perched on the step beside him as he picked up the rebab and began to play again, a slow quiet melody that trickled through the air in deep waves. I watched Afra as she woke up and unfolded herself from the blanket, feeling around with her hand to see if I was there. When she didn't find me, her features tightened and she called for me. I went over immediately and touched her hand and watched as her face softened. There was a part of me that was pleased to see this fear in her when she thought she'd lost me, because it meant that she still loved me, that even when she was locked inside herself she still needed me. I unwrapped the sandwiches that had been left for us and handed one to her.

After a while she said, 'Nuri, who is playing the music?'

'A man called Nadim.'

'It's beautiful.'

And as the hours passed the music washed over us, and when Nadim stopped playing and took a nap the absence of the music suddenly opened a door to other sounds: twigs snapping and breaking in the woods and murmurings and whispers and children playing. I wanted to wake him and tell him to play his music forever so that I would never hear anything else but the moving melody of the rebab until the day that I died. And if Angeliki was right, if we could never leave this place, then Afra and I would die here with the predators of the night and the heroes of a battle unknown to us.

When the sun set the campfire was lit and the place filled with smoke and the smell of burning wood. People gathered around its warmth and I was reminded of Farmakonisi. But the people were different on that island. Here it was as if we were all living in the darkest shadow of a solar eclipse.

Afra had been even more quiet than usual. I believed that she was listening to the sounds in the woods, that she could sense the danger there, but she didn't ask any questions. Most of the time she sat wrapped in a thick blanket.

Nadim had been gone for a while and he returned some time later, taking his usual place beneath the statue. But he didn't pick up his rebab, although I waited for the music; I needed it like water. My mind was so full of cracks.

The mother with the blue hijab was trying to breastfeed her baby; little Mahsa had her mouth around the nipple and she was sucking a bit but it seemed that there was no milk and the woman was pressing her breast with her hand, frustrated, with a flushed angry face. And then Mahsa gave up and went back to being listless. The woman began to cry and she wiped the tears away with the back of her hand.

Seeing the mother's tears and the ease with which they fell, I realised that Afra had not cried about Sami. Apart from that day in Aleppo when we were hiding in the hole in the garden, she had not shed a tear. She did not cry when Sami died. Instead her face had turned to stone.

Nadim came and sat next to me on the blanket and stared for a while at Afra. I wondered if he realised that his eyes were fixed on her, or if he was just lost in his own thoughts. Either way, I broke his gaze.

'So, where did you say you came from?'

Nadim's face suddenly changed and came to life. 'Kabul!'

'You liked it there?'

'Of course. Was my home. Kabul is very nice.'

'Why did you leave?'

'Because Taliban does not like us to play music there. They do not like music.' But there was more, I could tell by the way he stopped abruptly and picked up a pine cone for no reason, examining it before throwing it into the woods.

'That's the reason you left?' I said.

There was some hesitation as if he was contemplating whether to say more and at the same time inspecting me. After not too much time, and with a deliberately lower voice, he said, 'I was in Ministry of Defence. Then Taliban threaten me. I told them I cannot kill people. I cannot even kill ant – how do you expect me to kill people?'

And then he stopped again, and that was all. He had thrown me tiny fragments of a much larger and longer story. And then Nadim was quiet, but there was something uncomfortable in this man's silence, and so I was pleased when he spoke again, with that sing-song voice that seemed now to distract from something else.

'Do you know the name of this park?' he said.

'Yes, Pedion tou Areos . . .'

'Pedion means "square". Areos was god of war. He loved murder and blood. Did you know this? The old lady who bring food tell me.'

'I didn't know.'

'He loved murder and blood,' Nadim repeated these words slowly, placing emphasis on each. 'And look,' he said, 'they made a park for him!' He spread his arm, palm open, in the way Neil had done when he had presented me and Afra with our temporary room in the school, and the raw bloody wounds on the fine skin of Nadim's forearm glimmered like red ribbons in the firelight. A wind blew and clouds gathered and the darkness around us became more apparent, threatening to suffocate the light of the fire. I had a strange feeling that I needed to be nice to this man.

'When did you learn to play the rebab?' I said.

My question had the effect of producing a wide grin on Nadim's face and he leant forward with sparkling eyes. I had the odd sensation of watching someone sharpen a knife.

'Listen to story,' he said. 'My father, in Kabul, he was musician. Very good, famous. He play the tabla.' Nadim tapped his hands on invisible drums. 'So I sit and watch him. Every day I watch him play the tabla, I look and listen.' He touched his ear purposefully, followed by the edge of his eye. 'One day, when I was nine or eight, my uncle ask him for help outside and I sit at the tabla and begin to play. My father, he come inside with eyes and mouth open. He was so much shock! He say to me, "Nadim! How you learn to play, my son?" How learn to play?! Because I watch him. I watch him and I listen all these years. How I not learn to play? You tell me this!'

I found myself lost in the story, captivated by Nadim's sing-song voice, engrossed in the images of the boy in a house in Kabul playing the tabla, and I forgot for a moment the question I had asked, which remained unanswered. But Nadim was tapping his foot to a silent rhythm, pleased with himself. He rolled a cigarette and lit it, and although he leant back, his body seemingly relaxed, his eyes stayed sharp. They scanned people, they penetrated the shadows, looking and waiting, just like the men in the woods.

The crickets sang in unison, then fell silent for a brief moment, an interval, as if they were one breathing body that suddenly stopped, before the sound began again, a thick pounding buzzing noise that stretched far beyond and carved out the depths of the woods and the unknown.

Groups of men were hovering again by the trees, some sitting on benches smoking. There was banter and laughter tonight. Nadim was holding a lit cigarette without smoking it, his arm casually resting on his leg, and I couldn't help noticing again those wounds, the deep red lines in the fine skin of his forearms, like the violent scratch-marks of wild animals. He took his phone out of his pocket and was typing a message. I waited for him to finish and asked him if he had an Internet connection.

'I do,' he said.

'Would you mind if I checked my emails?'

Without hesitation, Nadim unlocked his phone and handed it to me. Then he sat there quietly and lit his cigarette. Once again, there were emails from Mustafa:

15/03/2016

Dearest Nuri,
I haven't heard from you in a while and I hope that you have made it to Athens safely.

It has taken me time to find my feet. I am waiting to find out if I have been granted asylum and in the meantime I have been volunteering at a beekeepers' association in the town where I am living. I have made some friends there, but I am a beekeeper without bees. I only need one hive to start, so I have posted an advertisement on Facebook asking if anyone has a hive to donate. I am waiting eagerly to see if there is a response.

I hope to hear from you soon. There is not a day that goes by that I do not think of you and Afra.

Mustafa

* * *

25/03/2016

Dear Nuri,
A woman from a town not too far from here replied to my advertisement! She offered not only a hive but a colony of British black bees, believed until recently to be extinct. This is like a treasure! I plan to split the hive

seven times. My aim is to cooperate with the community to improve the strain. Beekeepers from Britain usually have Italian honeybees exported from New Zealand, but these native bees are much more able to withstand the crazy climate here. There has been such a collapse of colonies; the European bee is not surviving well. I believe this black bee could be the answer, and I already know there are others who agree. And, Nuri, in this country there are rapeseed fields and banks of heather and lavender! Because it rains so much it is full of flowers. And so much green. More than you could ever imagine. Where there are bees there are flowers, and where there are flowers there is new life and hope.

Do you remember the fields surrounding the apiaries? They were beautiful, weren't they, Nuri? Sometimes I remember the day of the fire but I try not to think of these things. I do not want to get lost in that darkness.

I hope to hear from you soon, we have things to do together! I am waiting for you! The bees are waiting for you!

Mustafa

'The message has made you smile,' Nadim said.

For a minute I had forgotten where I was. I looked up to see the Athenian sun beaming through the trees.

'My cousin is in England,' I said. 'He is urging me to go there.'

'It is a difficult journey,' Nadim said, chuckling. 'He is a lucky man that he made it there.'

There was silence between us for a while and I could think of nothing else but the rapeseed fields and the banks of heather and lavender. I could see it all in my mind as clear and as vibrant as one of Afra's paintings. But the sounds of the crickets invaded my thoughts.

'It sounds like the woods go on forever,' I said.

'No. They don't. All around is the city. Civilisation.' Nadim grinned now with a kind of glee, and there was the sudden flash of a different personality, a kind of mocking or malice that comes from someone who knows more than he is letting on.

'Have you been here a long time?' I said.

'Yes.' But this word seemed final, and I didn't even know what 'a long time' meant anymore. Was it weeks or months or years or centuries like these heroes of antiquity cast here in stone?

Just then I noticed something very strange. It was so fast that if I had looked away for a moment I would have missed it. One of the men on a nearby bench, sitting with his back to us, turned his head, over his shoulder, and caught Nadim's eye. There was familiar acknowledgement, a quick nod, followed by a sudden change in Nadim's movements, a nervousness, a twitching of the fingers and the skin around the eyes. This made me pay more attention. Nadim waited a while, tapping his foot on the ground to his secret rhythm, and finally he got up, took a bottle of water from where he had been sitting earlier, poured some into his hands and ran his hands through his hair. This wasn't so unusual, but it was what happened after this that seemed the strangest of all.

Still running his hands through his wet hair, Nadim approached two teenage boys, twins, who had arrived the day before. They were sitting on a blanket beneath a tree, their clothes tattered, their skin dirty; they were new here and frightened, but there was a boyish playfulness between them; one would say something, and the other would laugh and they would nudge each other. I watched as Nadim sat down beside them on their blanket, introducing himself, shaking their hands.

By this time, the man beneath the tree, the one who had nodded at Nadim, had gone.

Nadim then put his hand into the pocket of his jeans and took out some money. He gave the twins about forty euros each, from what I could see. This was a huge amount for two boys who'd probably been living off food scavenged from bins.

'Nuri,' Afra said, drawing my attention away, 'what are you doing?'

'Just watching.'

'Watching who?'

'I don't like it here,' I said.

'Neither do I.'

'Something is wrong.'

'I know.' And just those words, coming from the mouth and the mind of my wife, calmed me. I held onto her hand, squeezed it, kissed it. With every kiss I said, 'I love you. I love you, Afra, I love you, I love you.'

I told her about Mustafa in England, what he had written about his beehive and the British black bees, and she lay on her back and listened to me and for the first time I saw a small smile appear on her lips.

'What kinds of flowers are there?'

'There are fields of lavender and heather.'

Then she was silent for a while. 'I think the bees are like us,' she said. 'They are vulnerable like us. But then there are people like Mustafa. There are people like him in the world and those people bring life rather than death.' She was silent again, thoughtful, and then she whispered, 'We will get there, won't we, Nuri?'

'Of course we will,' I said, though I didn't really believe it then.

That night I tried to imagine that the crickets were bees. I could hear them all around me. The air and the sky and the trees were full of bees the colour of the sun. I realised that I hadn't replied to Mustafa – something about Nadim had distracted me, something I couldn't explain that had drawn me away from what I had needed to do. And the crickets sang and I pushed the sound away and imagined the bees. I thought of my mother again, and her red silk fan. *Yuanfen. Fate. A force that draws two people together.*

It was my mother who had supported me when I wanted to become a beekeeper. My father's disappointment had made him shrink – in the weeks after I announced that I wouldn't be working in the shop, that I wouldn't be taking over the family business, he seemed to become a much smaller man. We'd been sitting in the kitchen after an evening meal. It was June, already very hot, and he was drinking ayran with salt and mint. The ice cubes clinked in the glass. My mother was emptying the leftovers into the bin. It was as if he knew I had something to say that he wouldn't like, for he kept looking at me over the rim of the glass, a frown on his face, his gold wedding band gleaming in the light of the setting sun. He was already a small man, hardly any fat on him, with bulging knuckles and a prominent Adam's apple that moved visibly when he talked, but his presence was big, his silence and contemplation often filled the room.

'Well?' he said.

'Well?' I replied.

'I want you to go to the wholesaler's early tomorrow morning – we need more of the yellow silk with the diamond pattern.'

I nodded.

'Then you will come to the shop and I will show you how to make up the curtains – you can watch me the first time.'

I nodded again. He drank his ayran in one go and held the glass up for my mother to refill. But my mother had her back to us at this point.

'I will do what you want for another month,' I said.

He put the glass down on the table, still empty.

'And what will happen after this month?' His voice was heavy with brooding anger.

'I will become a beekeeper.' I said this matter-of-factly, placing my hands on the table.

'So you are giving me a month's notice?'

I nodded.

'As if I am not your father.'

This time I did not nod.

He looked out of the window, the sun blazing in his eyes, making them the colour of honey.

'And what do you know about beekeeping? Where will you work? How will you earn a living?'

'Mustafa has taught me—'

'Ha!' he said. 'Mustafa. That boy is wild. I knew he would lead you astray.'

'He hasn't led me anywhere. He's taught me.'

He grunted.

'We will build beehives together.'

Another grunt.

'We will have a business.'

This time silence. A long silence and his eyes dropped and for the first time I felt his quiet disappointment and deep guilt in my heart that would haunt me for years to come. As my mother washed up she turned now and then to look at me, to nod, to urge me on, but I couldn't say anymore after this, and about fifteen minutes passed before my father spoke again.

'So the shop will die with me,' he said.

And that was the last thing he would ever say about it. According to him I had made my decision and there was nothing more to discuss. But in the days and weeks that followed I saw him become smaller, and less urgent, less purposeful in his actions, as he cut or sewed or measured. As if he had lost the fire that had driven him. And I thought in that moment, lying there looking up at the Athenian sky, that if I had sacrificed my father's happiness to become a beekeeper, then I had to find a way to make it to Mustafa. He had found me all those years ago, he had led me out of that dark shop and into the wild fields on the edge of the desert, and now I had to keep my promise to him. I would find a way to get to England.

I woke up in the dead of night. The fire was just a flicker now. The children were sleeping. A baby was crying; it was like the sound was coming from deep in the woods, but it couldn't have been. Angeliki was wrapped in a blanket, leaning against a tree beside us. Her eyes were wide open, her hands in her lap, her breasts still leaking. I wondered where she had come from, where her family was, who she had left behind. I wanted to ask her again: Angeliki, why did you leave? And what is your real name? And where is your baby girl?

I contemplated these questions here in the moonlit forest, surrounded by the buzzing of the crickets. Now there was a softness to the darkness, like night-time in the stories of the Arabian Nights, the kind my mother used to tell me in the days when she would look out of the window at a country that seethed with power and corruption and oppression, and I would see her frustration, her anger and sometimes her fear while she read.

There was something about the movement of time in these stories that I both loved and feared. Night after night, monsters came out of the sea. Night after night, stories were told in order to delay a beheading. Lives were broken up into nights. Night-time was filled with the cries of the grief-stricken.

Angeliki shifted her hands in her lap. The baby was still crying, but I couldn't tell where the crying was coming from. I didn't want to sleep again because this place was not safe. There was something very wrong here. I remembered how Afra's breasts used to leak when Sami cried. Hearing Sami, smelling him, sitting in the chair where she usually fed him, made Afra's breasts release milk, as if there was always an invisible cord between them. They communicated without words from the most primitive part of the soul. I remembered her laughing about this, saying that she felt like an animal, and how she realised that we are less human in our times of greatest love and greatest fear. In those early days of motherhood she didn't paint; she was exhausted and preoccupied entirely with Sami. Later when she took to the canvas again in the hours when Sami was asleep, these landscapes were the most beautiful, the most alive, with greater depth to the darkness and a luminous shimmer to the light.

When the crying stopped, Angeliki's eyes closed completely. I was thinking about Nadim now and the way he had slipped the money into those boys' hands. My thoughts turned to Mohammed, and now I was more afraid for him than ever before. And then, worst of all, I thought about Sami. First his smile. Then the moment the light fell from his eyes and they turned to glass. I didn't want to think about Sami. I never want to think about Sami. I looked up at the vast sky and stars and they morphed into images that I could not dispel from my mind.

Night after night, the predators came out of the woods. Nadim became more and more friendly with the two boys, and as the nights passed the boys disappeared and reappeared again, in the same spot, each time looking more troubled than before. But they had new shoes, and even a new phone, and they bantered with each other and fought and laughed, and they clung to each other, especially in the early hours of the morning when they returned from wherever they had been. Then they slept, late into the afternoon, even when the sun was beaming down on them, their bodies immovable, their minds switched off.

Night after night, Angeliki slept against the tree beside us. I think she felt safe next to us. I wondered if she still went to the old school. It seemed so far away now, so long ago, though it had probably been only a week or maybe two since we had come to this place.

I had given Afra the pencils and notepad, but she would not take them this time; she pushed them away, even in her sleep. Her mind was exhausted and preoccupied. She listened to the sounds around her, she responded to the children's playing and crying with facial expressions. She was afraid for them. She asked me sometimes who was hiding in the woods. I told her that I didn't know.

Some days people packed their few belongings and left, though I had no idea where they were heading. In Leros, people were chosen by their country of origin. There was a ranking. Refugees from Syria had priority; that was what we had been told. Refugees from Afghanistan and the African continent had to wait longer or maybe forever. But here in the park it seemed as if everyone had been forgotten. Some days new people arrived, dragged in by an NGO worker holding new blankets. Adults and children with startled eyes and sea-swept hair.

10

I TAKE AFRA TO THE GP for her appointment. It's a big clinic and there is a doctor here who speaks Arabic. Dr Faruk is a short, round man, probably around fifty. He has his glasses on the table in front of him next to a bronze plaque with his name on it, his eyes are lit up by the screen of the computer. He wants to record some details, he says, get Afra's history, before he examines her. He asks her questions about the type of pain in her eyes: Is the pain sharp or dull? Is it in both eyes? Do you have headaches? Do you see flashing lights? Afra answers his questions, and then he pulls up a chair and sits beside her. He takes her blood pressure and listens to her heart with a stethoscope and finally he shines a tiny flashlight into each eye. First the right eye, pausing there for a moment, then the left, pausing again, then back to the right. He repeats the procedure a few more times and then sits there watching her for a moment, as if in contemplation or confusion.

'Did you say you can't see anything at all?'

'Yes,' she says.

He shines the torch into her eyes again. 'Can I ask you if you can see anything now?'

'No,' she says, keeping very still.

'Can you make out any change? A shadow or some movement or light?'

'No,' she says, 'nothing at all.'

I can hear a tremor in her voice, she is getting upset, and the doctor may have also picked up on it, as he puts the flashlight down and asks no more questions. He sits again at his desk, scratching the side of his face.

'Mrs Ibrahim,' he says, 'can you explain to me how you became blind?'

'It was a bomb,' she says.

'Can you tell me a bit more about it?'

Afra shifts in her chair, rolling the marble around in her fingers.

'Sami, my son,' she says, 'he was playing in the garden. I let him play there beneath the tree, but I was watching him from the window – there'd been no bombs for two days and I thought it would be all right. He was a child, he wanted to play in the garden with his friends, but there were no children left. He couldn't be inside all the time, it was like a prison for him. He put on his favourite red T-shirt and jean shorts and he asked me if he could play in the garden, and when I looked into his eyes I couldn't say no, because he was a boy, Dr Faruk, a boy who wanted to play.' Afra's voice is strong and steady.

'I understand,' he says. 'Please go on.'

'I heard a whistle first, in the sky, and I ran outside to call him.' She stops talking and inhales sharply as if she has just surfaced from beneath water. I wish she would stop talking now. 'As I reached the door, there was a loud explosion and bright light, in the back of the garden, I'm sure, not right near Sami, but the force was strong. It was so loud the sky ripped open.'

I notice the sound of chairs moving in other rooms, the laughter of a child.

'And then what happened?'

'I don't know. I was holding Sami in my arms, and my husband was beside me and I could hear his voice, but I couldn't see anything at all.'

'What was the last thing you saw?'

'Sami's eyes. They were looking up at the sky.'

Afra begins to cry in a way that I have never seen her cry. She is bent over and crying from her chest and the doctor gets up from his desk and sits beside her, and I feel that I am far away, that there is a growing desert between me and them. I can see the doctor offering her a tissue, then giving her some water, and I can see Afra's body folded over, but I can't hear her, and he is saying something, gentle words, sorry words, but my heart is thumping too loud for me to hear anything on the outside and I am so far from them. His voice is louder now and I try to focus. He is sitting at his desk with his glasses on, looking straight at me. I can tell that he has said something I didn't hear. Then he looks at Afra.

'Mrs Ibrahim, your pupils are reacting to the light, dilating and constricting in exactly the way I would expect them to if you could see.'

'What does that mean?' she says.

'I'm not sure at the moment. You will need to have some X-rays taken. There is a possibility that the force of the explosion or the bright light damaged the retina in some way, but it is also possible that the blindness you are experiencing is the result of severe trauma – sometimes our bodies can find ways to cope when we are faced with things that are too much for us to bear. You saw your son die, Mrs Ibrahim, and maybe something in you had to shut down. In a way something similar happens when we faint out of shock. I can't tell you for sure. We will only have the answer when you have more tests.' For that brief moment, just as he finishes his words, he looks much smaller, hands clasped together, eyes darting now and then to the left of the room at a photograph on a cabinet of a beautiful girl in her twenties in a hat and graduation gown. He catches my gaze and looks away.

Then he scribbles on a piece of paper and says, 'And how are you, Mr Ibrahim?'

'Everything is fine with me.'

I notice out of the corner of my eye that Afra has straightened her back.

'Actually, Dr Faruk,' she says, 'I think my husband is unwell.'

'What seems to be the problem?' He looks from Afra to me.

'I'm just having a bit of trouble sleeping,' I say. 'I'm finding it difficult to get to sleep.'

I can see Afra shaking her head. 'No,' she says. 'It's more than that—'

'No, I'm fine!'

'Can you tell me more, Mrs Ibrahim?'

'Can nobody hear me?!'

She thinks for a while, searching her mind, and says, 'I can't explain what it is, Dr Faruk, but I know something is wrong. He is not my husband.'

Dr Faruk looks directly at me now. I laugh. 'Honestly, Afra, I'm sleep-deprived, that's all. I end up so tired that I fall asleep in all sorts of ridiculous places.' My laughter seems to be having no effect on either of them.

'Like where, for example?'

'The storage cupboard,' Afra says, 'and the garden.'

The doctor is frowning now and I can see that he is over-thinking this.

'Anything else unusual?'

They are both ignoring me. I look from the doctor to Afra. She quickly looks away.

'He changed in Istanbul. He . . .' Afra hesitates.

'He . . . ?'

'He talks aloud to himself, or rather to someone who is not there.'

'Dr Faruk, I would really appreciate some sleeping tablets to help me rest, and once I do I won't accidentally fall asleep in the storage cupboard again.' I am smiling too broadly.

'I am concerned about what your wife is saying, Mr Ibrahim.'

I laugh. 'What? No! It's just me running through things in

my head. Just memories. To-do lists. That kind of thing. It's nothing!'

'Have you experienced any flashbacks, Mr Ibrahim?'

'How do you mean?'

'Any repetitive or distressing images?'

'Not at all.'

'Trembling, nausea or sweating?'

'No.'

'How is your concentration?'

'Fine.'

'Do you feel numb, as if you have lost your ability to experience emotions such as pain or joy?'

'No, doctor. Thank you for your concern, but I am fine.'

The doctor leans back in his chair now, more suspicious than before. Afra's face has dropped, her eyes have darkened, and I feel a great sense of sadness watching her sitting there looking so burdened.

The doctor is unconvinced. Nonetheless, our time is up and he writes out a prescription for sleeping tablets, strong ones, and asks me to come and see him again in three weeks.

That afternoon Afra will not go into the living room. She sits on the edge of the bed for a long time.

'It wasn't the bomb that blinded me,' she whispers. 'I saw Sami die. And that's when it all went black.'

I don't know what to say to her, but I sit beside her for maybe an hour or more and we do not speak to each other.

Through the window I watch the sky change colour, the clouds and the birds moving across it.

We do not even move from where we are to get anything to eat. Usually the landlady brings a pot of stew or soup from her house, carrying it with oven gloves across the driveway, banging on the door with her elbow, and placing it in the middle of the dining table for us to help ourselves. I am sure that everyone has already eaten, that all this has happened without me noticing. I can hear footsteps and voices and the murmur of the TV in the living room, doors open and close, the kettle boils, the toilet flushes, water runs. The sky grows darker and I catch the moon, a crescent behind the mist of clouds. Sometimes I expect Mohammed, but he doesn't come. I move to the armchair and wait for

morning

of the fifteenth day, the mother with the blue hijab stood up suddenly, Mahsa in her arms, and ran over to where the old lady was tending to another young child. She grabbed the old woman by the shoulders. At first, I thought something bad had happened and I jumped to my feet. But then I saw that the mother had a smile on her face, and once she'd let go of the old woman's shoulders, she started pressing her own breasts with her palms.

'*Echeis gala!*' the old woman said. '*Eftichos! Echeis gala!*' and she crossed herself and kissed the mother's hands. The mother made herself comfortable now on a blanket, signalling to the old lady to keep watching as she held Mahsa in her arms, gave her the nipple and the baby girl began to feed. I smiled at this turn of events. A real smile, coming from my heart. The old lady saw this and she raised her hand to me in salute.

Having seen all this unfold convinced me that things can change, that hope can prevail, even in the most difficult of circumstances. Maybe we could get out of here soon. I remembered the money in my rucksack. I'd been guarding it with my life, using it as a pillow at night to ensure that nobody could get to it without waking me first. People spoke openly about the thieves. They were silent though about the other things that lurked in the shadows.

That night, when I saw the boys sitting on their usual blanket beneath the tree, I thought about approaching them, and when the strong smell of cologne wafted my way, I saw they were splashing aftershave onto their faces.

I wandered over and asked them if I could sit down. They were wary, their eyes darting to the woods, but they were too young and too naive to refuse. They shook my hand and introduced themselves as Ryad and Ali, twin brothers, not identical, about fifteen years old. Ryad was the taller and stronger of the two, Ali had something of the child in him still; together they were like puppies. I asked them questions and the boys answered, talking over each other at times.

They told me how they fled Afghanistan and their father's murderers. After their father's death the twins were themselves targeted by the Taliban and their mother urged them to leave before they were captured. She didn't want to lose her boys as well as her husband. They described to me how she had cried and kissed their faces a hundred times because she feared that she would never see them again. They told me about their journey through Turkey and Lesbos, and how they arrived in this strange city with no help and no idea what to do next. That was when a man advised them to head to Victoria Square, a well-known meeting point for refugees.

'We thought somebody there would help us,' Ali said.

'And we couldn't sleep on the streets anymore.'

'And all the benches were taken.'

'And there were too many gangs.'

'Ryad was afraid.'

'Ali was more afraid – he was shaking in the night.'

'So they told us to come here.'

'So, you know Nadim?' I said. 'Has he been helpful to you?'

'Who's Nadim?' Ryad said. They both stared at me without blinking, waiting for a reply.

'Maybe I got his name wrong.' I forced a smile. 'The man with the guitar. The man with the scars.'

They quickly looked at each other and their eyes became dark and unwelcoming.

'I think you mean Ahmed,' Ryad said.

'Oh, that's it! I knew I'd gotten it wrong. I've met so many people these last few weeks and I'm terrible with names.'

The boys remained silent.

'Did he help you?' I said. 'I've heard that he's very kind.'

'He helped us out quite a bit the first night,' Ali said, and Ryad nudged him. It was slight, on his thigh, but I saw it.

'I see. And then?'

Ali was reluctant to answer. He lowered his face to the ground, not looking at me or his brother.

'Does he want the money back?' I said.

Ali nodded. Ryad rolled his eyes, looked up at the sky.

'How much?'

'We are paying in instalments, OK?' Ryad spoke up now, he sounded defensive.

'How? Where do you find the money to make the repayments?' I must have looked at Ryad's new shoes because he tucked his legs under him, but it was Ali's reaction that disturbed me the most. I noticed that his body folded inward and he wrapped his arms protectively around himself, his face bright red. From nowhere there was a shadow that blocked out the sun and I saw that Nadim was standing over us, rebab in hand, a crooked smile on his face.

'I see you've all met,' he said, taking a seat beside us on the blanket, and he began to play, the soft sound washing through my mind, washing away the thoughts and worries, the melody warm, dipping lower and darker and becoming even more mesmerising. After an hour of music, Nadim put down his guitar and drifted away from us. I saw him head for the woods and decided to follow him, past a group of Greek men smoking by a bench, past two women loitering in the shadows. I followed him to a clearing with a fallen tree and as he sat down on the cracked log, he took something out of his rucksack: a small, sharp penknife. He placed its blade on his left wrist, paused for a second, then scanned his surroundings. I stepped back into the shadows to make sure that he wouldn't see me. Then without any more hesitation he ran the knife along his forearm. I could see the creases of pain on his face, his eyes rolling backwards, so that for a brief moment there was only white. His arm was bleeding and he took some tissues out of his bag and held them over the fresh wounds. But it was the look on his face that I remember the most; he seemed angry. Was this punishment?

I moved slightly and a twig broke and Nadim looked up and his eyes settled on me, narrowing. I stepped back, further into the darkness, and not knowing what else to do I began to run through the woods and back to the campsite.

'What happened?' Afra said when I sat down beside her.
'Nothing. Why?'
'Because you're breathing like a dog.'
'No, I'm not, I'm perfectly calm.'

She shook her head slightly in resignation and in that moment Nadim emerged from the trees and sat down on the step of the statue. He suddenly appeared emaciated again just as he did the first day I saw him – his strength had been drained from him. I waited to see if he would approach me, but he didn't even glance in my direction. He simply rolled one cigarette after another and sat there for an hour or more smoking.

The boys were on their blanket, playing a game on their phone and laughing. Sometimes Ali punched Ryad's arm, and then Ryad got fed up and took the phone, sitting with his back to Ali so that he couldn't see the screen.

Although Nadim seemed relaxed and preoccupied with his own thoughts, I could see that his mind was actually on the boys, his eyes constantly flicking towards them.

I lay down next to Afra and pretended to close my eyes, but I watched Nadim and the boys. At ten o'clock on the dot Nadim got up and went into the woods. Three minutes later the boys followed. I got up and followed them too, trying to keep enough distance between us so that they would not see me, while at the same time staying close enough so that I would not lose them.

They took sharp and unexpected turns, as if they were following an invisible path, and eventually reached a different clearing in the woods than before. Here, there was trash everywhere, piles and piles of it; a dried-up pond had become a rubbish dump. In the middle of a concrete well there was a stagnant fountain surrounded by the pipes of an ancient watering system. Just beyond this, all the bushes in a rose garden were dead. Drug addicts and dealers hovered around the well, syringes lay strewn on the ground. People sat on the roof of a maintenance building, and scattered around were mattresses and boxes – the remnants of a past life.

The boys stood by the well and they were soon approached by a man who slipped some money into Ryad's hand. Then the boys split up. Ali took the path to the right of the fountain, and Ryad waited until another man came shortly after to collect him, and they went off together in the opposite direction. I stood there for a while, and people started to notice me. Nadim was nowhere to be seen, he must have slipped away. I couldn't stay here too long. I had to leave this place, go back to the campsite.

So I began to make my way there, taking wrong turns and retracing my steps. When I heard the sound of children kicking a ball I knew I was close, and shortly after I saw the light of the campfire. I found Angeliki sitting by the tree again beside Afra. The notepad and colouring pencils were in her lap, her head pressed against the bark of the tree, fast asleep. Afra was also asleep, curled up on her side in a foetal position with her head resting on both hands. I could feel that someone was watching me, and when I turned around I saw that Nadim was back on the step of the statue, smoking and staring at me.

He raised a hand, signalling for me to come over, and I went and sat beside him on the step.

'I have something to give you,' he said.

'I don't need anything.'

'Everybody needs something,' he said, 'especially here.'

'Not me.'

'Just hold out your hand,' he said.

I watched him without blinking.

'Come on!' he said. 'Hold out your hand. Don't be scared. It's not bad, I promise.'

He took my hand and opened up my palm.

'Now close your eyes.'

This thing had gone too far now. I attempted to pull my hand away, but Nadim tightened his grip. 'Come on. Just close your eyes,' he said with a grin, his eyes sparkling in the firelight.

'No way,' I said, and attempted to pull my hand back with force, without making a scene. But what happened next was so sudden and unexpected that it caused my mind and my body to freeze. I felt intense pain across my wrist. He'd slashed me with his knife. I held my arm up like a wounded bird, the blood coming out fast, dripping onto my trousers.

I rushed away from him, stumbling over to Afra, pleading with her to wake up. She opened her eyes, frightened, and I led her hand to my wrist. She sat up sharply, the blood now running through her fingers. She began to feel the wound with her hands and she pressed down on it, attempting, in vain, to stop the blood. Then I could feel another pair of hands. Angeliki had taken off her green headwrap and was twisting it around my wrist.

'What happened?' Afra said. I looked back toward the statue, but Nadim had disappeared.

Angeliki exhaled and sat down beneath the tree, her face full of anxiety. The blood was seeping through the layered material of the scarf, my arm throbbing. I lay down from exhaustion, but Angeliki was sitting upright. The last thing I saw before my eyes closed was her long neck, her polished cheekbones sharp in the dying light of the fire.

When I woke up, hours later, in the middle of the night, I saw that she was still sitting in the same position, her eyes scanning the darkness and the shadows.

'Angeliki,' I whispered, and she turned to me, wide awake. 'Lie down here next to Afra. I'll take over for a bit.'

'You won't fall asleep again?' she asked.

'No.'

She was hesitant for a moment, but then she lay down on the blanket next to Afra and closed her eyes.

'Odysseus,' she said out of nowhere, 'he pass the island of Sirens. Do you know who the Sirens were?' This was not a rhetorical question – she waited for me to reply, and she opened one eyelid, halfway, to make sure that I was listening. But I was in pain and I found it difficult to concentrate on what she was saying.

'No,' I said, 'I don't.'

'They will try to entice men to death with their song. If you hear their song they will take you. So, as they are pass the island, the men put wax in their ears to no hear the song, but Odysseus want to hear the Siren song because he had been told it is so beautiful. So do you know what they do?'

'No.'

'This very important. The men tie Odysseus to the mast of the ship – they tie him on so tight. He says for them to leave him tied there no matter how much he begs, until they are safe, far from the Sirens and their song.'

I didn't respond. I held my bandaged arm, trying to ignore the heat of the pain, and looked out into the woods, into the things unseen lurking there.

Angeliki continued, 'Athens, this the place where people get caught in dangerous things – they are called to those things and they can't help it, so they go.'

I noticed that Ryad and Ali were not on their blankets. They still hadn't returned, and I didn't want to think about where they had gone and what they might be doing. I looked at Angeliki's blood-soaked green wrap on my arm, at her tufts of unruly frizzy hair, full of life, at Afra's hair spread out around her without her hijab. Angeliki had drifted off quickly and both women were sleeping now. I remembered what Angeliki had said about Odysseus when we had first arrived here, how he had travelled to all those places, made such a journey to distant lands, in order to find his way home. But there was no home for us.

I touched the letter that Mustafa had written to me, which was still in my pocket. I took out the photograph of us both and looked at it by the light of the fire.

Where was home now? And what was it? In my mind it had become a picture infused with golden light, a paradise never to be reached. I remembered one evening, about ten years ago, it was Eid, and to celebrate the end of Ramadan

Mustafa and I had organised a party for all our employees at the Martini Dar Zamaria Hotel in Aleppo. It was held in the inner yard – there were palm trees and lanterns and plants hanging from the balconies overhead. Above us a square of night sky, full of stars.

The hotel had prepared a feast of meat and fish dishes, with rice and grains and vegetables on the side. We prayed together and we ate with our employees, our friends and our families. Children ran around among the adults. Afra looked beautiful in a red and gold abaya, making her way around the room, holding Sami by the hand, greeting the people who arrived with a smile that held within it all the warmth in the world.

Firas and Aya and Dahab were there, and even Mustafa's father had made a trip down from the mountains; a quiet, unassuming man, nothing like his own father, but he was proud of his son's achievements and he relished the food and the company, speaking to me freely about his apiaries. The scene was magical – the leaves of the trees glistened, the smoke of the shisha rose into the night in ribbons of silk, the plants in the hanging baskets suddenly bloomed with glowing flowers, infusing the courtyard with their sweet scent. It became a place in a storybook, the type my mother used to read to me in the room with the blue tiles.

In the morning I woke up and I realised that I hadn't kept my promise, I did fall asleep on the tree, and Angeliki had left. The green headscarf was saturated with blood and the pain in my arm was worse. The old women were handing out food packages, and I noticed a few NGO workers walking around. I raised my hand and called to one, a woman in her early twenties. I held out my arm and she stood over me and flinched. She hovered there for a few moments, not knowing what to do, and then she told me to wait, to not go anywhere, that she would get someone who could help me, that she only worked with the children and had no medical experience, but she could find someone who would know what to do.

I thanked her and she left, and the day passed but the young NGO worker didn't return. So I took off the green headwrap and saw that the wound was deep and still bleeding. I cleaned it with some drinking water and then I wrapped it back up with the same headscarf.

It was later in the afternoon that I saw the NGO worker coming through the woods towards me. Behind her was an older woman with a rucksack on her shoulders. They stopped beside me and talked between themselves for a while in a language I didn't recognise. Perhaps it was Dutch or Swiss or German, I couldn't tell. The older woman then knelt down beside me and opened the rucksack, putting on some latex gloves, unwrapping the scarf and pursing her lips when she saw the wound.

'How did you do this?'

'Somebody did it to me,' I said.

She gave me a concerned look but said nothing. She spent a long time cleaning the wound with antiseptic wipes and then closing it with butterfly stitches, placing each one delicately over the cut with a pair of tweezers.

'I need to leave from here,' I said.

She said nothing.

'How do people leave?'

She gave me a long look, pausing with the tweezers in her hand, but then she continued with her task, lips tight. When she began to cover the wound with a clean bandage, her shoulders relaxed and she started to speak again.

'I would have told you to go to Scopje,' she said, blowing her hair away from her face, 'but people are fighting with the police there to cross into Macedonia. They've closed the borders. No one is getting through now. You'll get stuck there.'

'What else can I do?'

'You can take the coach to the villages. There is priority for people from Syria. It comes once a week.'

'And then what happens?'

'You stay there.'

'For how long?'

There was no response. She pushed her hair back, twisting it into a bun and releasing it. I noticed that she was wearing an identity badge around her neck. Her name was Emily. Underneath her handwritten name was a small logo.

She began to pack her things away.

'What about the woman from Africa, and there are two teenage boys in trouble. Can they go to the villages?'

'I don't know,' she said. Then, 'No. I don't think so. God, you really shouldn't be asking me. I can't take responsibility. There are advisors.'

'Where are they?'

I could see that she was struggling with herself, her eyes sparkling with grievance, her face flushed with anger.

'If you go to Victoria Square—'

'I've heard about Victoria Square.'

'If you go there, there is a centre on Elpidos Street – the Hope Centre. They help mothers and children and unaccompanied boys. They will advise you.' She said this in one breath and then forced a smile.

That night Angeliki returned. She sat down beside the tree and covered her face with talcum powder. She was wearing a black headwrap with silver sequins that sparkled in the light of the fire. She took small purposeful sips of water from a bottle and inspected the wounds on her arms. When Afra sensed her presence, she sat up, more alert, edging closer to her.

'What you doing?' Afra said.

'They say me to drink a lot of water,' Angeliki replied. 'Because of my poison blood.'

Afra shook her head.

'It is, I am telling you. I tell you all about it yesterday! I tell you, my breath it stop and it does not come back. My breath it stop, and they took it. Some people, they want to take your breath. And then they put something in my blood. They poison it, and now my mind is ill.'

Although Afra probably didn't understand all of what Angeliki was saying, I could see that she was moved by the words and her tone of voice, and when Angeliki stopped talking, Afra reached out and put her hand on Angeliki's arm.

Angeliki breathed slower now and said, 'I am glad you are here with me, Afra.'

From deep in the woods came the sound of the rebab, beautiful and full of light, even in the darkness. The notes seemed to touch the flames of the fire, causing them to flicker, and the music was carried away by the wind, deeper into the woods. The sound calmed my mind, but as soon as he stopped playing I was reminded immediately of Nadim's long nails, of the sharp edge of the knife and the heat across my wrist. The twins had not returned since last night and I wanted to go and find them. I contemplated going back to the empty well to see if they were there or to ask if anyone had seen them, but fear was stopping me from venturing into the woods again. I needed to stay alive for Afra. I waited instead, hoping that the boys would emerge from the shadows and return to their blanket beneath the tree.

It was Mohammed I saw in my nightmares that night, on the boat, his face serious and determined, between flashes of torchlight. Just like that night, there was a moment of darkness, and when the light came back on, he was gone.

It was almost exactly as it had happened that night. I was scanning the water, the black waves, as far as my eye could see in every direction, and then I jumped in, and the waves were high, and I was calling his name and I could hear Afra's voice from the boat. I went under into the black silence and stayed for as long as I could, feeling with my hands in case I should catch onto something, an arm or a leg. When there was no air left in my lungs, when the pressure of death was pushing down on me, I came back up, gasping into the darkness and the wind. But in my dream one detail was different: Mohammed was not saved by the man, he was not on the boat; in his place, wrapped up in the women's arms and headscarves, was a little girl with eyes like the night.

I woke up to the sound of shouting. A young boy was screaming something in Farsi, there was movement and noise in the darkness, people waking up and running towards the boy. I got up too, moved towards the commotion. The boy was crying and struggling to breathe and pointing into the woods. A group of men appeared with baseball bats as if they had been waiting for this moment, and they began to run in the direction the boy was pointing. I ran with them, and I soon realised that they were chasing someone. They pounced on him as if they were one huge animal, knocking him to the ground.

That's when somebody handed me a bat. I looked at this man squirming, trying to free himself, and I saw that it was Nadim. He looked so different there on the ground, his face full of fear. The men held him down and others took turns beating him. I stood motionless and watched as they beat him until his eyes were rolling in his skull and his face was broken, until his legs and arms twitched.

'Why are you just standing there?' one man said, nudging me. 'Don't you know this man is the devil?' And so I took a step closer to take my turn, and I heard the cheers of the men and then everything and everyone around me seemed to vanish and all I could see was Nadim's face looking up at me. For a moment his focus cleared, his eyes fixed on mine and he said something to me that I couldn't hear, while a voice from behind urged me on and I felt the throb of my wound and remembered the innocent faces of the twins and some other anger grew in me, one that I did not recognise, and I brought the bat down onto his skull.

Then he was motionless. I dropped the bat and stepped back. One man kicked him and another spat on him, and then they all ran off, in all directions, into the woods or back to the campsite.

I dragged his body deeper into the woods, where the trees were closer together, where the noises of the city and the noises of the campsite were far away, and I sat beside him until the sun began to rise.

By the dim light of dawn, I made my way back to the camp. I came upon two men having a heated discussion. I recognised them immediately and quickly stepped into the shadows. One of them was sitting on the splintered log where Nadim had once sat; the other was restless, pacing up and down, stepping over a baseball bat.

'What the hell are you feeling guilty about?'

'We killed someone.'

'He was taking those boys. You know what he was doing, right?'

'I know. I know that.'

'What if it had been your son?'

The man on the log didn't reply.

'I mean, can you imagine?'

'I don't want to.'

'He was evil. The worst kind of evil there is.'

'Did you not hear what happened to Sadik's son?'

This wasn't really a question, and the man sitting down lowered his eyes, running his hand over his face.

There was silence for a while and I didn't dare to move, to even take a breath. The wind picked up and leaves on the trees rustled above us and I could hear footsteps in the woods and the sounds of laughter and faint music.

The man sitting on the log stood up now to face the other man. 'What leads a man to do such things?'

I didn't hear the reply because a group of boys walked between us, about five or six of them. One held a football in his hands, another had an Arabic song playing on his phone and a few of the boys sang along to the chorus. The two men took this as their cue and began to walk back to the camp. I took their place on the log, and felt its ridges and grooves with my fingers. I imagined Nadim; I could see him, as if he was sitting right there beside me, penknife in his hand, slicing his skin, that look in his eyes, full of rage.

'What happened to you, Nadim?' I said out loud. 'What led you to do such things?'

And the wind replied, it lifted the fallen leaves, it tossed them about around me and then dropped them and the laughter and the music faded now completely, the boys lost to the depths of the woods.

Then I returned to the camp. Angeliki had gone now and I lay down beside Afra.

'Where did you go?' she whispered.

'There was a problem.'
'What kind of problem?'
'You don't want to know, trust me. It's finished now.'
I remembered a verse from the Qur'an:

Be merciful to others and you will receive mercy. Forgive others and Allah will forgive you.

I then recalled some words from the Hadith:

The prophet would not respond to an evil deed with an evil deed but rather he would pardon and overlook.

And I looked at my hands, turned them over as if I was seeing them for the first time: one wrapped in a bandage, the other that had held the bat. I began to feel that fear again, the kind that had consumed me in Aleppo, alert to every movement and sound, imagining danger everywhere, expecting that at any moment the worst would happen, that death was near. I felt exposed, as if people were watching me from the woods, and when the wind blew it brought with it whispers: *murderer, Nadim is dead, murderer.*

I placed my palm on Afra's chest, feeling her chest rise and fall, matching my breath to hers, slower, steadier. I recalled Mustafa's British black bees and kept my eyes closed tight until I could see purple fields and rolling hills of lavender and heather, spilling over the edge of the world.

* * *

When I woke up, it was the afternoon. I looked at the step where Nadim should have been sitting, rolling a cigarette. I looked at the white statue – the head and shoulders of a bearded man, the inscription in Greek and the date: 1788–1825, and wondered what kind of a man he was. In my anxious state, I remembered vaguely the stories my mother used to tell me. In these tales statues were not objects of art or reverence – they were evil-averting talismans or guardians of treasure, or human beings or animals who had been turned to stone. In some stories demons entered the statues and spoke through them.

Afra sat beside me and I wished that she could see, wished that she could be the woman she used to be, because Afra had always had a deep understanding of the world; she had a way of seeing things. Afra always knew too much, burdened with the ability to strip people and places of their masks, to find the remnants of the past in the present. I noticed that Nadim had left his rebab on the step of the statue. I walked over and picked it up. I strummed the strings and remembered the beautiful melody that had washed over me and through me like water, quenching the scorched cracks in my mind, like the feeling of the first drop of water on my tongue when the sun sets during the month of Ramadan. That was what Nadim's music felt like, and this thought alone twisted my mind, distorted my thoughts. I closed my eyes and focused instead on the sound of children playing, laughing, kicking a ball.

11

It is the day of our interview. Afra is sitting beside me on the train and I know that she is nervous. Diomande is standing, holding the rail; there is a free seat for him but he won't sit down. His tall distorted body is even more prominent in this public place. He looks like a character from a fairy tale, and I find it strange that out of all the people in the carriage I am the only one who knows his secret. Diomande is reading the advice in his notebook, muttering under his breath. 'This is not a history lesson,' he says in English, 'and they do not need to know too much about the last president, unless they ask.'

Eventually we arrive in a place called Croydon. Lucy Fisher meets us at the station and takes us to the centre. It is a tall building on a brown street. Inside we go through checkpoints, barriers, security, where they scan us, search us and get us to sign in. Then we sit in a waiting area with people who look as frightened as we do. And so we wait. Diomande goes in first. Next is Afra, and a few minutes later I am taken to a room at the end of a long corridor.

There are two people sitting in this room, a man and a woman. The man is probably in his early forties; he has shaved off his hair because he is balding on top. He doesn't look into my eyes, not once. He asks me to sit down, says my name as if he knows me, but his eyes wander. And yet there is an arrogance about him, a subtle smirk on his lips. The woman beside him is a bit older with curly hair. She is sitting very upright and trying to look welcoming. They are both immigration officers. He offers me tea or coffee and I refuse.

He runs through the procedure and says that the interview is being recorded. He reminds me that there will be a second interview. First, he asks me to confirm my name and date of birth and where I was born and where I was living when the war started. Then the questions start to become strange.

'Are there any landmarks in Aleppo?' he says.

'Of course.'

'Can you name some of these?'

'Well, there's the citadel. The Umayyad Mosque, Khan al-Jumruk, al-Firdaws Madrasa, which means "the school of paradise", al-Otrush Mosque, the Bab al-Faraj Clock Tower ... do you want more?'

'Thank you, that should be sufficient. Is the old souq in the north or east of the city?'

'It's central.'
'What do they sell at the souq?'
'Thousands of things!'
'Such as?'
'Fabrics, silks and linen. Carpets and lanterns and silver, gold and bronze, and spices and teas and herbs and my wife used to sell her paintings there.'
'What's your country's name?'
'Syria. Don't you want to know how I got here?'
'We'll get there soon. These are just standard questions, part of the procedure.'

He pauses for a moment and consults his papers. Then he scratches his shiny head.

'Have you seen Daesh?'
'No, not personally.'
'So you've never come in contact with anyone from this group?'
'No. Of course I've seen them on the streets or wherever, but I've never had any personal contact with them.'
'Were you ever held prisoner by Daesh?'
'No.'
'Did you work with Daesh?'
'No.'
'Are you married?'
'Yes.'
'What is your wife's name?'
'Afra Ibrahim.'
'Do you have children?'
'Yes.'

'How many?'

'One, a boy.'

'Where was he born?'

'In Aleppo.'

'Where is he now?'

'He died in Syria.'

He pauses for a moment and stares at the desk. The woman next to him looks sad. I'm starting to feel agitated.

'Can you say something special about him? Something you remember about him?'

'Who?'

'Your son. I understand this is difficult, Mr Ibrahim, but could you please try to answer the question. It's important that you do.'

'OK. Once, when he was riding his bike down the hill – I'd told him not to because there was such a steep hill going down to the city from our bungalow – well, he fell off it and broke his finger and it didn't really mend and he had this little bend in his finger.'

'Which hand?'

'Which hand?'

'On which hand was this injury? Right or left?'

I look down at my hands and remember Sami's hand in mine.

'It was his left hand. I know because his left hand fit into my right hand and I could feel his bent little finger.'

'What was his date of birth?'

'January 5th 2009.'

'Have you ever killed anyone?'

'No.'

'What's the national anthem of your country?'
'Is this a joke?'
'Is that your answer?'
'No! It's called "Guardians of the Homeland".'
'Can you sing it without the words?'
I hum a few of the lines through gritted teeth.
'Do you like reading?'
'Not particularly.'
'What was the last book you read?'
'A book about the crystallisation process of honey.'
'Do you read political books?'
'No.'
'What about your wife?'
'Not that I know of.'
'What does your wife do for a living?'
'She is a painter. Was.'
'What is the current situation in your country?'
'It's heaven on earth.'
'Mr Ibrahim, I understand that these questions may seem to be a bit unnecessary to you, but they are an important part of your screening.'
'The situation in my country is complete chaos and destruction.'
'Who is your president?'
'Bashar al-Assad.'
'When did he become the president?'

* * *

And the questions continue in this way. Do I have any association with the president? Where is Syria? What countries does it share borders with? Is there a river in Aleppo? What is its name? Eventually he begins to ask me about my journey here, and I tell him as much as I can remember in a straightforward, linear, coherent way, just like Lucy Fisher suggested. Except it's harder than I thought, because when I try to answer his questions he replies often with a question that I wasn't expecting, something that throws me and takes me to another part of the journey. I tell him as best I can about how we reached Turkey, about the smuggler's apartment, about Mohammed, and the trip to Leros, about Athens and all those nights we spent in Pedion tou Areos. I don't elaborate. I don't tell him about Nadim. I do not want him to know that I helped to kill a man, that I am capable of being a murderer. And finally I tell him about how we made it to England. But I don't tell him what happened to Afra before we arrived – I wouldn't even be able to say the words out loud.

He tells me the interview is over. The voice recorder is turned off and the files are closed. A bar of light from a rectangular window close to the ceiling falls across his smile.

When I stand my legs are numb and I feel that I have been robbed, somehow, of life.

Lucy Fisher is waiting for me. Afra and Diomande haven't yet finished. Seeing my face, she goes to the vending machine and returns with a warm cup of tea.

'How did it go?' she asks.

I don't reply. I cannot speak.

'Please,' she says, 'don't lose hope. That's the thing.' There is a tone of resignation in her voice and she is pulling at the strand of hair. 'This is what I always tell people, you see. Never, never, never lose

hope

was fading, dwindling like the fire in the night. I needed to find a way out. So the next day I ventured out of the park. I asked passers-by for directions to Victoria Square. The square was cluttered with people and litter, those who had nowhere else to go sat on benches beneath the trees and around the statues. I recognised a few faces from the park, some of the drug dealers hanging around by the station or outside the cafés beneath the canopies on the square. There were stray cats everywhere, scavenging in the bins. A dog lay on his side on the concrete with his paws outstretched; it was hard to tell if he was dead or alive. I remembered the wild dogs of Istanbul and standing on Taksim Square with some hope in my heart. Hope existed then in the unknowability of the future. Istanbul felt like a place of waiting, but Athens was a place of stagnant resignation, and Angeliki's words played on my mind: 'This is the place where people die slowly, inside. One by one, people die.'

This was the city of recurring dreams, with no way of waking up: a string of nightmares.

A man held up a bunch of worry beads. 'Twenty euro,' he was saying, 'very beautiful stone.' His voice was full of desperation and grievance, the sentence sounding like a demand, but there was a manic smile on his face.

'Do I look like I have twenty euros?' I said, and turned away from him.

I looked up at the buildings that lined the square and the streets running off it. There were balconies with canopies and a feeling that a better life had once existed here; in their shabbiness and fading beauty they told a story of abandonment. There was graffiti on the walls, angry slogans that I couldn't understand, and coffee shops, and a flower stall and book stall, and people trying to sell tissues or pens or SIM cards. These people were like flies buzzing around the entrance of the Metro, following people as they stepped off the escalators.

The man with the worry beads was still standing beside me, the same infuriating smile on his face.

'Fifteen euro,' he tried again. 'Very beautiful stone.' The colours caught the light. Marble and amber and wood and coral and mother-of-pearl. I remembered the prayer beads in the souq in Aleppo. The man pushed them closer to my face.

'Twelve euro,' he said, 'very beautiful!'

I pushed them away violently with the back of my hand, and I saw that the man had become frightened. He stepped back, lowering the beads.

I showed him both my palms. 'I am sorry,' I said. 'I'm sorry.' The man nodded and turned to leave and I stopped him.

'Can you tell me where I can find Elpida Street?'

'Elpida?'

I nodded.

'Zitas Elpida?' The man lowered his face and mumbled something in Greek. Then he said, 'Are you asking for hope? Elpida mean hope. No hope here.' There was sadness in his eyes now, but then he chuckled to himself, 'El-pi-*dos*,' he said slowly, emphasising my mistake. 'Elpidos Street.' He signalled to the right, to a street just off the square, and he continued along his way, worry beads held up like a prize, the smile on his face.

I crossed the square and turned onto a tree-lined street. At the end of this street was a long queue of refugees outside a building with glass doors. There were prams and wheelchairs and children, and locals weaving through the chaos with their dogs. The doors opened and some refugees came out holding bags, while some others went in. On the corner there was a crowd, some standing, others sitting on the steps outside another set of glass doors. People were greeting one another and talking among themselves. As soon as they saw their friends the children ran into the street to play. The sign on the entrance said: *The Hope Centre*. And there was something about all this that made me more determined to leave.

I noticed that the women and children were going inside, while the men stayed outside; some sat down on the steps, others looked in through the windows, some headed back to the square. I waited, hovering, and a man came to the door; he was wearing a pair of mirrored sunglasses on his head, which he lowered onto his nose as he stepped outside.

They reminded me of the police officers at the Leros camp and I was about to turn and walk away when the man greeted me warmly in Arabic. He explained that this was a centre for women and children only, a place where they could have a hot shower and a cup of tea, where the children could play and new mothers could nurse their babies.

I returned to the park and picked up Afra and together we walked to Victoria Square. She was quiet, sniffing the air like a dog, probably creating pictures in her mind – the coffee, the rubbish, the urine, the trees, the flowers.

At the Hope Centre we were greeted by the man with the mirrored glasses and Afra was given a number so that she could take her place in the queue for a shower. I was told to come back in a few hours. I peeked through the window; to the right, behind a wooden frame, children were playing. There were paintings on the wall, Lego and balls and board games on the floor, Afra was being guided to a chair, given a cup of tea and a plate of biscuits. She was smiling, so I left.

First I went back to the square and found an Internet café. I hadn't checked my emails for a while and was hoping to hear from Mustafa.

12/04/2016

Dear Nuri,
Last week I attended a dinner held for refugees and there I met a man and a woman. The woman works

with refugees in a nearby district, helping new arrivals to fit in. The man is a local beekeeper. I told them both that I had an idea to teach beekeeping to refugees and jobseekers. They were both very impressed! They are helping me to set it up with some local funding. I hope that soon I will be giving workshops to volunteers.

The beehives are thriving, Nuri! These British black bees are very different from Syrian bees. I thought that they would never work under 15 degrees Celsius, but these bees work at temperatures much lower and they even continue to work in the rain. The bees gather nectar from flowers along train tracks and private gardens and parks.

My dear Nuri, I don't know where you are. At night I open the map on the floor and I try to imagine where you might be. I am waiting for you.

Mustafa

Even in the email I could hear the excitement in Mustafa's voice again, that innocent boyishness that had carried him and moved him through life.

Dear Mustafa,
I am sorry that I haven't been in touch and that you have been so worried. I promise that I will find a way to make it to England. It has been a difficult time. Afra and I are staying in Pedion tou Areos, a large park in the city of Athens. I am struggling to find or even imagine a way out, but we will get out of here and be in England

before you know it. Most people are trapped here. So many come and not many leave. But I have the money and I have passports. I will need to do something soon because I fear that we cannot survive here much longer.

I think about you and your family. I think about the lavender and heather fields and the black bees in England. The work you are doing is amazing. When I am there we will work on these projects together.

I will find a way.

Nuri

I left the café and took a seat on a bench by the half-dead dog, who lifted one heavy lid, ever so slightly, and then went back to staring at people's passing feet. A man came and sat next to me. He had a phone and notepad on his lap. He tapped his fingers on this notepad and then glanced over at me. Then his eyes darted around the square and he looked over his shoulder. I noticed he was sweating a lot.

'Waiting for someone?' I said.

The man nodded, still distracted.

'Where are you from?' I said.

'Syria.'

'The Kurdish part?'

He looked at me and nodded. He smiled back, but his mind was elsewhere. Eventually a man and woman turned up.

'I thought you weren't coming,' he said. 'Did you bring everything?'

'Everything you told us to bring,' the man said.

'Let's go. He's been waiting a while – he won't be happy.'

I wanted to ask who they were meeting, but the man put his phone and notepad into his rucksack, and looked me right in the eyes, with confidence now. 'Nice to meet you,' he said. 'I wish you a day of morning light.' And before I could say anything the three of them headed off in the direction of the Metro station.

Afra came out of the Hope Centre smelling of soap, her face soft and gleaming with cream, and she had on a new headscarf. I suddenly realised how bad I smelt.

'Afra,' I said, as we walked back to the park, 'I stink.'

'Yes,' she said, trying not to smile.

'I need to find somewhere to shower.'

'Definitely.'

'It's bad.'

'Very.'

'You could at least try to lie!'

I sniffed at my armpits, surprised at how I'd become accustomed to the smell. 'I smell like the streets,' I said.

'You smell like sewage,' she said, and I leant in and tried to kiss her and she scrunched up her face and pushed me away laughing, and for that moment we were both the people we used to be.

As we entered the park and walked among the shadows of the trees, my limbs became heavy, my mouth dry with anxiety, remembering everything that had gone on in this place.

'This is the biggest sky I have ever seen!' a young boy said to the girl beside him. They both looked up and so did I. There were no clouds that day and no wind, the sun was strong and the area gleamed with green and yellow, a taste of the summer months to come; and through the leaves, far beyond, the sky was big and blue and bright, almost as big as the sky above the desert, and for this boy it held promises.

'When the night comes it will be full of stars,' he said to the girl. 'We will be able to make lots of wishes.'

And like a little boy, I made a wish to the blue sky. I wished to make it to England. I looked up and I let the wish fill my mind. I imagined the black bees and the hives. I thought of Mustafa's email. I remembered my response. I will find a way.

We made our way to our place on the blanket. The crickets were louder now. The twins still had not returned; their blanket remained where they had left it, umbrella still open and perched on its side, a pair of new trainers beneath it.

When night fell Angeliki arrived, wrapped in a blanket, taking a seat by the tree beside Afra. She was picking at the scabs on her arms; the tiny wounds had started to heal. As she adjusted the blanket, opening it up to wrap it more tightly around her shoulders, I noticed that her breasts had stopped leaking, only dry stains remained on her white top. She started to talk to me about Athens, stories she had heard about the ancient civilisation. She told me how she saw a team of young archaeology students digging for treasures by Monastiraki station, and she told me about the world hidden beneath the churches. Later she became quiet. She took the talcum powder out of her bag and smothered her face and arms with it, and then she sipped her water slowly and watched the children play, her hands in her lap.

The smell of the talcum and Angeliki's rhythms had become familiar to me. Afra was different when Angeliki was there. She sat up and listened to her even though she didn't understand everything she was saying, and every so often Angeliki would place a hand on Afra's arm, or nudge her to make sure that she was paying attention.

'Won't you ever tell me where you came from?' I said, once Afra had fallen asleep.

'Somalia, if you must know.'

'Why didn't you want to tell me?'

She untied her headwrap, readjusted it and tightened it again.

'I don't like to talk about it because it hurt my heart.'

I was quiet. Maybe she didn't want to talk to me because I was a man, maybe it was a man who had done something to her. I didn't want to force her story, but perhaps she sensed my acceptance and it helped her to relax, for she said, 'There was very little food. Bad famine. I had to leave and so I went to Kenya. I was pregnant, I didn't want my baby to be born at home, to suffer like I did.' She paused and I remained silent. 'In Kenya I was in a big camp called Dadaab but they were saying this camp was going to close. They thought al-Shabaab fighters from Somalia were using the camp for smuggling weapons. And there were so many of us. They wanted to get rid of us, to dump us. So I leave there and I make a long journey to here.'

She stopped and I saw that she was searching her bag for something. Eventually she pulled out a little pouch.

'They took my baby when I got to Athens. In here is a small lock of her hair. One night when I was sleeping in this park, somebody is take her from my arms. I know that they put drugs in my water, poison it so that I will not wake up, because usually I wake to every tiny movement and every tiny sound she make. How did they take her without me knowing? They poison me, I know it.'

Her voice cracked and I didn't ask any more questions, but I could tell that she was thinking about it now, that memories of both Somalia and her baby were filling her mind and her senses, in the way the memory of the heat and the sand of the Syrian Desert came back and engulfed me and filled my heart. The fire was bright now and her face was beautiful and sculpted in its light, but the talcum powder gave her a pallid complexion.

'You know, sometimes I remember that my country is so beautiful — there is the Indian Ocean and it sparkles blue and looks like heaven. There is golden sand and beach, rocks and some houses like white palaces. The city is busy with cafés and shops. But the situation there is so bad.' She looked at me now for the first time. 'I can't go back, because when I am in Somalia there is nothing forward, nothing goes forward. Now, in this place, there is forward.'

'There is? I thought you said there isn't?'

She considered for a few moments, and then said, 'This is what I believed.'

She was silent for a while and then she said, 'I want to find job, but nobody want me. English is no good here. People here don't like me. Even Greek people can't get job. They sell tissues on the street. How many tissues will people need to buy? Maybe this is a city of crying?' She laughed now, and I was reminded suddenly of the laughter I had heard through the window back at the school.

The following morning, Angeliki had gone and Afra was drawing. She was sitting cross-legged on the blanket, using both hands to create an image. In her right hand she held the pencil, and with the fingertips of her left hand she followed the grooves of the marks on the page. An image was emerging and it looked like a place from a dream, a desert meeting a city, the lines and dimensions distorted, the colours mixed up, but I could see Afra's soul in the lines on the paper, the way they appeared to move with light and life.

'This is for Angeliki,' she said, and when she'd finished she asked me to put it under the blanket so that it wouldn't blow away.

We made our way to the Hope Centre. I left Afra there and headed to the square, hoping I would see the man from yesterday. I sat on the same bench and waited. At one point the man with the worry beads passed through, heading towards the Metro. He saluted me by lifting the beads.

'You find Elpidos?' he called.

'I did, thank you.'

'Elpida mean hope,' he said again, as he had last time, throwing a stale bit of bread on the ground for the dog, but the dog didn't move.

About an hour later I spotted the man I was looking for standing by the statue on the square with a group of other young men and women. They were smoking and laughing and there were two female NGO workers among them, wearing green T-shirts and carrying rucksacks. I waited until most of the group had dispersed and the young man was sitting on a low wall; he had the notepad open now and was writing. He looked more relaxed than he had the previous day.

I got up and sat down beside him. The man was occupied with his writing for a long time but eventually glanced up to see who was sitting beside him.

'Can I ask you something?' I said.

'Of course,' he replied but continued to write.

'I want to find a smuggler. I was wondering if you could help me. I had a feeling that that was where that couple were going yesterday.'

The man closed his book now and adjusted his position on the wall so that he was facing me. He smiled. 'You're very observant.'

'So I'm right? You can help me?'

'Most of the good ones live in the school,' he said. 'I can introduce you. Where do you want to go?'

'England.'

He laughed, like everybody did. 'Are you crazy? Or maybe very rich? It is the most expensive and most difficult place to get to.'

'Why is it so expensive?' I say.

'Because it is more difficult to get to. Also, people think they will be safer there and there is a good chance of being helped, as long as you are granted asylum.'

I became aware of the money in my rucksack. If anyone knew about it, they would kill me for it.

'My name is Baram,' he said, offering his hand. 'Are you serious about it?'

'Yes.'

'Would you like me to set something up for you?'

'Definitely.'

He took a phone out of his rucksack and walked several metres away, talking to someone for a few minutes before returning.

'How many of you?'

'Two.'

'Can you meet tomorrow at 1 p.m. at a coffee shop in Acharnon?'

I nodded, but I was beginning to feel sick and my T-shirt was soaked through with sweat.

Baram put his phone back into his rucksack and sat down again beside me. 'I will meet you here at twelve forty-five tomorrow and take you to the café. Make sure you bring your passports and please don't be late – he won't like that.'

'Shall I bring money?'

'Not yet.'

* * *

That night two women carrying many bags claimed the twins' blankets and umbrella for themselves. I was about to stop these new refugees from sitting down, from making these blankets their new home, when it occurred to me that the twins were probably not returning. I'd been expecting them to reappear, to come and sit down again, laughing and fighting and playing on their phones. To my surprise, the women did not look nervous to be here; they glanced around with some satisfaction, as if they had just come from somewhere far worse. They took off their shoes before stepping onto the blanket, and after about half an hour, after making a few phone calls and eating some apples, they started to make something out of colourful threads. They sat opposite each other and one of the two began to weave, while the other held the ends.

Elsewhere, a few men were playing cards and laughing. Then they began to sing songs in Urdu, a few Arabic words thrown in. The wind blew and brought with it the smell of spices and warmth, the fire was crackling, and someone was cooking. Pedion tou Areos was becoming like a new home to people: shoes lined up next to the blankets and tents, clothes hanging from trees, games of cards and music and singing, and although I should have found some comfort in this, instead I felt suffocated by these glimmering remnants of an old life.

I pulled the rucksack close to my chest. This money was our only way out, and the next day we would be meeting the smuggler. Because of this I could not sleep. Instead I sat up all night beside Afra, listening to the sounds in the woods, waiting for the sun to rise and turn the leaves gold.

The following day Afra and I made our way to Victoria Square, and although we arrived half an hour early, Baram was already there, sitting on the bench, the notepad on his lap, writing. He stood up when he saw us and said that we should wait there for a while, so that we wouldn't get to the café too early – the smuggler wouldn't like that either. He sat back down and continued to write. I tried to read it, but his handwriting was too small. Tucked into the binding of the notebook was a photograph of a young woman in an army uniform.

'Who is the woman in the picture?' I said.

'My girlfriend. She died. I am rewriting my diary.'

'Rewriting?'

He didn't speak for a very long time and I watched the half-dead dog, who was now looking up at me and moving his tail.

'When I got to Turkey the army caught me,' Baram said finally, releasing the words in one breath. 'There were thirty-one of us altogether. They captured us and searched us all. They took three of us and let the rest of the people continue on their journey.'

'Why?'

'Because we are Kurdish. I was writing a diary. I had been writing it for two years, and they found it in my bag and they saw one word, only one word: "Kurdistan". They took me to jail and they said, "What is that word?" and I said, "Kurdistan." I had to say it because they already knew. So they locked me up for one month and three days. Then they let me go. But they took my passport and nine hundred euros and they burned my notebook. The money and the passport were not important to me, but the notepad had my life in it, and I cried when they burned it. They took my fingerprints and scanned my eyes, and I paid two hundred euros for the guard to let me go, and I ran to a Kurdish town. And from there I called my father.' He closed the notebook, resting a hand over it.

'How come you are still here?' I said.

'I'm trying to make enough money to leave. My brother is in Germany. I want to get there before he gets married.'

At the entrance to the Metro, the man with the worry beads approached people as they came off the escalators.

'I hope you will go to your brother's wedding,' Afra said.

The three of us walked together to Acharnon. When we got to the café, Baram discreetly pointed out a man sitting alone in the far-left corner. He was wearing a black polo-neck and a black leather jacket and drinking cold coffee from a plastic glass with a straw. There was something immediately ridiculous about this man, but when I looked back to ask Baram if this was the right person, he was no longer there, and that would be the last time I ever saw him.

Reluctantly I led Afra to the table where the man was now slurping the last of his coffee.

'Good afternoon,' I said in Arabic.

The man looked up as if he hadn't been expecting anyone. Then without saying anything he took the lid off his coffee and stuck his fingers into the plastic cup, trying to get an ice cube.

'I'm Nuri and this is Afra. You're supposed to be expecting us.'

The man managed to get hold of the ice cube and threw it into his mouth, biting down on it.

'Do you not speak Arabic?' I said.

'Sit down,' he said in Arabic.

We both took a seat, and maybe I was nervous, or maybe there was something about this man's silence, but I began to ramble. 'We met Baram in the square, he said you could help us, he called you yesterday and he said to bring our passports, which I have done, they're right here.'

'Not yet,' he said abruptly. His words stopped my hand in its tracks. He smiled, probably at my sudden obedience, then crunched harder into the ice cube, grimacing in a way that made his face take on the appearance of a nine-year-old boy. It was amazing how much power this man-child had; in normal life he would probably have been struggling to make ends meet in some back-alley greengrocer's in Damascus. There was a glint of something dark and desperate in his eyes, like the men in the woods.

'This is your wife?' he said.

'Yes, I am Afra.'

'You're blind?'

'Yes,' she said simply, but with a hint of sarcasm in her

voice that only I could pick up on, and I could almost hear her follow it with: 'Clever man.'

'That's good,' he said. 'Poor blind woman – less suspicious. You'll have to take off that hijab and dye your hair blonde. Not much we can do with you,' he said to me, 'but you're not a complete lost cause. Good shave, clean shirt. Work on your expression.'

On the table the man's phone vibrated and flashed. He glanced at the screen and his face changed, a twitch in his cheek, a clenched jaw. He turned the phone face down on the table.

'So where is it you want to get to?'

'England.'

'Ha!'

'Everybody laughs,' I said.

'Ambitious. Expensive.'

I lowered my face, the money in my rucksack making me nervous. It felt as if I was carrying a bag full of eggs.

'Two thousand euros for Denmark. Three thousand for Germany,' the smuggler said. Then he paused. 'You're much better off going to one of those.'

'How much to England?'

'Seven thousand for both of you.'

'Seven thousand!' Afra said. 'That's crazy! How much does it cost to get a flight from here to England?'

The man laughed again, and she scrunched up her face and turned away.

'This isn't a trip to England,' he said. 'You are paying for our services. England is a special place – you will be safer, and it's harder for us to get you there; that's the additional cost.'

Afra looked as if she wanted to spit on him. I nudged her foot with mine.

'That's why we want to go there,' I said. 'We're tired, really tired now. But we just don't have that kind of money.'

'How much do you have?'

'Five thousand.'

'In cash?'

I looked over my shoulder.

The man raised his eyebrows. 'You're walking around with that amount of cash on you?'

'No,' I said. 'I have some in cash and the rest is in a private account. I'll do anything, I'll find work to make up the money. I'll pick up rubbish, clean cars or windows or anything.'

'Ha! Where do you think you are? Even the locals can't find work.'

'I've had enough of this,' Afra said, standing up to leave. I grabbed her arm. Seeing my desperation, the man smiled.

'You can do some work for me,' he said.

'What kind of work?'

'Just deliveries.'

'Just?'

'The others are kids, can't drive yet. I need someone who can drive. Can you drive?'

I nodded.

'You can work for me for three weeks. If you behave yourself, then we'll say five thousand euros for the two of you.'

'OK,' I said, and held out my hand to shake his, but instead he gave me a huge grin and chuckled.

Afra was quiet again, but I could feel her anger.

'You'll have to come and stay with me,' the man said.

'Why?'

'To ensure that you don't run off with the car and the packages.'

The rest of the ice in the plastic cup had melted now and he leant forward, taking the straw in his mouth and slurping as he'd done before.

'And that way I'll know you won't run off because I'll have Afra – that was your name, wasn't it?' Before she could reply, he raised his hand and asked the waiter for a piece of paper and a pen to write down an address.

'Meet me here tomorrow at 10 p.m. If you don't turn up, I'll assume you've changed your mind.'

It was early afternoon when we got back to the park. Children were playing with a ball in the open area between the tents and blankets. Others were squabbling over marbles. Two children had made a village on the ground with stones and leaves. The thought of leaving this place filled me with energy, gave me hope, but later I found myself scanning the crowds of children, hoping to see Mohammed among them. Those black eyes, the way they filled with fear and questions, I could almost see him in front of me. It was Sami who had disappeared in my mind, and no matter how much I tried to bring him to life, to conjure an image of him, I couldn't.

Angeliki was already sitting beneath the tree, waiting for us. Her face was covered in talcum powder again and her hands were resting in her lap. There was a stillness to her when she was like this, an aloneness that I couldn't stand to see. Somewhere in the distance a baby was crying and I saw that her breasts were leaking again; the strong smell of sour milk hung around her.

Afra asked me to fetch the picture from under the blanket and she handed it to Angeliki.

'You draw this?'

Afra nodded. 'It's for you.'

Angeliki stared at the picture and back at Afra, a long look, and I could see the questions in her eyes but she didn't say anything more for a while; she sat with the picture in her hands, glancing down at it from time to time and then looking up again, either at the children playing or at something in her own mind.

'In here,' she said, 'they hide everything they don't want world to see. But this picture, it will remind me of another world, better world.' And maybe she knew we were leaving, for she started to cry, then she stayed all night right beside Afra, lying down next to her, resting a hand on her arm, and they slept there together all night, like sisters or old friends.

12

It is the morning after the interview. Diomande and the Moroccan man are in the living room drinking their new favourite beverage: tea with milk. They must have heard me get up, because there is a steaming mug on the dining table waiting for me. I join them, as Afra is still asleep.

With the tea warm in my hands I step up to the glass doors to look outside. Today the courtyard is glowing with sunlight. The cherry tree in the middle with the twisted roots is full of birds, there must be about thirty in there, all chirping and chattering. The landlady's garden behind is spilling over the wooden fence, red and purple flowers, fallen petals on the flagstones. I find the key behind the curtains and open the doors to let in the air and the distant smell of the sea.

Diomande is telling the Moroccan man about the interview.

'I think it go very well,' he says, his smile so wide it fills his whole face.

The Moroccan man high-fives him.

'I told them what you said. Mother, sister, difficult life. But they ask me some very strange questions.'

'Like what?'

'What the national anthem is. They ask me to sing it.'

'And did you?'

Diomande stands up and with his hand on his chest he begins to sing, still with that same broad smile on his face:

'We salute you, O land of hope,
Country of hospitality;
Thy full gallant legions
Have restored thy dignity.

'Beloved Ivory Coast, thy sons,
Proud builders of thy greatness,
All not mustered together for thy glory,
In joy will we construct thee.

'Proud citizens of the Ivory Coast, the country calls us.
If we have brought back liberty peacefully,
It will be our duty to be an example
Of the hope promised to humanity,
Forging unitedly in new faith
The fatherland of true brotherhood.'

'You know it in English?'

Diomande nods.

'Did you sing in English for them?'

'Yes.'

'Why? What's the problem?' I say.

'The words paint a very positive picture!'

Diomande sits down again, dejected. 'But I tell them. I tell them life so hard. I tell them about Libya and prison and being beaten till I think I will die. I tell them my sister and mum's life difficult because of civil war. I have no job and my mum she sent me to find better life. I tell them all this. I tell them that here there is hope. Here maybe I will find work. I can clean, I can cook, I can teach, I have many skill.'

The birds have silenced now and Diomande's back is so hunched over that the wings under his T-shirt look as if they are opening up. 'I also tell them how beautiful it is there, my country, how much I love being there.'

The Moroccan man is thoughtful, staring out into the courtyard, sometimes glancing over at me with a question in his eyes, but whatever it is he doesn't ask.

Diomande decides that he wants to go to the fair. 'I can hear it,' he says, 'this crazy music all the time and see the lights over sea. Can we go?'

The Moroccan man gets excited at the prospect of having company. 'Geezer,' he says, 'let's go! When we see the lights and the sea and hear the music, all our troubles and worries will be like a small grain of sand.'

They insist that I go with them. They drag me, one hand each, to the stairs so that I can go upstairs and get ready.

When I go to our room I see that Afra is already dressed and sitting again on the edge of the bed, but this time she is crying. I kneel down in front of her. The tears are streaming out of her eyes like dark rivers. 'What's wrong, Afra?' I say.

She wipes her face with the back of her hand but the tears keep coming.

'Since I told the doctor about the bomb, it's all I can think of. I can see Sami's face. I can see his eyes looking up at the sky. I wonder what he felt. Was he in pain? What did he feel when he looked up at the sky? Did he know I was there?'

I take her hand in mine but I can't hold on to it for too long because I feel heat rising up through my spine and along my neck and into my head. I let go and stand away from her.

'I'm going to go for a walk with the Moroccan man.'

'But . . . I . . .'

'I'm going for a walk with him and Diomande.'

'OK,' she says quietly. 'Have a nice time.' I can still hear her words — there was so much sadness in her voice — even as we walk along the wooden pier and enter the fairground, swept up in a tornado of slides and roller coasters and bumper cars. 'Have a nice time' echoes in my mind, even when Diomande is talking about the Ivory Coast.

'The sea is like the crystal,' he says, 'not like this one. This one look like shit. No! Sea there is like the sky. So clear! You could see all the little fishes swimming. Is like glass. And when sun set everything is red — the sky, the sea. You should see this! Everything red.' He sweeps his hand across the sky and I remember Afra's paintings. We walk by the seawall, so that we're close to the water.

We sit in a café in the arcade. It smells like vinegar and sherbet. The Moroccan man has some change in his pocket so he buys us all a bright red drink so that we can think about the sky of the Ivory Coast. The drink tastes like cherry-flavoured plastic and is made of crushed ice.

'You be very quiet,' Diomande says to me, his dark eyes illuminated by the sun so that they are a warm brown now.

'What is the sea like in Syria?' the Moroccan man asks.

'I live by the desert,' I say. 'The desert is as dangerous and as beautiful as the sea.'

Then the three of us sit there silent for a long time, staring out across the water, imagining our own homes, I guess, what we have lost, what has been left behind.

By the time we head back, the sun is setting and a strong wind blows across the pier so that its foundations squeak and rattle.

At the B&B, Afra is not in the living room or the kitchen. I find her in the bedroom, lying on the bed this time, her face still wet with tears. She is holding the marble in her fingers and twirling it around. Sometimes she rolls it over her lips, or along her wrist.

She doesn't speak to me when I enter the room, but when I lie down next to her she says, 'Nuri, have you heard from Mustafa?'

'Won't you stop asking me?' I say.

'No. He is the reason we are here!'

I don't say anything.

'You are lost in the darkness, Nuri,' she says. 'It is a fact. You've got completely lost somewhere in the dark.'

I look at her eyes, so full of fear and questions and longing, and I had thought it was her who was lost, that Afra was the one stuck in the dark places of her mind. But I can see how present she is, how much she is trying to reach me. I stay there until I know she is asleep and then I head downstairs.

The living room is quiet tonight, the Moroccan man is in the kitchen on the phone, pacing, and now and then raising his voice. Diomande took a shower after the fair and has stayed in his room. There are two or three residents sitting around the dining table playing cards. I sit down at the computer. The light of the TV is flickering in the room.

I log into my emails quickly before I have a chance to change my mind. There is a message there from Mustafa.

11/05/2016

Dearest Nuri,
I wonder if you made it out of Athens. It is hard for me to sit here not knowing if you and Afra are safe. I hope that you are making your way to us. It was raining today, all day, and I miss the desert and the sunshine. But there are good things here too, Nuri, and I wish that you were here to see. It is a colourful place, full of flowers now in spring. I have just given the third of my weekly workshops to volunteers. One was a Syrian woman who arrived here with her mother and son, another a Congolese refugee who has memories of gathering honey in the jungle, and an

Afghan student is already asking how to get her first queen!

At the moment I have six hives to demonstrate beekeeping and the project is growing week by week. These bees are gentle, not like the Syrian bees. I can even collect the honey without protective gear – I know when they are about to get aggressive because their tone changes. It is a wonderful experience to stand among them exposed like that, and I am getting to know them. Their humming is beautiful – when you hear their song it will fill your heart to the brim with sweetness.

But sometimes this sound reminds me of everything we have lost and I think always of you and Afra. I hope to hear from you soon.

Mustafa

I type a reply and press send.

Dear Mustafa,
Afra and I have made it to the UK. We have been here for over two weeks now. I am sorry that I wasn't in touch sooner. It was a very difficult journey. We are staying at a B&B in the far south of England by the sea. I must stay here until I have my interviews and until I find out whether we have been granted asylum. I am worried, Mustafa. I am worried that they will make us leave. I am so pleased to hear about your project. I wish I could be there with you.

Nuri

I think about the cold tone of my email, the fact that I have been here so long and had not contacted my cousin. I am here because of Mustafa, I escaped Athens because of the hope and the will he gave me, but somehow the darkness inside me has swallowed me up.

I send another message:

Mustafa, I believe I am unwell. Since I got here my mind is broken. I think I am lost in the darkness.

I am about to log out when an email comes through:

Nuri! I am so pleased to hear that you are in the UK at last. This is amazing news! Please send me the address of where you are.

I find the address on a letter in the bedroom and return to the computer, where I copy it out and press send. I say nothing else to Mustafa and there is no reply after this.

I fall asleep in the armchair and when I wake up it is dark and the living room is empty. But I can hear the marble rolling across the wooden floor. At first, I can't see Mohammed but then I realise that he is sitting under the table in the same red T-shirt and blue shorts that he was wearing last time.

I crouch down to meet his eye. 'What are you doing under there, Mohammed?'

'This is my *house*,' he says. 'It's a wooden one, like in *The*

Three Little Pigs – do you remember when you told me that story?'

'Did I tell you that story? There was only one story I ever told you – the one about the brass city. The only person I read that story to was Sami, because I found the book one day on a stall at the souq.' He is not listening to me; he is busy pushing the marble along the cracks of the wood, then he tucks it under the rug.

'Do you like my house? This house doesn't break like the houses at home. Isn't it nice, Uncle Nuri?'

There is a sharp pain in my head, so sudden and intense that I have to stand up and close my eyes and press my forehead hard with my fingers.

Mohammed tugs at my jumper. 'Uncle Nuri, will you come with me?'

'Where?'

He slips his hand into mine and takes me to the front door. As soon as I open it I realise something is wrong; ahead, beyond the buildings, the sky flashes white and red; from somewhere not too far away there is a wild screech, metal on metal, like a creature being dragged to death, and when the wind blows it brings with it the smell of fire and things burning and ash. I walk across the street, Mohammed's hand in mine. The houses are bombed-out and they look like carcasses with the light of the flashing sky behind them. We continue along the road. Mohammed is dragging his feet in the dust. It is so thick, like we are walking through snow. There are burnt cars, lines of washing hanging from abandoned terraces, electrical wires dangling low over the street, trash piles on the pavements. It all stinks of death and burnt rubber. In the distance smoke rises, curling into the skyline. Mohammed pulls me by the hand, all the way down the hill, until we reach the Queiq. There are waves on the river and it is darker than usual.

'This is where the boys were,' Mohammed says, 'but I was dressed in black so they didn't see me, they didn't drown me in the river. Allah looked after me.' He looks up at me with those wide black eyes.

'Yes,' I say. 'He must have.'

'This is where *all* the children are,' he says, 'all the ones who died. They're in the river and they can't get out.'

When I look more closely I notice that there are limbs in the water, and faces. I can make out only blurred outlines in the darkness, but I know what they are. I take a step back.

'No,' Mohammed says. 'Don't be scared. You have to go in.'

'Why?'

'Because it's the only way to find us.'

I take a step forward. The water is almost opaque and yet I can see those shadows slithering beneath the surface.

'No, Mohammed, I'm not going to go in there.'

'Why? Are you scared?'

'Of course I'm scared!'

He laughs, 'It's usually me who is scared of the water! How have we swapped places?'

He kicks off his shoes and starts to wade in.

'Mohammed, don't!' He ignores me, going further, the water rising above his knees and hips and to his chest.

'Mohammed! If you don't come back now I'm going to get very angry!' But Mohammed keeps walking. I take a step forward, then another and another until the water is up to my thighs. Something slips past me like a fish or a snake. Just ahead, a small object glimmers on the water's dark surface, I scoop it into my hands. It is

a key

was placed in my open palm. 'Make yourselves at home,' the smuggler said, and grinned, and I saw that he had a silver tooth in the back of his mouth. His flat was a little way out of the centre of Athens, not too far from the sea. We walked up three flights of stairs because the lift was broken. It was a tiny place that smelt of stale spices.

At the end of a narrow corridor there was an odd-shaped asymmetrical living area with three rooms leading off it. Every single window faced the brick walls and ventilation systems of the surrounding buildings. The smuggler introduced himself properly as Constantinos Fotakis. I was surprised that his name was Greek as he spoke Arabic like a native, but as I looked at his features and the colour of his skin, it was difficult to know where he was from.

The key he'd given me was for the bedroom. The room had a double mattress on the floor and an old fur rug which was to be used as a blanket. There was a damp smell, and green mould lined the walls. We could hear the buzz and whir of the vents. The wall of the opposite building was an arm's length away and the heat and steam from the other flats gathered in the space between the buildings and settled in the room.

It wasn't a comfortable place to sleep, but it was better than the park. I wasn't sure if it was safer though – something about Mr Fotakis made me uneasy; maybe it was his deep throaty laugh, the gold signet ring on his little finger. He was even more confident now than he had been at the café. But he was also friendly; he welcomed us into his flat as if we were family, even insisting on carrying our bags and taking them into the bedroom. He showed us where the shower was, how to use the taps because the hot water sometimes turned cold, he went through the contents of the fridge and told us to help ourselves to anything we wanted. We were treated like special guests. On a small green and bronze coffee table were the stubbed-out butts of cannabis cigarettes and rolled-up twenty-pound notes, which confirmed to me what kind of deliveries I'd be making.

Later that night Mr Fotakis had friends visiting. There were two of them, and they both slumped into the sofa and bickered for a while over the remote control, as if they were children. To me they looked like brothers, one a bit plump, the other much taller, but their features were the same, both with deep frowns and long noses and eyes that were a little too close together so they always looked a bit startled.

At around 10 p.m. Mr Fotakis gave me instructions for my first delivery. There were five white boxes and they all needed to be taken to different parts of Athens. He gave me the addresses, the order in which the deliveries needed to be made and the names or nicknames of the people who would be receiving the packages. He also gave me a brand-new iPhone, which I was to use only for work; if I called any other number he would know. He gave me a charger for the van and made sure data roaming was switched on so that I could use Google Maps.

'Drive carefully, now. Don't kill anyone,' he said, with a smirk on his face. 'You have no insurance and no licence.'

As I was getting ready to leave, Afra was lying down on the bed holding the room key in her hands, close to her chest. When I went over to kiss her on the forehead and to tell her to stay safe, she handed me the key.

'Why are you giving me this?' I said.

'I want you to lock me in,' she said.

'Why don't you lock it from the inside? That way you can get out if you need to.'

But Afra was shaking her head. 'No,' she said. 'I want you to lock me in.'

'I know the men are dodgy,' I said, 'but I don't think they'll try anything.'

'Please,' she said, 'I don't want the key. I want you to keep hold of it. I want to know that you have it.'

'Are you sure?' I said.

'Yes. I'm certain.' I didn't really understand her, but I agreed. I put the key in my back pocket and all through the night I kept checking to make sure it was still there. The key made me think of Afra, reminding me that she was in that damp room alone waiting for me. It reminded me of the brick walls and the vents and the men in the living room. The key gave me a determination to keep going, especially during those long hours in the early morning, before the sun had even begun to rise, when I was driving for miles along unfamiliar carriageways, past the shadows of distant villages and towns. I wonder now if she gave me that key to make sure that I remembered her, to ensure that I didn't drive away and leave her there forever.

It was a clear night, the sky full of stars. My first delivery was by the port of Piraeus, not too far from where the ferry had dropped us off when we'd come from Leros. The satnav took me off the main road into a residential side street, where the apartments were neat and all had canopies. There was a man already waiting for me, beneath an olive tree, smoking a cigarette. I got out, opened the doors of the white van and gave him the box. He told me to wait there. He went into one of the apartment blocks, stayed there for around ten minutes and came out again, this time holding a white bag which had another package inside. He said I was not to touch or open anything. Mr Fotakis would know if anything at all went missing.

It was 5 a.m. when I started to head back to central Athens and the sun was rising across the sea, the mountains on the islands blue-grey in the distance. I had the window open so that I could listen to the whisper of the wind and the water, but soon I turned away from the shimmering shoreline and right into the city, with its graffiti and blocks of flats and the dark shadow of the mainland mountains.

When I got back to the smuggler's apartment everyone was asleep. I could hear snoring from the master bedroom, and the two brothers were asleep on the sofa, their arms sprawled over each other. I unlocked the door and entered the bedroom. Afra was sitting upright in bed waiting for me.

'Have you not slept at all?' I said.

'No.' She was holding her knees.

I sat down on the bed next to her. 'I'm here now,' I said. 'Why don't you lie down?' She lay back and I saw that she was shivering even though it was warm and humid in that room. I didn't bother to get undressed. I stretched out beside her with my hand resting on her chest and, listening to her heartbeat, I fell asleep.

We both slept into the early afternoon. I woke up a few times to sounds of plates and cutlery in the kitchen, but I forced myself to go back to sleep. I didn't want to be awake in this world – my dreams were better than reality, and I think Afra felt the same, because she didn't move to get up until I did.

The following night was almost exactly the same, except one of the packages was collected by a man on a boat, who then set off into the dark sea towards one of the islands.

The days passed like this, sleeping next to Afra by day, with a view of the brick walls through the window and the sounds of the ventilation systems, and then travelling around Athens and its suburbs at night delivering packages to strange men.

Three weeks came and went. We lived like this for a month. It was taking much longer than Mr Fotakis had promised. He said he was trying to sort out our passports and flights. There were times when I didn't believe him, when I thought that one day he'd throw us out and we would end up stuck forever in Athens, back in Pedion tou Areos, which for me was the equivalent of hell.

Then one day he knocked on the bedroom door. It was early afternoon and I'd been dozing next to Afra. When I got up and went into the living area, he had a plastic bag for me. Inside was peroxide hair dye for Afra and some scissors and clippers and good shaving foam for me. 'I want you to sort yourselves ready for the passport photos,' he announced.

In the bedroom, I took off Afra's hijab, released her black hair from its bun and followed the instructions on the box, dividing her hair into sections and coating it in the foul-smelling mixture. We left it on for three-quarters of an hour before going into the bathroom and washing it off over the sink. I gave her a towel and waited for her in the living area. Mr Fotakis had made us all some fresh mint tea – he had some pots of herbs on the windowsill which seemed to thrive in the humid air – and we both sat there sipping the tea from small glasses.

When Afra came out of the bathroom she looked like a different woman. The blonde hair somehow made her look taller, her cheekbones rounder, and although the lighter hair should have made her skin look darker, it somehow created a paler complexion, so white it reminded me of ashes and snow. The grey of her eyes had deepened and there was a shimmer in them as she sat down beside us.

'I smell mint,' she said, and Mr Fotakis put a glass in her hand. He couldn't keep his eyes off her.

'You look so different!' he said, laughing. 'Amazing how one thing can change a person so much!' But there was something else in his voice, the same tone that had made me uneasy from the first day we came here. It was the lust and greed that crackled through his phlegm when he spoke, almost hidden, but not quite.

I cut my hair and shaved well and then I put on a crisp white shirt that belonged to Mr Fotakis. The taller of the two brothers came to take the photos. He positioned us in the light of the window and clicked away until he was satisfied.

In the evenings I continued to make the deliveries. There were so many packages and as the days passed I would often meet the same people again; they got to know me and trust me, and sometimes they would offer me cigarettes. I was awake only at night, I no longer saw the sun. Afra and I existed in darkness.

About a week later the passports arrived. Our new names were Gloria and Bruno Baresi.

'You're Italian,' Mr Fotakis said.

'What if they ask us questions? We don't know any Italian.'

'I'm hopeful that won't happen. You will be going from here to Madrid, then from Madrid to the UK. No one will know that you don't speak Italian. Just don't speak Arabic! Keep your mouths shut as much as you can!'

So the date was set and the tickets were booked. Mr Fotakis bought Afra a red dress made of the finest material and a grey scarf that had been hand-woven with tiny red flowers the same colour as the dress. It was beautiful but casual. He also gave her a jean jacket, a handbag and a new pair of shoes. I got a pair of jeans, a leather belt, a new white shirt and a brown jumper. He wanted us to put the clothes on to make sure that we looked authentic.

'You are a beautiful couple,' he said smiling. 'You look like you have stepped out of a magazine.'

'What do I look like?' Afra said to me later as I was getting ready to make my deliveries.

'You don't look like you.'

'Do I look horrible?' she said.

'No,' I said. 'Of course not. You are always beautiful.'

'Nuri, now all the world can see my hair.'

'Really they can't,' I say, 'because it is a different colour.'

'And they can see my legs.'

'But they are the legs of Gloria Baresi, not yours.'

Her lips smiled, but her eyes didn't.

We were due to leave the next day, and that night there were more packages than usual. I locked Afra in the room and I put the key down on the coffee table for a second to count the boxes and tick them off the list. At that moment Mr Fotakis came in to tell me about the travel arrangements to the airport. He then helped me to carry the boxes downstairs to the van. It wasn't until I was halfway across Athens that I realised that I'd forgotten the key. I couldn't turn back to get it – I had ten people to meet and they all had their designated time slots; if I was late for one, I'd be late for all of them. So I kept going and I tried not to think about Afra; I remembered her again only when I was heading back into the city in the early hours of the morning.

When I got to the apartment I rushed up the winding staircase and into the living area, but the key was not on the coffee table where I'd left it and the door was locked. I knocked and there was no answer.

'Afra,' I whispered, 'are you asleep? Can you open the door for me?' I waited like that with my ear to the door, but I could hear nothing, no answer and no movement, so I resigned myself to catching a few hours' sleep on the sofa. I was just lying down when I heard the key in the lock and the door open. Afra stood there. I looked at my wife's face and I immediately knew something was wrong. The morning light that reflected so coldly off the walls of the other buildings revealed a scratch on her face, red and raw, running from her left eye to her jawbone. Her blonde hair was a tangled mess around her face. In this moment, she was not my wife. I could not recognise her. I could not find her. Before I could say anything, she turned away and went back into the bedroom. I sprang up and quickly followed her, closing the door firmly behind me.

'Afra, what happened?' I asked. She was curled up on the bed with her back to me.

'Won't you tell me what happened?' I put my hand on her back and she flinched, so I lay beside her without touching her or asking any more questions. It was early afternoon by the time she spoke again. I hadn't slept at all.

'Do you really want to know?' she said.

'Of course.'

'Because I'm not sure you really want to know.'

'Of course I want to know.'

There was a long pause, and then she said, 'He came in here – Mr Fotakis. I thought it was you because you'd locked the door. I didn't know he had the key. He came in here and he lay down beside me, just where you are lying now. I realised it wasn't you because of the smell of his skin when he came closer to me, and I called out and he put his hand over my mouth and his ring scratched the side of my face, and he told me I should be quiet or you would come back and find me dead.'

She didn't need to say any more.

13

THE SKY IS BIG AND blue and full of seagulls. They sweep across and dip down into the sea, and up again, up and up and up, into the heavens. There is a cluster of multicoloured balloons above me, rising and becoming smaller until they fade into the distance. There are voices around me and then someone has my wrist in his hand. He is checking my heartbeat.

'Strong heart,' the man says.

'What's he doing here?' A woman is standing in the sunlight.

'Maybe homeless.'

'But why is he in the water?'

Neither of them asks me, but I don't think I could speak anyway. The man lets go of my wrist and drags me by the arms so that I am on the dry sand. Then he heads off somewhere. The woman stands there still, looking down at me as if I'm a seal. She takes her coat off and lays it over me, tucking it in around my chin. I try to smile at her but I can't move my face.

'It's OK,' she says. There is a catch in her voice, a shimmer in her eyes, as she looks at me upside down, and I think maybe she is crying.

The man returns shortly with some blankets. He takes off my wet jumper and wraps the dry blankets around me. After a little while I see blue flashing lights and people are lifting me onto a stretcher and then I am inside and warm and we are moving fast through the streets, the siren screaming. My eyes close as the paramedic beside me begins to check my blood pressure.

When I wake up I am in a hospital bed, wired to a heart monitor. The bed next to mine is empty. A doctor comes to see me because she would like to know who I am and what I was doing sleeping on the beach with my body in the water. She tells me that when they brought me in I was suffering from hypothermia.

'My name is Nuri Ibrahim,' I say. 'How long have I been here?'

'Three days,' she says.

'Three days!' I bolt upright. 'Afra will be worried to death!'

'Who is Afra?'

'My wife,' I say. I try to search my pockets but I'm no longer wearing trousers.

'Please can you tell me where I can find my phone?'

'We didn't find a phone,' she says.

'I need to contact my wife.'

'I can contact her for you, if you give me the details.'

I tell her the address of the B&B and the landlady's name, but I don't know the number. The doctor asks me a lot of questions: Do you have thoughts of killing yourself, Mr Ibrahim? How is your memory? Do you find that you are forgetting important events? Do you forget little everyday things? Do you feel confused or disorientated? I try to answer as best I can. No. My memory is good. No. No. No.

I have a brain scan. Then they bring me some lunch, which is peas and mushy potatoes and a bit of dry grilled chicken. I eat all of it as I'm starving by now and then I sit up in bed and hum a song that my mother used to sing to me. I can't get it out of my head. I don't remember the words but the melody is a lullaby. Some of the other patients look at me as they pass my bed. There is an old lady with a Zimmer frame who keeps going up and down. I think she has started to hum the song too. I fall asleep and when I wake up there is a woman in the next bed; she is pregnant and is resting her hand on her bulging belly. She is singing the song too and she knows the words.

'How do you know the lyrics?' I say.

She turns her face towards me; it is dark and clear and shiny under the halogen lights.

'I knew it when I was a child,' she says.

'Where are you from?' I say.

She doesn't reply. She is lying on her back and moving her hand in circular motions over her belly, singing the song as a whisper to her unborn child.

'I claimed asylum,' she said, 'and they denied me. I'm appealing. I've been in this country seven years.'

'Where are you from?' I say again, but my mind blurs and I hear only the faint sound of her voice and see the gentle flicker of the light above me fading into black.

The following morning it is quiet on the ward and the bed next to mine is empty. A nurse approaches and tells me I have a visitor, and I see the Moroccan man walking towards me.

He sits down in a chair by my bed and puts his hand on my arm. 'Geezer,' he says, 'we've been so worried about you.'

'Where is Afra?'

'She is at the B&B.'

'Is she OK?'

'Why don't you just get some rest? We'll talk about it later.'

'I want to know how she is.'

'How do you think she is? She thought you were dead.'

Neither of us says anything for a long time. The Moroccan man doesn't leave anytime soon; he stays there by my side with his hand on my arm. He doesn't ask me where I went or why I slept on the beach, and I don't tell him that I walked into the sea at night. He doesn't ask me anything, but he doesn't leave either, which annoys me at first because all I want to do is hum the lullaby, but after a while his presence soothes me. There is something about his solidity and silence that brings some peace to my mind.

He takes his book out of his pocket and begins to read, chuckling to himself now and then. He stays there until the very last visitor leaves and then he returns again the next morning to pick me up. He comes with a bag of clothes. I take off the hospital gown and put on the things he has brought me.

'They are pyjamas,' he says. 'Diomande calls them tracksuit. He said you will be comfortable in these. I don't understand it. You will have to walk in the streets now in nightwear.'

Just before we leave the hospital the doctor comes to see me again. I am perched on the edge of the bed and she sits opposite me on the visitor's chair with a clipboard in her hands. The Moroccan man is by the window, looking down at the car park.

'Mr Ibrahim,' she says, hesitating, tucking her brown hair behind her ear, 'the good news is that your brain scan was clear, but from what happened and from the information that I have from you, I believe you are suffering from post-traumatic stress disorder. I advise you strongly to seek some counselling from your GP.' She says all this slowly and clearly, looking at me straight in the eyes, and then she glances at her clipboard and I hear a small sigh before she checks her watch. 'Can you reassure me that you will do that?'

'Yes,' I say.

'Because I wouldn't want you to put yourself in danger again.' There is real concern in her eyes now.

'Yes, Doctor, I promise that I will take your advice.'

* * *

We get the bus back to the B&B. It is mid-morning by the time we arrive and the landlady is dusting the living room. She clomps across the wooden planks in her platform shoes to greet us. She is wearing bright yellow rubber gloves.

'Would you like a nice cup of tea, Mr Ibrahim?' She almost sings these words, and I don't reply because I am distracted by something in the courtyard. Afra and the Afghan woman are sitting on deckchairs beneath the cherry tree, by the bee. When Farida sees me she says something to Afra, then gets up to let me sit down.

Afra is silent for a very long time. She has her face tilted towards the sun. 'I can see shadows and light,' she says. 'When there's a lot of light I can see the shadow of the tree. Look!' she says. 'Give me your hand!'

I put my hand in hers and she sits forward into the light and positions my hand across her eyes. Then she tells me to move it from left to right, making a shadow sweep across her face.

'Now it's light,' she says, smiling, 'now it's dark.'

I want to show her that what she is saying is making me happy, but I can't.

'And I can see some colour!' she says. 'Over there.' She points at a red bucket in the corner of the garden. 'What is that? A rose bush?'

'It's a bucket,' I say.

She lets go of my hand and her face drops. I see that she is rolling that marble in her fingers, running it along her palm and wrist. The red blade in the middle catches the light and becomes translucent. There is a gentle buzzing in the distance that gradually becomes louder, as if a swarm of bees is making its way to this concrete courtyard.

'I missed you,' I hear her say. 'I was so scared.' And the wind blows and shakes the blossoms and sends them swirling around her. 'I'm so glad you're here.' Her voice is full of sadness. I watch the marble.

'You have forgotten Mustafa,' she says.

'No, I haven't.'

'Have you forgotten about the bees and the flowers? I think you've forgotten about all that. Mustafa is waiting for us and you haven't even mentioned him. You're lost in a different world. You're not here at all. I don't know you anymore.'

I don't say anything.

'Close your eyes,' she says.

So I close my eyes.

'Can you see the bees, Nuri? Try to see them in your mind. Hundreds and thousands of them in the sunlight, on the flowers, the hives and the honeycomb. Can you see it?'

In my mind I picture first the fields in Aleppo and the golden yellow bees in the apiaries, and then I see the fields of heather and lavender, the black bees that Mustafa described.

'Can you see it?' she says.

I don't reply.

'You think it's me who can't see,' she says.

We sit in silence for a long time.

'Won't you tell me?' she says. 'Won't you describe to me what's wrong?'

'Why do you have Mohammed's marble?' I say.

Her hands become suddenly still.

'Mohammed's?' she says.

'Yes. The little boy we met in Istanbul.'

She leans forward as if she is in pain and exhales.

'This marble was Sami's,' she says.

'Sami's?' I say.

'Yes.'

'But Mohammed was playing with it.'

I'm not looking at her now but I hear her exhale again.

'I don't know who Mohammed is,' she says. She hands me the marble.

'The boy who fell off the boat. Don't you remember?'

'A boy did not fall off the boat. There was a girl who kept crying and when her dad went into the water she went in after him and they had to pull her out and wrap her in the women's scarves. I remember it very well. Her mother told me all of it later when we were on the island by the fire.'

She pushes the marble towards me, urging me to accept it.

I take it, reluctantly.

'The boy who came with us from Istanbul to Greece,' I say, 'Mohammed. The boy who fell off the boat!'

She ignores what I am saying, just gives me that look. She has already answered these questions.

'Why didn't you tell me before?' I say.

'Because I thought you needed him,' she says. 'This marble, I took it from the floor of our house the day before we left, the day when the men broke everything and threw all his toys on the floor. Do you remember?'

I remember her last words as I make my way through the

dark living room and up the stairs, along the corridor to our bedroom. I remember her words as I look at her from the window, sitting there beneath the blossoms of the tree with the sun on her face.

'Do you remember?'

I don't know what I remember anymore. I shut the curtains. I lie down on the bed. I close my eyes and hear the sound of the bees deep in the sky.

When I open my eyes and sit up in bed, I see that there is a gold key on the rug. I pick it up and head to the door at the end of the corridor, put the key in the lock and open it. I am high up on the hill again. The noise is louder now; it fills my mind completely. I am on the hill with my house behind me and there is Aleppo stretched vast and wide below, the wall around the city is made of golden jasper while the city is pure glass, the buildings shimmering outlines, every single one of them – the mosques, the markets, the rooftops, the citadel in the distance. It is a ghost of a city in the setting sun. To the left there is a flash – a child running down the hill to the river's edge. I can see him on the path in his blue shorts and red T-shirt.

'Mohammed!' I call. 'Stop running from me!'

I follow him all the way down to the river, and on as he zigzags through the lanes, round the bends and through the arches and beneath the vines, and then I lose him for a while, but I keep walking until I see him sitting beneath a narenj tree by the water. The tree is alive and laden with fruit. He has his back to me. I approach him and sit down beside him at the river's edge.

I put my hand on his shoulder and he turns now to face me and his eyes, those black eyes, begin to change, becoming lighter, turning grey, and transparent, so that there is a soul in them now, and his features soften and morph like a swarm of bees, then settle, until I can see his expression and his face and his eyes more clearly. The boy sitting next to me, looking at me fearfully, is not Mohammed.

'Sami,' I say.

I want to hold him, but I know that he will disappear, like paint in water, so I sit as still as I can. I realise now that these were the clothes he was wearing the day he died, his red T-shirt and blue shorts. He is holding the marble in his hand and he turns now to face the city of glass. He takes something out of his pocket and hands it to me: a key.

'What's this for?' I say.

'It's the key you gave me. You told me it opened a secret house that didn't break.'

I see that in front of him are pieces of Lego.

'What are you doing?' I say.

'I'm building a house!' he says. 'When we go to England we will live in this house. This house won't break like these do.'

I remember now. I remember him lying in bed, afraid of the bombs, and how I had given him an old bronze key that once opened a shed at the apiaries. I had tucked it beneath his pillow so that he could feel that somewhere in all the ruins there was a place where he could be safe.

Ahead, the glass city shimmers in the sunlight. It looks like a city in a drawing that a child has made, a sketch, pencil outlines of mosques and apartments. He puts his hand in the river, scoops out a stone.

'Will we fall in the water?' he says, and he looks up at me with wide eyes. He was asking me this for months before he died.

'No.'

'Like the other people?'

'No.'

'But my friend said that to leave here we have to cross other rivers and seas, and if we cross those rivers and seas we might fall into the water, like other people did. I know stories about them. Will the wind take the boat? Will the boat turn over into the water?'

'No. But if it does we'll have life jackets. We'll be all right.'

'And Allah – have mercy on us – will he help us?'

'Yes. Allah will help us.'

These were Sami's words. My Sami. He looks at me again, his eyes wider, full of fear. 'But why didn't he help the boys when they took their heads off?'

'Who took their heads off?'

'When they stood in a line and waited. They weren't wearing black. That's why. You said it was because they weren't wearing black. I was wearing black. Don't you remember?'

'The day we went for a walk?' I say. 'The day we saw the boys by the river?'

'Yes,' he says, 'I thought you didn't remember. But you said if I held the key and wore black I would be invisible, and if I was invisible I could find the secret house.'

I have an image of walking with him by the river and how we had seen the boys lined up along its bank.

'I remember,' I say.

He is silent now. His face sad, as if he is about to cry.

'What are you thinking?' I say.

'Before we leave I would like to play with my friends in the garden one last time. Is that OK?'

'Yes,' I say, 'of course it is. And then we will go

away

to the moon, away to another place, another time, another world, anywhere but here. But we cannot escape this world. We are bound to it, even in death. Afra stood still by the window while I dressed her. She was like a doll. Her face had lost all expression now. Only her fingers trembled, ever so slightly, and I could see her eyelids twitching. But she said nothing as I put her in the red dress, as I tied the scarf around her neck and slipped on her shoes, and then she stood there like a different woman.

If I had seen her in the street I might have walked right past her without knowing who she was. Inside the person you know there is a person you do not know. But Afra was entirely changed, inside and out. I avoided touching her skin, and as soon as I had finished dressing her I stepped away from her and she dabbed her wrists and her neck with the rose perfume and the familiarity of it made me feel sick. This time we were really going somewhere, we were going away. Away from the war, far from Greece and further away from Sami.

Mr Fotakis had arranged for someone to take us to the airport. This man wasn't just a driver – he would be escorting us in and introducing us to the man who would give us the tickets and passports. While we waited, Mr Fotakis made us

Greek coffee in tiny cups, as if nothing had happened. I watched him as he heated it on the stove, and it took everything I had not to open one of the kitchen drawers and take out a knife. I wanted to kill him very slowly. I wanted him to feel every inch of the knife entering his flesh. But, if I took this revenge Afra and I would never be able to leave. If I let him live, we would still have this chance to escape, even though something of me would always be left behind, trapped within the dank walls of this apartment. I'd helped to kill a man before, and I knew I would be able to do it again. I stared at the drawer, I imagined opening it and taking a knife. It would be easy.

'So you ended up being a hard worker. Very obedient.'

My eyes moved up to his hand and I watched as he stirred the coffee. He smiled as he poured it into three cups.

'And I guess now you have your dream. Amazing what determination and a strong will can do.' He handed me one of the coffees and took the other two into the living room, placing them on the low table. His eyes rested on Afra. She was sitting on the sofa and I wished she would do something, scratch her arms, or pick up the cup, or even cry, but she just sat there as if she had died inside and only her body was alive. I felt as if her soul had left her.

There was a buzz at the door and Mr Fotakis helped us to take our hand luggage downstairs, then he placed the bags in the boot of a silver Mercedes. The driver, a tall, muscular Greek man in his forties, introduced himself as Marcos. He leant on the bonnet and smoked a cigarette.

It was a beautiful day, the rising sun illuminating the

buildings. Behind was the misty shadow of the inland mountains, a wispy halo of clouds above them. There was a slight chill in the air, but the flowers in the courtyards of the apartment blocks were blooming.

'I'm going to miss having you around.' Mr Fotakis chuckled.

We would leave. He would live.

We got into the back of the car and set off and I watched Mr Fotakis from the back window of the car, standing there watching us leave. I turned towards the front and tried to block his face out of my mind. We drove through the streets of Athens and it was strange to see the city in the sun – for weeks I had known it mostly at night, or in the early hours just as the sun was melting the darkness. Now I could see some of its normality, the cars, the traffic, the people going about their daily lives. Marcos was playing Greek music on the radio; when the news started at 9 a.m. he turned the volume up and shook his head or nodded as he listened. He had his window rolled down, his elbow resting out of it, his fingers touching the steering wheel, and I was amazed at how relaxed he seemed, but when the news finished he glanced at me in the rear-view mirror with anxious eyes.

'When we get to the airport,' he said, 'I will open the boot and you take your bags. Then I would like you to follow me, but make sure you stay about ten metres away at all times. Don't get too close and don't lose me. This is very important. I will lead you to the men's toilets. Afra will wait outside. There will be someone else waiting for you there. I want you to wait in the toilets. When they are empty, and only then, knock on a door three times.'

I nodded. He didn't see as he was checking the mirror to change lanes.

'Do you understand? Or would you like me to go through that again?'

'I understand,' I said.

'Good. Now if you make it to Heathrow, throw your passports and boarding passes in the nearest bin. Wait three hours, and then hand yourselves in to the authorities. Understood?'

'Yes,' I said.

'You must not forget to throw them away. And you must wait three hours, maybe more, but not less. Do not tell them which flight you were on.'

He took a packet of chewing gum from the glove compartment and offered me a piece. I refused.

'Your wife?' he said. But Afra was sitting very quietly, with her hands in her lap, a bit like Angeliki, her lips tight, and if you didn't know she was blind you would think that she was looking at the streets through the window.

'You're lucky you're rich,' he said. His eyes in the mirror were smiling now. 'Most people have to make a terrible journey through the whole of Europe to reach England. Money gets you everywhere. This is what I always say. Without it you live your entire life travelling, trying to get to where you think you need to go.'

I was about to tell him that I didn't agree, that we had already made a terrible journey, much worse than he could have even imagined, and that our journey had stolen Afra's soul. But in some ways he was right. Without that money we would have had a much longer road ahead of us.

'You are right, Marcos,' I said, and he tapped his fingers on the steering wheel and inhaled the air as we edged past the sea.

At the airport we did as Marcos said. We walked through crowds of people; all the while I kept my eye on Marcos's grey suit. Then I saw him from a distance, standing outside the men's toilets. He stayed there until he was sure that I had seen him, and then he walked away. I went into the toilets. There was a man pissing, and I saw that one of the cubicles was occupied. I waited for the man to finish – he took his time washing his hands, checking his face in the mirror. Then another man came in with his young son. They took a while and I thought for a moment that there would be a constant stream of people and that I'd be stuck in there for hours. But soon enough the toilet was empty. I knocked on the door three times, as instructed, and a man came out of the cubicle. I hardly got a chance to see him.

'Nuri Ibrahim?' he said.

'Yes,' I confirmed.

Then he handed me the boarding passes and the passports and that was it, he was gone.

We were on our own after that.

We didn't speak to each other at all as we made our way through the airport, first to check-in, then to security. We passed through the metal detector and put our luggage on the conveyor belt so that it could be screened. I was frightened at this point and I became self-conscious, too aware of the expression on my face. I didn't want to seem afraid, I didn't want to look at any of the security guards, in case they picked up on something, but I think this made me look guilty. Afra slipped her hand in mine, but the feel of her skin, and the fact that she was standing so close to me, made me uncomfortable, so I took a step away.

Soon we had our bags and we made our way to duty free, and there we had an hour's wait and another half-hour delay. I bought us each a coffee and we strolled around, as casually as we could, pretending to window-shop until we were called to gate 27.

At the gate we took a seat next to a couple with two children who were playing games on their phones. For a moment I let my shoulders relax and I thought everything would work out OK. I watched the little boy so engrossed in his game; he was a bit younger than Sami would have been, wearing a colourful rucksack which he didn't take off even though he was sitting down.

Afra was so still and so quiet I almost forgot that she was there. There was a part of me that wished she would just disappear, that the seat next to me was empty. The boy's game ended and he threw his arms up in the air and that's when I noticed a disturbance by the gate entrance. There were five police officers talking to a flight attendant, who was looking more and more distressed. I saw that one of the officers was scanning the area. I looked down. I whispered to Afra to act normal. Then I glanced up, unintentionally, and for a second the officer caught my eye and I thought that was it. We had been found out. We would be going back. But back where? Back to what?

The officers came through the entrance into the waiting

lounge and I held my breath and prayed as they walked towards us and then past us, to the last seats by the windows, where a group of four young men and women suddenly stood up, startled, afraid, grabbing their bags, looking as if they wanted to make a run for it, but there was nowhere to go. We all tried not to stare as the four were escorted out, and I noticed as they walked past me that one young man was crying, wiping his face with the backs of his hands, so many tears that he could barely see where he was going. He stumbled over my bag and paused to look at me. The police officer pulled him on. I will never forget the look of pain and fear in his eyes.

Afra and I showed our boarding passes and passports at the gate exit. The woman checked them, glanced at us both in turn and wished us a safe and pleasant journey.

So we boarded the plane and took our seats and I sat there with my eyes closed, hearing the noises and conversations of the people around me, listening to the safety instructions and waiting for the sound of the engine. Afra grabbed my hand and held it tightly.

'We're going,' I heard her whisper. 'Nuri, we're going to Mustafa and we will be safe.' And before I knew it we were off, up into the big, blue sky. We were finally going. Going away.

14

When I wake up it is night-time and I am in the storage cupboard, my head pressed up against the vacuum cleaner, coats above me, shoes and boots digging into my back. I stand up and head along the corridor. I can hear the sleep sounds of the other residents. The Moroccan man is snoring loudly, and as I walk past his room I see that the bronze pocket watch is hanging from the door handle. I take a closer look at the etchings of flowers on the casing and the mother-of-pearl face, the initials engraved on its underside: *AL*. The time is stuck at four o'clock. Diomande's door is wide open. He is sleeping on his side, the covers draped loosely over him. I walk quietly into the darkness of his room and place my hand on his back, expecting to feel the wings, those tightly scrunched-up balls curling out of his dark skin. But instead

I feel ridges of distorted skin, large protruding scars running along the blades like burn marks. My eyes fill up with tears and I swallow them. I think about him, so full of dreams.

He sighs and turns on his side. 'Maman,' he says, half opening his eyes.

'It's Nuri,' I whisper. 'Your door was open and the covers were off. I thought you might be cold.'

I pull the covers over him, tuck him in as if he is a child. He mumbles something and falls back asleep.

I head downstairs and I unlock the glass door and stand outside in the moonlit courtyard. The sensor catches me and the light comes on. The bee is sleeping on one of the dandelions. I stroke her fur, very gently so that I will not disturb her. I am amazed that she has survived in this little garden she has made into a home. I watch her resting among the flowers with her saucer of sugar water by her side; she has learnt to live without her wings.

I now know that Mohammed will not be coming – I understand that I created him, but the wind picks up and the leaves rustle and there is a chill in the air that gets beneath my skin, and I imagine his tiny figure in the shadows of the garden. The memory of him lives on, as if somehow, in some dark corner of my heart, he had had a life of his own. When I come to this realisation it is Sami who fills my mind. I remember tucking him into bed, in the room with the blue tiles, and sitting beside him to read the children's book I had found at the market. His eyes lit up, full of anticipation. I translated as I read, from English to Arabic.

'Who would ever build a house made of straw?' he had

said, laughing. 'I would have used metal, the hardest metal in the world, like the type they use for spaceships!'

How he loved to look up at the stars and make up stories. The sensor light goes off and I sit for a while in the darkness and look into the dark sky. I have only memories now. The wind blows and I can smell the sea. The leaves on the trees move and I can see him again, in my mind, Sami, playing beneath the tree in the garden in Aleppo, in our house on the hill, putting worms into the back of a toy truck so that he could take them for a drive.

'What are you doing?' I'd said to him. 'Where are you taking them?'

'They have no legs so I'm helping them. I'm going to drive them to the moon!'

There was a full moon in a blue sky that night.

I go to our room. Afra is asleep with her hands tucked beneath her cheek. On the bedside table there is another picture. I pick it up and for a moment I cannot breathe. She has drawn the cherry tree in the concrete garden, with its crooked branches and soft pink petals. This time the colours are correct, the lines and shading less distorted. The sky is bright and blue with wisps of clouds and white birds. But beneath the tree, a grey sketch, almost invisible: the gentle outline of a boy, the pencil marks soft and swift, making him appear as though he has been captured in movement. He is part of this world and yet not quite in it. There is a slight shimmer of red on his T-shirt where Afra has started to colour him in and stopped. Although he is a half-ghost, he is clear enough for me to see that his face is tilted toward the sky.

I climb in next to her and look at the gentle curve of her body and remember the shimmering outline of the buildings.

I reach out and touch her for the first time, run my hand along the length of her arm, then down over her hips. I touch her as if she is made of the finest film of glass, as if she might easily break under my fingertips, but she sighs and edges closer to me, though she is asleep. I realise how afraid I have been of touching her.

The sun is rising and her face in the dawn light is beautiful, those fine lines around her eyes, the curve of her chin, the dark hairs on the sides of her face, the slope of her neck, soft skin down to her breasts. But then I imagine him on her, forcing her, the look in her eyes, the fear, the scream locked inside her, the hand over her mouth. I remember the key that I forgot on the coffee table of the smuggler's apartment, I remember driving through the streets of Athens and not turning back. I am shaking now. I fight it, push the thought out. I realise I have forgotten to love her. Here is her body, here are the lines on her face, here is the feel of her skin, here is the wound across her cheek that leads into her, like a road, all the way to her heart. These are the roads we take.

'Afra,' I say.

She sighs and opens her eyes ever so slightly.

'I'm sorry.'

'What for?'

'I'm sorry I forgot the key.'

She doesn't say anything but she wraps her arms around me so that I can smell the roses, and then I can feel her crying on my chest.

I move back so that I can look at her – sadness and memories, love and loss, blooming from her eyes. I kiss her tears, I taste them, I swallow them. I take in everything that she can see.

'You forgot about us,' she says.

'I know.'

And then I kiss her face and her body and I feel with my lips every inch of her, every line, every scar, everything that she has seen and carried and felt. Then I rest my head on her stomach and she puts her hand on my head and strokes my hair.

'Maybe we can have another child,' I say, 'one day. They won't be Sami, but we will tell them everything about him.'

'You won't forget him?' she says.

She is silent for a while and I can feel her heartbeat in her belly.

'Do you remember how he loved to play in the garden?' I say.

'Of course I do.'

'And how he pushed that worm around in his toy truck like he was actually taking him somewhere?'

She laughs and I do too. I can feel her laughter rippling through her body like falling coins.

'And when I bought him a map of the world,' I say, 'and he made a family with stones and sent them out of Syria. He'd been watching Mustafa and me planning out our journey on the globe.'

'And he didn't know how to get the stones across the water! How afraid he always was of the water.' she says.

'I even had to wash his hair in the sink!'

'And how about the way he always waited for you at the window when it was time for you to come home.' And with that last word she sighs and falls asleep and her inner world softens and sounds like water.

Early in the morning the doorbell rings. When nobody answers, it rings again and again. After a while I hear footsteps crossing the landing – they are the footsteps of the Moroccan man. He pauses at the top of the stairs and makes his way down, the floorboards creaking with each step he takes. The door opens and there is muffled conversation. It seems to be a man with a deep voice. I make my way to the top of the stairs and I hear my name, my full name, loud and clear.

'Nuri Ibrahim. I am here to see Nuri Ibrahim.'

In my pyjamas and with bare feet I go down the stairs and standing there, with the full light of the morning sun behind him, is Mustafa. And the memories flash before my eyes: his father's house in the mountains, his grandfather spreading honey on warm bread, the paths that led us into the woods where the bees found the flowers, the shrine to his mother and that glittering smile, the way we used to stand exposed in the apiaries with the bees all around us, my father's sad face and shrinking body, my mother with the red fan: *Yuanfen – the mysterious force that causes two lives to cross paths* – and our apiaries, the open field full of light, thousands of bees, employees smoking the colonies, the meals beneath the canopies – it all flashes before my eyes as if I am about to take my last breath.

'Nuri,' he says simply, and his voice shakes. And that's when I begin to sob, my body shaking, and I think that I will never stop, and I feel Mustafa moving, coming over to me, resting his hand on my shoulder, a strong grip, and then he embraces me and he carries the smells of an unknown place.

'I knew you would come,' he says. 'I knew you would get here.'

Then he steps back to look at me, and through my blurred vision I see that his eyes are brimming with tears, and that his face is paler than before and older, the lines around his eyes and mouth much deeper, his hair more grey. And there we both stand, battered by life, two men, brothers, finally reunited in a world that is not our home. The Moroccan man stands to one side of us, watching this scene. I notice him now, the sad look in his eyes, the way he is winding his fingers around one another as if he does not know what else to do.

'Would you like a cup of tea?' he says in his own Arabic. 'Where have you come from? It must have been a long journey.'

'I have come from Yorkshire,' Mustafa says, 'in the north of England; I took the night coach. But I have travelled much further than that.'

I lead Mustafa into the living room and we sit in silence for a while – Mustafa on the edge of the armchair, wringing his hands, me on the sofa. I see that he is looking out into the garden and then at me. He opens his mouth to speak but then remains silent, until we both talk at the same time.

'How have you been, Nuri?' he asks.

'You will be coming, won't you?' He sounds anxious.

'Of course.'

'Because I can't do it on my own – it's not the same.'

'If I made it this far,' I say, 'then I will make it to Yorkshire.'

'When do you find out?' he says, and, 'You said in your email that you're not well?'

Just then there are footsteps in the hallway and Afra appears, standing motionless in the doorway. Mustafa's eyes light up, and he rises, at first to take her hand in his and then he puts his arms around her and holds her for a long time. I hear her exhale, as if Mustafa's presence has lifted a heaviness in her heart.

It's a warm day so we go out into the courtyard.

'I can see the green of the tree,' Afra says, her eyes smiling. 'And over there –' she points to the heather plant by the fence – 'I can see a soft pink. There are times when things are clearer.'

Mustafa is happy for her. He is reacting in all the ways that I couldn't. The Moroccan man brings out the tea and Mustafa tells us about his beehives.

'Afra,' he says, 'you will like it there. Dahab and Aya are waiting for you, and there are so many flowers, lavender and heather fields, and the bees also collect nectar from private gardens and allotments and along the train tracks. You will be able to see the colours – I will take you myself; we will walk when it is warm and I will take you to the places where the bees go. And we have found a shop that sells halva and baklava!' He speaks with the enthusiasm of a child again, but

I can detect an undertone of desperation – I know him, and what he is really saying is this: This is how the story must end; our hearts can bear no more loss.

Then he lights a cigarette, biting and sucking the end of it while he tells us about the workshop groups and his students and about the beekeepers' association.

'When you come, Nuri will help me with the groups, and we will split the colonies and build new hives.' He glances over at me as he talks, as he creates pictures with his hands and his words. He wants to give me something to hope for, I can tell. Mustafa has always given me something to hope for.

I am standing a little away from them by the glass doors, watching them, and I think about the little boy who never existed and how he had filled the black void that Sami had left. Sometimes we create such powerful illusions, so that we do not get lost in the darkness.

'One day,' I hear Mustafa say. 'One day we will go back to Aleppo and rebuild the apiaries and bring the bees back to life.'

But it is Afra's face that brings me to life, standing here in this tiny garden like she stood in Mustafa's courtyard in Aleppo, her eyes so full of sadness and hope, so full of darkness and light.

She is looking up at something. Among the blossoms of the cherry tree, three hoopoe birds perch on a branch, checking out their surroundings, with their majestic crown of feathers and curved beaks and stripy wings. Here they are, migrants from the east, in this small town by the sea.

'Do you see them?' I hear her say. 'They have come to find us!'

We are all looking up now, and, all at once, they open their black and white wings and set off together into the unbroken sky.

Acknowledgements

Thanks to all the people who told me their stories; the refugees who opened my eyes. Thanks to the beautiful children at Faros who showed me what real courage means. I will never forget you. To Faros Hope Centre in Athens, for the wonderful work you do, and for welcoming me and accepting my help. Thank you Elias, for sharing the story of your difficult journey with me that day in Brighton. Thank you Professor Ryad Alsous, for being such an inspiration; to you and your family, for the lovely meal we had, and for introducing me to the bees and The Buzz Project. Thank you to my Arabic tutor, Ibrahim Othman, you went above and beyond, listening to me read, and offering invaluable advice.

Thank you to all my family, friends and colleagues who supported and encouraged me to continue to write. To Dad and Yiota, Kyri and Mario, for your unending support. To Marie, Rodney and Theo, Athina and Kyriacos, for everything – there are no words. To Antony and Maria Nicola, for your suggestions. To my great friend, Claire Bord, for your insight, advice and constant support. To Mariana Larios for being there through it all. Thanks to Louis Evangelou, for listening to me and for all your creative ideas, and to my uncle Chris for your patience and help. Thank you to Dr Rose Atfield and Celia Brayfield for being brilliant mentors to this day. To Bernadine Evaristo, Matt Thorne, and Daljit Nagra, for your support. Thank you Richard English, for the great conversations about writing and life and all that stuff. Thank you to my family who helped me in Athens – Anthoula, Thanassis, Katerina and Konstantinos Cavda, Maria and Alexis Pappa, for your warmth and generous hospitality. Thank you Matthew Hurt for the advice you gave me on the flight to Athens. A big thank you to Salma Kasmani for reading and re-reading the manuscript, for your excellent suggestions, and for the insight you gave me. Thank you, Stewart, for being there through the twists and turns, the ups and downs.

Thank you to my publishers at Bonnier Books UK, especially to Kate Parkin, for all your unwavering passion, your enthusiasm, for everything. To Margaret Stead, Felice McKeown, Francesca Russell and Perminder Mann. Thank you Arzu Tahsin for your sharp editor's eye and editorial suggestions.

And, finally, thank you to my agent, Marianne Gunn O'Connor, for believing in me, for never letting me give up, for your love and support and for this journey we have been on. Thank you Vicki Satlow, for all your help and for bringing light and honey and flowers to the darkness. Thank you Alison Walsh, for your advice on the manuscript.

All the experiences I had along the way, the people I met, the things I saw and heard, have changed the way I see the world, forever.

Dear Reader,

In the summer of 2016, and again in 2017, I found myself in Athens, working as a volunteer in a refugee centre. Every day, new people were flooding into Greece, families, lost and afraid, mostly from Syria and Afghanistan. The experience of being there for these people, during the most horrific circumstances of their lives, opened my eyes.

I began to realise that people wanted to tell their stories, there were language barriers, but they wanted to speak, they wanted others to hear, to see. The children drew pictures. They would draw balloons and trees, and below them a tent and a dead body. I was disturbed by these images and by the stories. But it was their reality; it was what they had experienced.

I returned to London, and I hoped that the horror of what I had seen and heard would fade, but it didn't. I couldn't forget any of it. And so I decided that I would write a novel as a way of telling the stories of these children, these families.

The question I kept asking myself was what does it mean to see? And so Afra came to life, a woman who has seen her son die, and who has been blinded by the explosion that killed him. Then I met a man who had once been a beekeeper in Syria. He had found his way to the UK and was building beehives and teaching refugees about beekeeping. Bees are a symbol of vulnerability and life and hope. My protagonist,

Nuri, was once a proud father and a beekeeper. Now, he is trying to connect with his shattered wife, Afra, seeking her in the dark tunnels of her grief, but she will not leave Aleppo, she is frozen in her grief. Nuri knows that they must leave in order to survive. It is only when they allow themselves to see, to feel the presence and love of one another, that they can start to make the journey towards survival and renewal.

The Beekeeper of Aleppo is a work of fiction. But Nuri and Afra developed in my heart and mind as a result of every step I took beside the children and the families who made it to Greece. I have written a story as a way of revealing the way we are with the people we care about most in the world when we have suffered so much loss. *The Beekeeper of Aleppo* is about profound loss, but it is also about love and finding light. This is what I saw and heard and felt on the streets and camps in Athens.

Christy Lefteri

Reading Group Questions

- What do you think are the main themes of the novel?
- What impact does the war have on the lives of the main characters?
- Do you agree with Afra's need to remain in Syria at the beginning of the novel? What might this suggest about her state of mind?
- Which of the two characters seem stronger at the start of the novel? Does this impression change by the end?
- Are there similarities and differences in the way in which Nuri and Afra deal with the obstacles they face?
- What do you think the author's intentions were by introducing the character of Mohammed? What could the relationship between Nuri and Mohammed reveal about Nuri's state of mind?
- What do you think the bees and beekeeping represent and symbolise in the story?
- At the end of the novel Nuri says, 'Mustafa has always given me something to hope for.' To what extent does Mustafa influence the decisions that Nuri makes in his life and during his journey with Afra? In what ways might the friendship between the two men give the reader something to hope for?

- It is because of Mustafa that Nuri strives to reach the UK. Why do you think Nuri does not make contact with Mustafa as soon as he arrives?
- Nuri contributes to the murder of Nadim. Do you condemn or agree with his actions?
- Do you consider Nuri to be a strong or weak man?
- Which character do you think changes the most during the course of the novel?
- Why do you think Nuri finds it so difficult to make emotional and physical contact with Afra?
- What might Afra's blindness reveal about her state of mind?
- We never really meet Sami, but in what way do we learn about his character and the type of boy he was?
- How does Nuri and Afra's relationship change during the course of the novel?
- At the end of the story Afra says to Nuri, 'You think it's me who can't see.' What do you think she means by this? And how far do you agree with what she says?
- Which character in the novel do you think displays the greatest emotional resilience?
- What do you think happens after the end of the novel?
- Can reading a novel about the experience of refugees offer a different perspective or have a different emotional impact to that of the media and news bulletins?

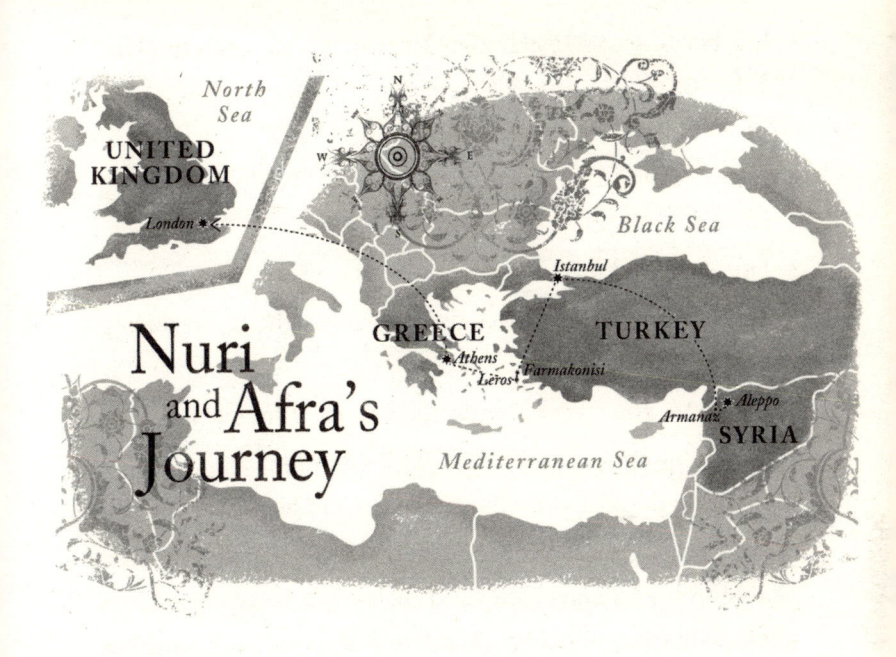

Nuri and Afra's Journey

North Sea
UNITED KINGDOM
London
Black Sea
Istanbul
GREECE **TURKEY**
Athens
Leros *Farmakonisi*
Armanaz *Aleppo*
SYRIA
Mediterranean Sea

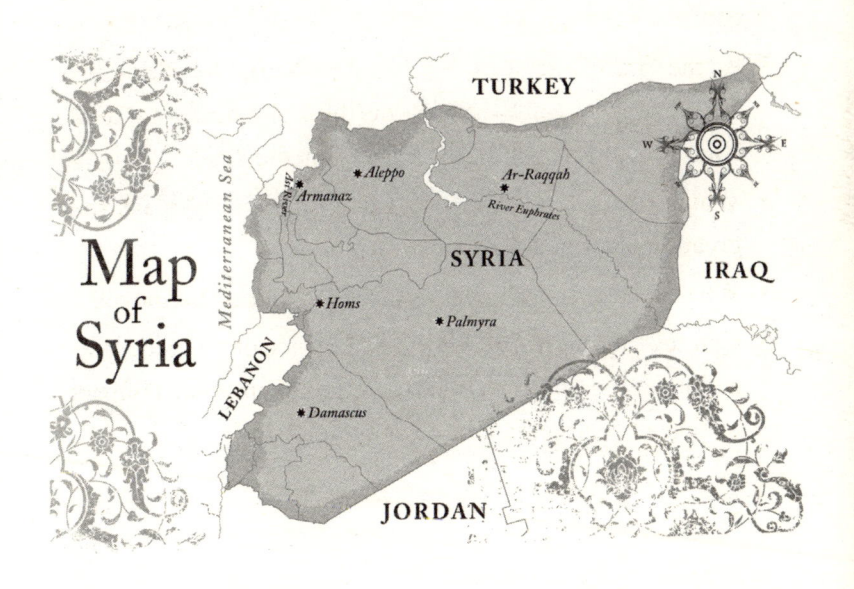

Map of Syria

TURKEY
Aleppo *Ar-Raqqah*
Armanaz *River Euphrates*
SYRIA **IRAQ**
Mediterranean Sea
Homs *Palmyra*
LEBANON
Damascus
JORDAN

If you would like to be more involved, please see the below information about some smaller charities in the UK and Europe who work with refugees and asylum seekers at a local level.

* * *

Open Cultural Center is an NGO and informal education & integration project in North Greece. They work to create community, reduce isolation, and develop skills for displaced people in Nea Kavala camp and the surrounding area. Their team of refugee and non-refugee volunteers work together to provide language lessons, sports, and social/cultural activities for children, adolescents and adults.

Learn more about their work at:
www.openculturalcenter.org

* * *

Faros (The Lighthouse) is a Christian non-profit organization that provides humanitarian care and individual support to unaccompanied refugee children and young adults in the centre of Athens. They help unaccompanied children and young adults find safety, discover their worth, and build a future perspective. They do street work to identify vulnerable minors, run a shelter for minors and provide skills development training (design, wood work, 3D printing, electronics, sewing) in their two educational centres for young men and women.

Learn more about their work at:
www.faros.org.gr

* * *

Salusbury World is a grass-roots charity supporting refugees of all ages to rebuild their lives in the UK. In 2019, it is celebrating 20 years of painstaking work, much of it with children who have gone on to achieve great things. Based in north-west London, they provide clubs, mentoring and more for children and young people, and careers advice, guidance and practical support for new arrivals of all ages. Working with schools and creative arts organizations, Salusbury World also seeks to challenge prejudice and build understanding across communities.

Learn more about their work at:
www.salusburyworld.org.uk

* * *

The Buzz Project at the Standedge Tunnel Visitors Centre, Marsden, West Yorkshire, is a charity organisation founded in 2017 and led by apiarist Professor Ryad Alsous. Himself a refugee, Professor Alsous was a beekeeper in his native Syria for more than forty years, and taught modern beekeeping and food quality control at Damascus University. The Buzz Project teaches refugees and jobseekers and aims to save native British bees in the UK. Alongside a team of dedicated volunteers, he brings his skills to the project, teaching the young people to keep bees, tend to a growing garden of flowers and vegetables, and make honey.

To learn more about The Buzz Project, visit the Canal and River Trust Website, www.canalrivertrust.org.uk and The Buzz Project Facebook page

* * *

From the bestselling author of
The Beekeeper of Aleppo

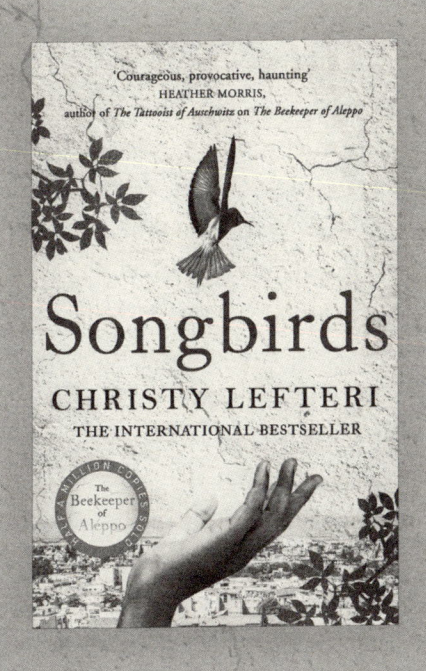

Songbirds
CHRISTY LEFTERI
THE INTERNATIONAL BESTSELLER

A powerful story about what it is to migrate in search of freedom, only to find yourself trapped. *Songbirds* is a triumphant exploration of loss, the strength of the human spirit and the unbreakable bonds of courage, and of love.

COMING JULY 2021

For more news on *Songbirds*, join
Christy Lefteri's Readers' Club at:
www.beekeeperofaleppo.com/readersclub

Read on for an extract . . .

Yiannis

Before Nisha vanished, before I realised she had gone, I saw, in the forest, a Mouflon Ovis. I thought it was odd, as these beautiful creatures are wild and rare. They're usually alone in secluded parts of the mountains. I'd never seen one on flat terrain, never this far east. I should have known from that moment that something was wrong. I knew a long time ago that sometimes the earth speaks to you, finds a way to pass on a message if only you look and listen with the eyes and ears of your childhood self. This was a lesson my grandfather taught me. But that day in the woods, by the time I saw the golden Mouflon, I'd forgotten the lot.

It began with a crunch of leaves and earth. Late October morning. So early, so cold, the branches shone with ice. I'd returned to collect the songbirds. I'd put out the lime-sticks while it was still dark, a hundred of them strategically placed in the trees where the berries are and the birds feed. I'd also hidden three devices amongst the leaves, recordings of birdsong to attract my prey. Then I found a secluded spot and lit a wood fire.

I used olive branches as skewers and toasted haloumi and bread. I had a flask of strong coffee in my backpack and a book to pass the time. I didn't want to think about Nisha, the things she had said the night before, the stern look on her face as she left my flat, the way I could see the tightness of the muscles in her jaw.

These thoughts fluttered around me with the bats and I waved them away, one by one. I warmed myself and ate and listened to the birdsong in the dark.

So far, it was a normal hunt.

I fell asleep by the fire and dreamt that Nisha was made of sand. She dissolved before me like a castle on the shore.

The rising sun was my calling. I had a shot of coffee to wake myself fully and threw the rest on the fire, then stamped out the remaining flames and forgot about the dream. The thick woods began to stir, to wake. I usually make thousands of euros for each hanging, and this one was a good one – there were around two hundred Blackcaps stuck on the lime-sticks. They are worth more than their weight in gold. Tiny songbirds migrating from Europe to Africa to escape the winter. They come in from the west, over the mountains, stopping here along the way before heading out to sea, towards Egypt. In the spring, they make the return journey, flying in from the southern coast. So small, we can't shoot them. Endangered, protected species.

I was always frightened at this point, looking over my shoulder, expecting that this time I would be caught and thrown in jail. This was always my weakness – the fear, the anxiety I felt before killing the birds. The woods were quiet, no sound of footsteps. Just the birdsong, the breeze and the leaves.

I removed one of the birds from the stick, gently prying its feathers from the glue. This one had tried hard to free itself, it seemed. The more they try to escape, the more stuck they get. I held it in my palms and felt its tiny heart racing. Then I bit into its neck until I could taste warm blood and dropped it, lifeless, into a bin-liner. This is how we kill them – a quick, deep bite to the neck. I'd filled up the first bag and begun to remove the feathers and berries from the lime-sticks with my teeth so I could reuse them, when I heard the crunch of the leaves.

I froze for a moment and held my breath. I didn't move an inch, just scanned the surroundings with my eyes. In a clearing between the bushes I saw the Ovis, calmly staring at me, as if it knew something that I didn't. It stood in the long shadows of the trees and it wasn't until the light shifted that I saw the most extraordinary thing. Instead of red and brown, its short-haired coat was gold. Its curved horns, bronze. Its eyes were the exact colour as Nisha's – the eyes of a lion. I thought I must be dreaming, I must still be asleep by the fire before the sun began to rise.

I took a step forwards and the golden Ovis took a small step back, but its posture remained straight and strong and its eyes were fixed on mine. Without moving too much, I removed my backpack from my shoulders and took out a slice of fruit. The Ovis shuffled its feet and lowered its head so that its eyes now looked up at me. Half wary, half threatening. I placed the slice of peach in my palm and reached out my hand. I stayed like that, as still as a tree. I wanted it to come closer, so that I could take a better look at this magnificent creature.

Seeing the beauty of its face, a memory came to me, sharp and clear. Last March, Nisha and I had gone to the Troodos Mountains. She loved to go for long walks with me on Sunday mornings, her day off. She'd often come with me into the forest to pick mushrooms, wild asparagus, blue mallows or to collect snails. On this day, I wanted to see if we could spot the magnificent Mouflon Ovis, native to the land. I hoped that we would see one in the depths of the woods or the verge of the mountains, at the threshold to the sky. We were so high up and she slipped her hand into mine.

'So, we're looking for a sheep?' she'd said.

'Technically, yes.'

'I've seen plenty.' There was a mocking smile in her eyes.

'I told you, it doesn't look like a sheep!'

'So. We're looking for a sheep that doesn't look like a sheep.' She was holding her hand over her eyes, scanning the environment, pretending to look.

'Yes,' I said, matter-of-factly.

This made her laugh and her laughter escaped into the open sky. I felt in that moment that she had never been a stranger.

We'd been walking around for hours and were about to turn back as the evening was closing in, when I suddenly spotted one standing at the edge of a steep cliff. I could tell it was female as it had smaller curved horns and no gruff beneath its neck. I pointed so that Nisha could see.

The Mouflon saw us and faced us straight on. Nisha stared at it in amazement.

'It's so pretty,' she said. 'It looks like a deer.'

'I told you.'

'Nothing like a sheep.'

'See!'

'Its fur is smooth and brown ... and such a gentle look on its face. It's like it's going to speak to us. Doesn't it look like it wants to say something?'

I didn't reply and she stood there in silence watching it for a while, her eyes wide with curiosity, and I stood beside her and watched her.

There was a flash in her eyes, as if the colours of the forest shone through them, as if some secret energy, some nimble animal hiding in amongst the trees, had suddenly come to life. She let go of my hand and took a few steps towards the animal. Strangely, it stepped away from the edge of the cliff and came slightly closer. These are wary, solitary animals, and I had never seen one approach a human before. Nisha was so gentle in the way she stretched out her hand, so still and gentle in the way she waited for the animal. But there was a restlessness in Nisha that I'd never noticed before. It was all in her eyes, which burned with an emotion that I didn't recognise. In that moment, I felt such a distance from her and the animal, so far away. Like they were sharing something I couldn't understand or had long forgotten.

The animal was about to come forward, I could tell, but maybe the moment was too much too bear. Nisha turned to face me. Something strange happened then. It was as though the previous moment continued in spite of the movement of her body. As though part of Nisha remained facing the Mouflon, transfixed by this animal, in whatever world or whatever place she had escaped to. When she turned to me, she was no longer with me.

She kissed me slowly on the lips. One soft kiss. And as she stepped away from me, I could see a darkness in her eyes, as if the sun had set within them.

The sun set behind the mountains and the beautiful animal looked out to the sky, at the blazing colours of dusk.

Now, dawn in the forest, and the memory of that day brought a sharp pain to my heart. The Mouflon Ovis gazed at me, transfixed, tilted its head slightly, making a sound which was like a question. A question of a single word.

'I won't hurt you,' I said, and realised suddenly how loud my voice was in the woods, how it shattered the peace. My voice was unnatural and the Mouflon knew this. It shook its head and took another step back.

'Sorry,' I said to it, this time softly.

For the first time, it broke its gaze. First it seemed to rest its eyes on the bucket beside me, and then up, into the branches, where the live birds were still hanging from their wings. Then it bought those eyes back to me.

'Sure,' I said, 'I don't blame you. Basically, a murderer, offering you a peach.' I laughed a bit, at the irony of it, as if this creature might share the joke.

The Mouflon made another sound and looked at me with a seriousness that sent a shudder through me. I pressed my heels into the ground to feel the certainty of the earth. I dug my nails into my palms. Strangely, it took a step towards me. In that spot, it now stood directly in a beam of light and its eyes and its fur and its horns shone gold.

I threw the slice of fruit on the ground, and this time I walked backwards, retreating into the shadows and the trees. I watched it from there for a while, this magnificent animal, strong and beautiful. It was very still, then it looked at something over to the left and turned its back to me and walked away, deep into the forest.

I removed the rest of the birds from the lime-sticks as quickly as I could so I could go back home, find Nisha, and tell her what I'd seen. I was hoping that telling her about the Mouflon Ovis would make her shine again.

Petra

THAT DAY WE'D MADE A trip to the mountains. It was a chilly Sunday in October. The three of us put on our hiking boots and waited for the bus that goes up to Troodos, which comes by just twice a day. Nisha would normally go out on her own on Sundays, but this time, for the first time, she decided to come along with Angela and me. Oh, it was beautiful up there, because the autumn mist rested gently on the ferns and pines and golden oaks. If you have ever been to these mountains you might have heard that they once rose from the sea when the African and European tectonic plates collided. You can see the earth's oceanic crust. These rock formations, with their veins and lava pillows, look like they are wearing snake skins. Byzantine monasteries and churches were built on its peaks, far from the threatened coastline.

Angela played with the leaves as Nisha and I sat beneath the heater at one of the taverns and drank coffee. I remember our conversation clearly. Nisha had been unusually quiet, stirring her coffee for some time without drinking it.

'Madam,' she said, eventually, 'I have a question to ask.'

I nodded and waited while she shifted in her seat.

'I would like to take tonight off to . . .'

'But Nisha, that's unexpected!'

She didn't speak for a while. Angela was gathering armfuls

of leaves and placing them on a bench. We both watched her. Nisha had decided to spend her day off with us, to join Angela and me on this trip. I shouldn't be expected to give her more time off. She stirred the coffee; she hadn't taken a single sip.

'Nisha,' I said, 'you have all day off on Sunday. In the evening, you have things to attend to. You need to help Angela get her bag ready for school and then put her to bed.'

'Madam, many of the other woman have Sunday night off too.' She said this slowly.

'I know for a fact that other women are not allowed to go gallivanting around at night.'

She acted like she hadn't heard this and said, 'And I don't think Madam has plans tonight,' giving me a sly look before returning her gaze to the coffee. 'So maybe Madam could put Angela to bed just for tonight? I will do extra duties next Sunday to make up for it.'

I was about to ask her where she intended to go, what was so important that she was causing a disruption to our routine. Perhaps she saw the disapproving look in my eyes, but there was no time for either of us to say anything, because at that moment an avalanche of leaves was released over our heads. Nisha screeched, making a pantomime of it, raising her hands in the air and chasing Angela, who was slipping away down a path which led into the woods. I could hear them after a while in the forest, like two children, laughing and playing, while I drank coffee.

Nisha didn't mention going out again; she seemed to have forgotten about it, and that night when we got back to the city, she made dhal curry. The house filled with the smell of onions and green chillies, cumin, turmeric, fenugreek and curry leaves. I looked over her shoulder as she sautéed the onions and combined the spices with the split red lentils, finally adding a splash of coconut milk. My mouth was watering. Nisha knew this was my favourite dish, and I lit the fire in the living room. It had rained earlier that afternoon and from the living room window, I could see that Yiakoumi opposite had his canopy open and the cobbled streets around glimmered beneath the warm lights of his antique shop.

We do not have central heating, so we sat as close as we could to the flames with the bowls of dhal on our laps. Nisha bought me a glass of sweet *zivania* – the aromatic type with caramel and muscat, so warming on this chilly night – and tested Angela on the seven times table, as she had an exam the following day. I remember all this very well, the way that Angela was munching and yawning and shouting out the answers, the way that Nisha kept her attention on Angela, saying hardly a word to me. The TV flickered in the background. The news was on with the volume right down: footage of refugees, rescued by coast guards off one the Greek islands. An image of a child being carried to the shore. I would have forgotten all this, but I have been over it again and again, like retracing footsteps on the sand when you have lost something precious.

Angela lay on her back and kicked her legs up in the air.

'Sit up,' Nisha scolded, 'or you will be sick in your mouth. You've just eaten.'

Angela made a face, but she obeyed. She perched on the sofa and watched TV, her eyes moving over the faces of people as they scampered out of the water.

Nisha refilled my glass, for the third time, and I was starting to get sleepy. I looked at my daughter then, a monster of a child, she'd always been too big for me; even her curly hair was too thick for me to get my hands around.

Then, in the light of the fire, I noticed that Nisha's face was pale and weary. Looking at her eyes was like opening a door into an empty room. She caught my eye and smiled, a small, sweet smile, but her eyes were still blank. I shifted my gaze over to Angela.

'Do you have your bag ready for school?' I said.

Angela's attention was on the screen.

'We are doing it now, Madam.' Nisha got up hastily, gathering the bowls from the coffee table.

Angela never spoke to me anymore, she never called me 'Mum', never addressed me. Instead, she talked to me through Nisha. I watched Nisha as she licked a tissue and wiped a stain off Angela's jeans, and then took the bowls and spoons to the kitchen. Maybe it was the alcohol, or the trip up to Troodos, but I was feeling more tired than usual, a heaviness in my mind and my limbs, and so I announced that I was going to bed early, I had a long day approaching.

I fell asleep straight away and didn't even hear Nisha putting Angela to bed.

I woke up suddenly in the middle of the night. I thought I'd heard a crashing noise, it was loud and clear, like a window smashing or a glass dashed on the floor with force. The sound had come from the garden, I was sure about that. The clock on my bedside cabinet showed midnight. Could it be the wind? But the night was still and apart from the sound I had heard, there was a deep silence. Or maybe a cat?

I put on my slippers and opened the shutters and the long glass doors to the garden. It was a clear night with a full moon. My house is a three-storey venetian property in the old part of the city, east of Ledra and Onasagorou, on a street that reaches the end of the world. At least this is what I thought when I was a little girl. We live only on the ground floor, each of our bedrooms looking out onto the garden. Two years ago, I rented out the storey above me to a man called Yiannis. The top floor is empty, or full of ghosts, as my mother used to say, which would make my father scoff at her and respond always with the same words: *ghosts are memories. Nothing more, nothing less.*

In the garden, there is boat. There were times in the past, on long nights when I couldn't sleep, that I would see Nisha sitting out in my dad's tiny fishing boat, *The Sea Above the Sky* painted in pale blue on its hull. Its paint is peeling and the wood is crumbling. It's a boat that has made many journeys. Nisha would sit in it and stare out into the darkness. The boat has one oar; the other has been missing for as long as I can remember, but someone placed an olive tree branch in its place. Because my bed is next to the window, I would sit up and watch her for a while through the slits of the shutters, and wonder what was going through her mind, alone like that, in the middle of the night.

But on this night, she wasn't in the boat. I looked around to try to determine the cause of the crashing noise. I was half expecting the crunch of glass beneath my feet. But there didn't seem to be anything broken or out of place.

The moon illuminated the pumpkins, the winding jasmine and vines, the cactus and fig tree to the far right near the glass doors of Angela's room, and, in the middle, on a slightly raised bit of earth, where the roots have cracked through the concrete, the orange tree – like a queen on her throne. I always felt, growing up, that this tree quietly commanded the garden.

Behind the garden there is an empty field with overgrown weeds and, in summer, wild greens. In the centre of the field sits a copper bird, about the size of a small child, its feet hidden amongst the weeds. Before Nisha arrived, the copper had turned green, and in the spring, we could barely see the bird camouflaged amongst the foliage. Nisha cleaned and polished it until it shone.

She told me once that she believed the bird carried the burden of time, that it needed to be renewed, brought to life again. She would go out into the field once a week and rub the copper as if she might be releasing a genie from a lamp. I had preferred it before, when it was exposed to the elements, when the pale green verdigris deepened in the creases of its metal wings, when it bore the signs of the passage of time and the changing of seasons. It made the bird seem more alive and part of this world. Now it was fiery, its steely eyes looking up, forever, to the sky – and yet, it made my bones go cold. Although Nisha took such great care of it, it now, strangely, seemed so untouched.

I suppose, now, that this glimmering bird reflected something back to me, something it would take me a long time to understand.

I didn't know who made this bird, or why it was displayed in the middle of this abandoned field; it had been there since I first came to this house as a child, forty years ago. But I do know that the copper came from deep underground, from the mines that run silently, like black rivers, beneath the city.

Everything was so still. So still and quiet. Hardly a leaf moved. I walked around the garden in the moonlight. By the steps that lead up to Yiannis's flat, I discovered the source of the noise: a ceramic money pot that I'd had since I was a child – it lay smashed on the ground, its white shell broken, hundreds of old Lira scattered about, making tiny pools of gold.

It was the kind of money box that you have to break one day in order to retrieve the treasure inside. I remembered dropping in the coins throughout my childhood, imagining a day when I would rediscover them. My aunt, Kalomira, had made it for me in the village of Lefkara where she lived with her husband. I had watched her spinning the clay on the wheel. Later, she had painted it white with a funny sketch of a dog. It was ready for me and waiting on a shelf when I returned with my mother to see her many weeks later.

I never broke it; the time was never right. So, I left those coins safely inside, like wishes or secret dreams collected from childhood.

But who had broken it now? How had it fallen from the garden table?

I decided to go back to bed and ask Nisha to deal with it in the morning. I pulled the covers over me and in the dark and quiet of my room, I remembered my mother by my side.

'What will you do with all that money?' she had said.

'I will buy wings!'

'Like the wings of a bird?'

'Not really. More like the wings of a dragonfly. They will be transparent, and when I wear them I will fly around this garden at night and glow in the dark.'

She had laughed and kissed me on the cheek. 'You will be beautiful as always.'

The memory faded and I suddenly felt the deep pain of guilt for the absence of words and dreams and laughter with my own daughter. How had I lost her? Or had she lost me?

It was 6.30am when I woke up. Nisha would have just had a shower and gone out into the garden with long damp hair, picking oranges and collecting fresh eggs. After collecting the eggs, she would fry or boil them. When we had courgette flowers or wild greens from the field with the copper bird, she would scramble the eggs over them, adding lots of lemon and pepper. This was always Angela's favourite.

On this morning, Nisha was not outside. A silvery mist rested over the leaves, as if the garden had exhaled. The Lira on the floor now glimmered in the sun.

In the kitchen, Angela was sitting at the table, still in her pyjamas, swinging her legs and playing a game on her iPad. Her loose hair, heavy and tar-like, hung around her shoulders. By this time, it was usually in a neat ponytail and she should have been wearing her school uniform and finishing off her orange juice.

'Where is Nisha?' I said.

Angela looked up from the screen and shrugged.

'Have you eaten?'

She tutted, no, but said nothing more, and sank down into her seat. I saw a stroke of uncertainty in her eyes.

I went into Nisha's room. It was empty, and her bed looked like it hadn't been slept in.

Returning to Angela, and with as much cheer as I could, I said, 'Why don't you go and get changed and I'll make breakfast? Then I'll take you to school.'

She got up, reluctantly, but did as I'd suggested. In the meantime, I called Nisha's mobile a few times, but it went straight to voicemail.

'Nisha,' I said, 'What are you playing at? Where are you? Call me back.'

I began to boil the eggs and make toast, opening all the cupboards to find where Nisha kept the fig jam. I was beginning to get more irritated; the fear hadn't gripped me yet. It was Angela who had the deeper instincts that I lacked. After I peeled the eggs and laid the table, Angela still hadn't come to the kitchen, so I went to her room and found her sitting in front of the mirror, crying. She'd put on her uniform but she'd been unable to tie up her hair. The elastic band was stuck in a knot of curls.

I told her to sit on the bed and I perched beside her and gently untangled the band, making sure not to hurt her. Then, with a wide hairbrush, I tried to bring all that hair together into a high ponytail, like Nisha did. But the curls were wild and unruly. As I bought one side up, the other side fell out of my grip and tumbled back down to her shoulder.

I could feel her shifting, uncomfortable and impatient.

'I'll tell you what!' I said. 'Forget the ponytail. Let's do something different.'

I plaited her hair and she pulled the thick black braid over her right shoulder and stood to look at herself in the mirror. Her patio doors were open and the room was full of sunlight and music from the birds. Even the mist came in like a lost spirit.

Such a crisp autumn morning, and it should have been a happy morning, like every other. But what I saw in Angela's eyes as she stared at her reflection was a broadening expanse of fear. It suddenly reminded me of how I had felt at her age, standing on the street that led to the end of the world.

After work, I collected Angela from school and heated up the leftover dahl for supper. Nisha still hadn't returned, so I went in search of her. Outside, Yiakoumi was bringing in the antiques, which he'd displayed on a table, in order to shut shop for the night. To the right, a little further down, Theo's Restaurant was starting to get busy, it was close to dinnertime. His two Vietnamese maids dashed about in their rice hats, holding drinks or trays of dips.

Right next door, on a deck chair placed just outside her front door sat the Paper Lady (as Angela called her). Indeed, her skin was so white and creased that she looked as though someone had scrunched her up into a ball and opened her up again. Even her hair was like tissue paper. She sat there most of the day, late into the evening, sometimes until midnight, watching the day go by, the seasons change, and she remembered everything – her mind was like a journal, full of pages and pages of the past, or at least every bit that had passed her way. It was a well-known fact that her hair had turned white overnight, during the war, when the island was divided. That's when she started storing everything in her mind, so that nobody could take her soul from her. This is what she told me once, many years ago.

She sat there now, perched on her deck chair, watching the TV, which had been brought outside, the wire stretched to breaking point, plugged into a socket in the living room. She spat phlegm into a handkerchief, inspected it, then shouted at the TV. She was furious, it seemed, about a decision the president had made. I decided to ask her if she'd seen Nisha the night before.

I watched as her maid came out with a tray of fruit and water, placing it on a small table by the old lady's side.

'I don't want any,' she said, flicking her snow-white wrist in dismissal, and the maid mumbled something in her own language before returning to whatever she was doing inside.

This maid was new, hadn't yet learnt a word of Greek or English, so they communicated with their respective mother tongues, plus gestures and rolls of the eyes. As usual the Paper Lady was surrounded by cats, all of which Angela had named. One of the cats was sitting to attention, staring at her, meowing.

'What is it my dear?' she said with a sigh. 'What is it my darling Sesame Dough? You want to drink? You want to eat? Come to me and I'll kiss you!' In response, the cat turned its back to her. Then, without even looking my way, she lowered the volume on the TV, and said, 'Petra, come over and have some fruit.'

I approached, with usual pleasantries about the weather, taking a slice of orange out of courtesy, and then I asked whether she had seen Nisha the previous night or in fact, earlier that morning.

Sitting there with her fingers laced together, she searched her mind, her head tilted slightly to the right towards the light of Yiakoumi's shop. She fixed her gaze on the window display. 'According to seven clocks it was nine thirty when I saw her. According to one, it was midnight.'

I waited for her to say more, but instead she scooped up one of the cats and placed it on her lap. This black cat's eyes were gold with an area of patchy blue that looked like the earth from a great distance. Angela had named it The Cat with the World in its Eyes.

'Did she say where she was going?'
'She was in a hurry. She said something about meeting a man.'
'Who?'
'Do you think if I sniff my nails they will tell me the answer?'

She stared at me for a while, as if she was waiting for me to stop chewing. When I swallowed the last bit of orange, she tapped the plate with her finger,

'Have some more.'

I could see that her attention would remain on the plate until I obliged, so I took another slice. She watched me bite into it, wiping the juice from my chin.

'Was there anything unusual . . .' I began.

'My daughter is coming next week from New Zealand. She's coming to see me from the other side of the world.'

'That's wonderful.' Through the crochet curtain I could see her maid's silhouette, she looked like she was bending down to wipe the coffee table, the glow of an orange lamp behind her. She was shaking her head, talking to herself, about the old lady, no doubt – unless there was something else that had angered her that day. Just at that moment the Bouzouki started playing in the restaurant and the cats, as if on cue, scurried off in that direction.

'Did she say anything at all?' I said. 'Nisha, I mean.'

'No, she said nothing more.'

'Which way did she go?'

She pointed to the right. 'Then she turned left at the end of the road.'

I knew that way was a dead end. What would Nisha be doing going down that way? It only led to the Green Line, to the military base and the buffer zone. Nobody went that way.

'But that way's a dead end,' I said.

She was looking up at me, examining me. From her corneas, triangular films of tissue threatened to take over her eyes.

'What's the problem?' she said

'I don't know where Nisha is. I'm sure it's nothing to worry about, she probably just—'

She interrupted me. 'Just what? You mean to tell me she hasn't returned?'

I nodded.

'I presume you've tried her phone?'

I nodded again and she looked up to the sky, her silvery eyes restless in their cloudy prison. She looked so worried that I suddenly had the urge to reassure her.

'Honestly, I'm sure it will be fine. There has to be a reasonable explanation.'

'No,' she said

'Maybe she went to see a friend or . . .'

'No,' she said again. 'Nisha would never take off like that, even for a day. You must know that? She is an extremely conscientious young woman.'

She picked up a slice of orange, bought it to her lips and – seemingly remembering that she didn't want any – tore it up into sections, throwing the pieces on the floor for cats.

Then she reached out and placed a sticky hand on my arm. 'Petra,' she said, staring at me hard, like she was trying to see me through a thick mist, 'there is something not right here. Don't be complacent.'

* * *

I thought I would check on Angela and I found her sitting on her bed in the dark. She was in her pyjamas on top of the covers, sipping a small glass of warm milk which she cradled in her hands. Her school bag was at the foot of the bed and her uniform was hanging ready on the back of her chair by the desk. If I hadn't known better, I would have thought Nisha had been here.

She glanced at me over the rim of the cup.

'You're OK?' I said and she nodded.

I went over and gave her a kiss on the forehead. The Cat with the World in its Eyes was cradled up on the bed beside her, at first just a gleam in the moonlight, its shiny black fur oily in the darkness, then it opened its eyes and there was a flash of gold and blue. I was about to say that she knew very well that cats weren't allowed in this house, but I thought better of it and I left the room.

I kept seeing the Paper Lady's face in my mind, her concern, the way she had looked at me, her sticky hand on my arm. With that one touch, some cold anxiety had passed into me, through my flesh, into my blood. I felt so cold. I couldn't rest. I couldn't sit still. I kept looking out of the window. The Paper Lady had finally gone inside and the street was dark and empty. Further along, the music at Theo's continued to play, the ovens and candles continued to burn.

I made myself some tea and toast and went to Nisha's room. I looked around, without knowing what I was searching for. Her makeup was on the dressing table, neatly lined-up. The brushes sparkled with rouge. I noticed a notebook, and resting on top of it, a gold engagement ring. I had never seen her wearing this before – it was simple, with a decent sized diamond in a raised clasp. I placed the ring on the dresser and opened the notebook. On the first page was a rough sketch of this garden – there was the boat and the orange tree. In this picture, however, the copper bird was flying free in the sky above the field beyond the boat. The rest of the pages were full of writing in Sinhalese. I held the book open in my palms and heard a noise outside again. It wasn't the sound of anything breaking, but someone talking.

This time, when I looked out of the glass doors of Nisha's room, I saw Angela sitting in the boat. The sky was empty of moon or stars and her hair shone in the dark. She was saying something, talking to herself, as if there was someone sitting opposite her in the boat. I was about to go outside and ask her why she wasn't asleep, tell her that it was a school night and she should be in bed. But she looked so content sitting there in the dark, that I hesitated. Angela took the oar and the olive branch and pretended to row, as if she was on some beautiful calm ocean that I couldn't see.

If you enjoyed *The Beekeeper of Aleppo*, look out for . . .

A moving, unforgettable story, inspired by true events.

'Absolutely breathtaking . . . It will remain engraved in my heart and mind forever'
Christy Lefteri

Discover the international No. 1 bestseller, available now.

The Phone Box at the Edge of the World is an unforgettable story of the depths of grief, the lightness of love and the human longing to keep the people who are no longer with us close to our heart.

We all have something to tell those we have lost . . .

On a windy hill in Japan, in a garden overlooking the sea, stands a disused phone box. For years, people have travelled to visit the phone box, to pick up the receiver and speak into the wind: to pass their messages to loved ones no longer with us.

When Yui loses her mother and daughter in the tsunami, she is plunged into despair and wonders how she will ever carry on. One day she hears of the phone box, and decides to make her own pilgrimage there, to speak once more to the people she loved the most. But when you have lost everything, the right words can be the hardest thing to find . . .

Then she meets Takeshi, a bereaved husband whose own daughter has stopped talking in the wake of their loss. What happens next will warm your heart, even when it feels as though it is breaking . . .

'Moving and uplifting'
Sunday Times

'A striking haiku of the human heart'
The Times

'It will break your heart and soothe your soul'
Stacey Halls

'Mesmerising . . . a joy to read'
Joanna Glen